ALIEN HUNTERS

ALIEN HUNTERS

ALIEN HUNTERS, BOOK I

DANIEL ARENSON

CHAPTER ONE
MIDNIGHT'S FLIGHT

They're after me. I have to escape. They're going to catch me. They're going to break me.

Midnight grimaced and leaned forward in her cockpit. Her small blue starjet buzzed across the vastness of space. Behind her, the hulking warship roared in pursuit. The stars streamed around them, and Midnight's heart pounded almost as loudly as the engines.

"Midnight!" The voice boomed out of the speakers on her dashboard. "Midnight, surrender yourself. You cannot escape us. Surrender now!"

Tears burned in Midnight's eyes. She flipped switches madly, but they had seized control of her starjet's communicator. The sound of their breathing filled the cockpit; she could almost smell it. She cried out and pounded her fist against the speakers, trying to shatter them, to silence them, but she only bloodied her fist.

"Midnight!" The voice rose again, deep, grainy, lusting for blood. "Turn around now, Midnight!"

Midnight ignored the voice. She cursed, leaning forward in her seat, sneering. Sweat dampened her brow. She shoved the throttle so far forward it banged against the dashboard. Her starjet was small, only large enough for one person, not meant for the depths of open space. The slick metal vessel felt more like a coffin than a true starship.

"Come on, faster!" she shouted, shoving against the throttle as if her will alone could speed up the starjet.

She had to make it to the humans' planet.

Earth, the old man had called it.

I have to get there. I have to or the galaxy will fall.

She stared forward out of the cockpit. Earth still lay light-years away. Even at this velocity, streaming through hyperspace at many times the speed of light, she would not reach Earth for days, maybe even weeks.

Is it hopeless?

The headlights of the warship behind her blasted across her vessel. The light streamed into the cockpit, and Midnight caught sight of her reflection in the glass. Her long imprisonment had been cruel to her. Her indigo hair seemed thinner than before. Her yellow eyes seemed huge in her gaunt, purple face. Across the galaxy, travelers called her kind--the mysterious pirilians--beings of beauty. They had obviously never met a pirilian who had just escaped both a burning planet and the most ruthless prison in the known cosmos.

"Midnight, surrender yourself now, or we will blast you apart!" The deep, rumbling voice roared out from the speakers, deafening. "Your jet is low on fuel, Midnight. Turn around now and we will spare your life."

Midnight shuddered. Yes. Yes, they would spare her life. She knew that was true. But the fate they planned for her was far, far worse than death.

Fear flooded her belly like ice.

If they catch me, she thought, *they're going to harvest what's inside me. They're going to tear me apart, dissect me, install me into their ships, turn me into a million cyborgs screaming in anguish.* She trembled. *And they're going to use what's left of my soul to conquer the cosmos.*

She panted and bared her teeth.

She would not let them.

She would escape.

Her starjet flitted onward, buzzing madly, slicing through the darkness as stars streaked in white lines around her.

And still the warship roared behind.

Midnight glanced over her shoulder. Her cockpit afforded a view in all directions, a view that right now she regretted. She did not want to see this starship pursuing her. She could not imagine a more terrifying sight. And yet she looked . . . and felt the blood drain from her face.

The skelkrin vessel was massive, a hundred times larger than her own. While her starjet was slender and smooth, this ship was a mass of spikes, claws, and cannons. It looked like a great crab from the dark depths of the sea. There was no elegance to its design, but oh, there was cruelty. There was malice and bloodlust and ruthless strength to this ship. As there was to those who lurked within its craggy metal hull.

The skelkrins. Midnight shivered. The most infamous predators in the galaxy. The beasts who had destroyed her planet. The creatures who had captured her, tortured her, who would rip her apart if they caught her.

And they were gaining on her.

"Surrender now, renegade vessel!" rose the booming voice again. "You cannot escape."

No, Midnight realized. *I cannot.*

A strange calmness filled her.

But I will not let you take me alive.

She grabbed the starjet's joystick. She yanked it left. She roared out her pain and fury as her ship spun in space, turning to face the warship. Teeth bared and heart pounding, she thrust the throttle forward again--as far as it would go. The engines roared as she charged toward the towering skelkrin vessel.

If I cannot escape you, I will take you head on.

She jabbed the two red buttons on her joystick. Blasts of plasma roared out of her jet, streamed across the darkness, and slammed into the skelkrin starship.

Fire blazed against the spiky iron hull.

Midnight screamed, tugged the joystick backward, and shot up in a straight line, skimming the edge of the skelkrin warship. Its metal claws snapped, grazing her tail. Her ship rattled madly. Sparks flew around the cockpit. She blasted upward, made it past the top of the warship, then spun and swooped.

She was as small as a baby attacking a giant. Yet she fired her weapons again, and again fire exploded across the skelkrin hull.

For a moment Midnight dared to hope. Dared to dream that she could defeat them, at least damage them enough to escape.

And then the skelkrin vessel fired back.

Midnight screamed.

Its weapons were a terror, a nightmare of black fire and smoke and blazing white light. The skelkrin cannons bellowed with the sound of shattering bones, collapsing planets, the cries of dying races, dying suns. They screamed with the sound of Midnight's own people blazing in the nuclear inferno. They roared with the sound her heart had made when her planet had burned.

And those weapons slammed into her starjet with the fury of gods.

The black fire blazed around her. She could no longer see the streaming stars. Her jet tumbled. She tore free from the seat, smashed against the cockpit glass, crashed against the controls. Glass cracked around her. One of her jet's engines tore free; she saw it whip through the smoke outside, still sputtering out flame.

With a scream and *pop* and the smell of burnt metal, she crashed out of hyperspace.

The stars, previously white lines streaming all around her, slammed into tiny dots.

Down in the distance, perhaps only ten thousand kilometers away, a small green planet slowly turned. A strange planet. Still light-years from Earth.

With a flash of light followed by looming shadow, the skelkrin ship slammed out of hyperspace behind her. It towered above Midnight's crippled jet, as large as an expanding sun spreading toward a fragile moon.

The cockpit was cracked around Midnight. Floating in the darkness, her body bruised, Midnight stared up at the hulking warship. She had hoped that her weapons had crippled it, but the damage seemed so minimal now; her blasters had left only a few pocks. The bulk of the warship--its cannons, spikes, thrusting mandibles--remained untouched, glittering black.

A mouth yawned open in the ship.

Midnight's jet shook as the tractor beam grabbed her and began sucking her in.

She growled. With her jet's last ounce of power, she managed to spin it around to face the enemy again. She pressed her two red buttons, prepared to fire her plasma.

Only sparks left her jet's guns.

Damn it! The weapon systems, like her hyperdrive engine, were fried. The hatch opened wider on the warship ahead, and the tractor beam kept tugging her closer and closer.

Fear flooded Midnight.

She closed her eyes, struggling to breathe.

Again, in her mind, she saw it--her planet burning, turning from a lush forested world into an inferno. Again she felt it--the skelkrin knives cutting her, probing, trying to extract her power. Again she screamed, thrashing against her bonds, trying to escape, to free herself, and their needles driving into her, and--

She sucked in air.

She opened her eyes.

"Will this be my fate again?" she whispered, eyes damp.

The human with the long white beard had saved her. He had smuggled her out from the skelkrin prison. He had given her this starjet, told her to seek the Earth, to find shelter there with his son.

"You are important, my child," he had whispered, helping her into the starjet. "Perhaps more than you know. You cannot let the skelkrins catch you."

"Come with me!" she had begged her savior, a man with many names in her people's lore. The traveler. The wizard. *Aminor.*

He had only shaken his head. "There are other tasks for me. Other battles to fight. Now fly! Fly to Earth. Find my son. He will care for you."

She had flown away--by the gods, it had been only yesterday.

And already the skelkrins were reeling her back in.

Midnight growled and spun her jet toward the planet. She shoved down on the throttle, engaging her thruster engines. They roared out flame, and she blasted forward a few hundred meters. Within an instant, her jet slammed to a halt, and Midnight flew forward and banged against the cockpit glass. She cried out in pain. Her engines thrummed, but the tractor beam was too powerful.

Shadows fell around her.

The skelkrin warship swallowed her starjet like a whale swallowing a fish.

The hatch slammed shut, sealing her within the belly of the warship. Her engines gave a last sputter and died. The bottom of her jet slammed against the hangar floor.

For a moment, everything seemed so silent.

Midnight shoved the cockpit open and leaped outside into the hangar, her black cloak fluttering around her. She found herself in a towering square cavern, feeling like a fly in the belly of a behemoth. The walls, floor, and ceiling were black and craggy, carved of iron. Red lights blinked, offering the only illumination. She saw nobody.

But they're here somewhere. Midnight's heart tried to leap out of her throat. Her fingers trembled. *The skelkrins.*

She winced to remember them strapping her down to their table, cutting, puncturing, studying, dissecting.

"Never again," she whispered.

She looked deep into herself, seeking her power, the source of power all pirilians had. The mystical energy some called magic. The power the skelkrins wanted to harvest from her. The power that might, just might, let her still fight.

A round door in the back of the hangar dilated.

Three skelkrins entered.

Midnight hissed and raised her fists.

They were towering creatures, over eight feet tall--a good three feet taller than her. While her skin was purple, theirs was crimson like old blood. While her eyes were golden and gleaming, theirs were blazing white, smelters of molten steel within their faces. Their fangs jutted out, wet with saliva. Their claws creaked as they flexed their long, knobby fingers. They wore armor of charcoal iron, the plates sprouting spikes and hooks. An acrid stench wafted from them, and they raised iron rods tipped with crackling balls of electricity.

One among the three, a crimson spiral painted on his helmet, stepped forward. His lips peeled back in a lurid grin. Saliva dripped down his chin, and his white eyes burned.

"Hello again, Midnight." His voice was a hiss, the scrape of metal on bone. "It's time to come home."

Midnight stared at him, the hatred flaring inside her. She knew him.

"Skrum," she whispered.

The skelkrin lord who had burned her planet. Who had murdered her family. Who had locked her in the dreaded prison that floated above the charred remains of her home world.

The creature she would kill.

Midnight screamed and lashed forth her hands. Blue balls of *qi* energy hurtled across the hangar, lighting the shadows, and slammed into the skelkrins.

The power blazed across their armor, cracking the iron. They roared and charged toward her, claws swinging.

Midnight raised her chin and channeled a deeper, older power. The power they wanted from her. The power they had tortured her for.

With a deep breath, she *ported.*

She snapped out of reality.

For an instant, she saw white and blue lights, a foreign realm beyond existence.

She snapped back into the hangar, appearing behind the charging skelkrins.

She blasted forth more *qi* from her palms.

The skelkrins never even had the time to spin around. Her power slammed into their backs, cracking armor. One skelkrin fell facedown, blood gushing from him. The other two--the cruel Skrum and a drooling female--had survived the attack. They turned and raised their iron rods. They swung the weapons. Electricity crackled toward Midnight.

She ported again.

She vanished from reality a split-second before the electricity could hit her. She reappeared behind her charred blue starjet. She reached over the vessel and shot more *qi* toward her enemy, a blast from each palm.

One blast hit the towering female skelkrin. The creature wailed, clutched her chest, and crashed down to the floor.

The second ball of *qi* slammed into Skrum's shoulder, cracking a plate of armor, driving the creature back a step. But Skrum kept standing. The skelkrin came walking toward her, his grin widening, revealing many wet fangs.

Midnight raised her palm again, struggling to summon more *qi*.

Skrum thrust his rod, and a bolt of lightning slammed into Midnight's chest.

She cried out and fell, writhing. Smoke and electricity rose across her black cloak.

"Yes, scream for me." Skrum stepped forward, his boots thumping against the hangar floor. "You will scream much more back in your prison." He licked his chops. "How you will scream as we tear you apart, grow you into a million prisoners, suck up your power like a glutton sucking marrow from a bone! Oh yes. Your screams will be so sweet."

The lightning died across Midnight. She lay, shuddering, smoke rising from her, then screamed and held out her palms.

But she was too weak. Only a soft flow of *qi* left her. It dispersed across Skrum's armor, no more harmful than waves against a breakwater.

He stepped closer, rod raised.

"I will drag you back to your prison myself," he said. "But first . . . first I will hurt you some more."

He pointed his rod toward her.

Summoning every last bit of power inside her, Midnight ported again.

She blinked out and back into reality, appearing by a console at the hangar wall. She slammed her fist against it, shattering the tractor beam controls.

She ported again, appearing by the hangar's hatch. She tugged down a great lever. With a roar, the hatch began to open, exposing a clear view of open space. Stars shone and the planet turned in the distance. The air roared, streaming out into space.

Skrum roared too. He came charging toward her, lashing his rod. Lightning slammed into Midnight, but she ported once more.

She reappeared inside the cockpit of her charred starjet.

"Please, stars and gods and angels above," she whispered, "please let there be just a drop of fuel left."

As the hatch kept opening, Midnight shoved down her starjet's throttle.

Skrum raced toward her.

Her engines sputtered, then blasted out flame.

She glanced behind her to see the inferno crash into Skrum, shoving him back. He flew through the hangar and slammed against the distant wall. Her starjet screeched across the floor, raising sparks. She blasted out the hangar door, and then she was free--out in open space.

She blazed across the emptiness.

Her starjet was seared, missing part of its tail, missing one engine. Its cockpit was cracked, its guns shattered. It could barely fly. Midnight tugged madly at the joystick, directing the little ship down . . . down toward the distant planet.

She did not know what world this was. It was smaller than Earth, light-years away. It could be a land of beasts or a land of lifeless emptiness.

Right now, it was a land of hope.

Bolts of plasma shot around her, lighting the darkness. She flew madly, darting like a bee. The skelkrin ship was firing all its guns, and Midnight screamed as a blast hit her jet, knocking her into a tailspin. She righted her jet. She kept racing forward. To the planet. To hope. To a chance to live, to keep her power from the enemy.

The planet grew closer before her, looming ahead, a great green sheet that covered her vision. Clouds appeared below. Fire blazed around her. She entered the atmosphere with shrieking air, a fountain of sparks, and fear that pounded against her chest.

She screamed, diving through fire.

Blue skies opened up before her.

Water and forested islands spread below.

Bits of metal tore off her vessel. Screws. Panes. Another engine. The cockpit finally shattered and showered shards across her.

All Midnight knew was flame, roaring air, blue water and blue sky. And then darkness.

CHAPTER TWO

THE BLUE STRINGS

Raphael "Riff" Starfire, blues musician extraordinaire, was playing his guitar onstage when the men who had murdered his mother walked into the club.

At least, he considered himself an extraordinary musician. Throughout the night, the crowd had seemed to think otherwise, pelting him with beer bottles, chicken bones, and once even a dwarf. But it was that kind of club. A place in the dregs of sprawling Cog City. Many folks claimed that the entire planet Earth was now the dregs, that the best of humanity had long since departed to the stars.

If Earth is a stain of puke on a rug, Riff thought, *The Blues Strings club is a coughed-up furball in its center.*

In addition to his guitar prowess, he also thought himself quite good at metaphors.

All sorts of sleaze filled the club most nights. Smugglers and bounty hunters sat at the back tables, faces scruffy and hair greasier than the burgers the Blue Strings served. Boozehounds hunched over the bar, their office clothes ruffled, their faces flushed and their cups going from empty to full and back again.

Old men in corduroy sat closer to the stage, smoking and sipping rye, bobbing their heads to the music. The old-timers--retired bootleggers and moonshiners--were usually the only ones who appreciated Riff's playing. Something about the blues, shuffleboard, and prune juice just seemed to appeal to the elderly.

But this night it wasn't just the usual assortment of riffraff that filled the shadowy club. This night, for the first time since Riff had begun playing here, Cosmians stepped into the Blue Strings.

Riff's playing died with a discordant note.

All across the club, men turned toward the new arrivals and fell silent. The dwarf, only just recovering from being tossed onstage, hid behind a chair.

"Cosmians," Riff muttered. "I hate these guys."

There were five of them, all clad in black robes and hoods. They could have passed for monks, if not for the heavy guns they carried, nasty things larger than the exhaust pipes of most starjets. The emblem of their order, a black planet with three moons, was embroidered on their chests--the distant planet of Skelkra.

Bloody nutters, Riff thought. The Cosmians were human, but they worshiped the skelkrins, ancient aliens that were probably just a myth. Riff had never been a religious man. His idea of a spiritual experience was hearing the music of his idols, legendary blues duo Bootstrap and the Shoeshine Kid. The idea of worshipping bloody *aliens* was downright disturbing.

His mother had thought the same.

His mother was now dead.

"Carry on, everyone!" said one of the Cosmians, his voice grainy. "We're only here to enjoy the music."

The man who spoke walked ahead of the other Cosmians, presumably their leader. With every step, metal clinked and machinery buzzed. Riff squinted, peering through the haze of cigarette smoke, and lost his breath.

Oh gods of blues, he thought.

A mechanical arm, tipped with steel claws, emerged from the Cosmian's sleeve. Within his black hood gleamed one human eye, one red mechanical orb.

"Grotter," Riff whispered.

He grimaced. The room spun around him. Riff was there again, thirty years ago. Only a boy. Only a terrified child. That mechanical claw was grabbing his mother, tugging her away. Riff screamed--only he wasn't Riff then, only a boy named Raphael. He tried to attack the Cosmian, to free his mother, yet that claw slammed against his face, cutting him, knocking him down, and his mother cried out and tried to reach him, but they dragged her back, and--

Riff clenched his fists.

But I'm no longer a child.

He touched the scar on his cheek--the scar Grotter's metal claws had left thirty years ago--then let his hand stray down toward Ethel, the gun he always kept on his hip.

Before he could draw, the ten Cosmians raised their heavy blasters toward him.

Riff let both hands return to his guitar.

"That's better," Grotter said, smiling thinly. "Now, Mr. Starfire, how about I buy you a drink and we talk?"

"Riff," he grunted.

Grotter took a step closer toward the stage. The light fell into his hood, revealing his disaster of a face. Half that face was missing, overlaid with metal, the eye a red lamp.

"Riff?" said the cyborg, raising his one eyebrow.

"My name. It's Riff. Nobody calls me anything else."

Riff doubted that Grotter remembered him. Thirty years ago, Riff had been only a kid, barely old enough to tie his own shoelaces. For decades now, Grotter and his goons had been terrorizing the poor neighborhoods of Cog City, preaching their worship of the skelkrins and, sometimes, visiting those who dared criticize their faith. Those people, like his mother, tended to disappear. To Grotter, Riff would have been just another pipsqueak kid.

But I never forgot you, Grotter.

Two Cosmians stepped forward, guns still raised, and grabbed Riff's shoulders. They dragged him off the stage to the sound of scattered applause. As the next performer stepped up-- an old saxophone player with one leg--the Cosmians manhandled Riff toward the bar and sat him down on a stool. Grotter reached down and pulled Riff's gun--the beloved old Ethel--out of its holster. The cyborg tucked the gun into his own belt.

"How about I buy you a drink, *Riff,* and we talk?" Grotter said, sitting down beside him.

Riff snorted. "They don't serve engine oil here."

The cyborg's red eye narrowed with clicking sounds like a camera's shutters. "Ah . . . a joke at the expense of my handicap."

Riff pointed a thumb over his shoulder toward where burly construction workers were tossing dwarves again, this time at Velcro targets. "In case you haven't noticed, we're not exactly politically correct at the Blue Strings. What do you want, Grotter? Don't you and your goons have any rally to shout at or books to burn?"

Grotter gestured toward the bartender, a blind old man in a rumpled suit and a fedora. Old Bat Brown had been a blues bassist before his fingers had begun to shake too much; he now poured drinks to the patrons. The nice thing about Bat Brown was that, with him blind, you never quite knew what drink you were going to get. Bat's method involved grabbing the first couple of bottles he could paw at. Tonight Riff found himself drinking a Memory Killer, a cocktail of Earth's most powerful spirits, which suited him fine. Memories were the last thing Riff needed now.

"You all right, Riff old buddy?" Bat Brown asked, cigarette dangling from his lips.

Riff passed a hand through his hair. "Yeah, Bat. Say, do me a favor, will you? Can you go make my bed for me?"

Grotter leaned forward on his stool, his mechanical parts creaking. "You have a blind bartender make your bed?"

Riff nodded. "Better than a maid, he is."

Bat Brown grinned, showing only four yellow teeth. "Prettier too. Off I go." With that, the old man grabbed his cane, left the bar, and made his way upstairs.

Grotter and the other Cosmians moved in closer, surrounding Riff. One of their guns poked him in the back. Riff felt a little like a stress ball in a cabbie's fist at rush hour--squeezed beyond comfort.

"Now, Riff," said Grotter, half his mouth smiling thinly; the other half was hiding behind metal. "It would be quite easy for my associates here to put a ball of plasma the size of my fist through your back. It would also be quite easy for you to walk out of this alive and well, back to your life of booze, shadows, and bad jazz."

"Blues," Riff said. "I play the blues."

"Quite." Grotter's smile flickered just the slightest. "All you must do to return to your . . . *blues* . . ." He spoke the word as if it were from a foreign language. ". . . is hand over the woman. We don't want you. We want her."

Riff raised an eyebrow. He looked over his shoulder, then back at Grotter. "*Woman?* Do you see any ladies in this place? Bloody hell, we haven't had a woman walk in here in twenty years. We even got that potpourri here on the bar--lovely jasmine scent, smell it!--and we put on pants and everything, but still no women stop by. Unless you mean Bubba over there." Riff pointed at a burly, bearded trucker who sat nearby, wearing a polka dot dress; the man waved back hopefully. "But I don't think he counts."

Grotter raised his mechanical hand. Joints creaked as the metal fingers flexed; each looked less like a human finger and more like the claw of a velociraptor. Riff winced, sure that Grotter would drive those claws into his throat. Instead, the cyborg thrust the mechanical hand down, closed his claws right around Riff's most sensitive bits, and began to squeeze.

Riff's eyes widened. "Let go! That's inappropriate, man!" He winced. "Though Bubba might appreciate it."

"Do you know, I lost half my face and my arm," Grotter said, squeezing tighter.

Riff winced. "Really? Haven't noticed."

Grotter's claws tightened just a smidgen further. Riff was starting to abandon any hope of ever producing mini-Riffs.

"Yet I kept the parts that make me a man," Grotter continued. "If you do not lead us to the woman, you will not be as fortunate. I know that your father sent the woman here."

"My father?" Riff laughed bitterly. "I haven't seen my father in a year. And I told you, there ain't no women here. I--ow!" His voice rose an octave. "The woman. Right! Uhm . . . I'll lead you to her. If you could just . . ." He gently pried the claws loose. "That's better. The woman. Follow me."

Riff rose from his barstool, gently pushed his way between the Cosmians, and made his way through the dingy club. Gristle Scotch was up on stage now, blundering his way through "Ain't Got No Moonshine Left," while Rumple McNally sat at his usual table, smoking ten cigarettes at once while tapping his feet to the beat. As Riff walked between the tables, the Cosmians marched behind him, and Riff was keenly aware of the guns pointing at his back.

His mind raced and cold sweat trickled down his back. Who was this woman? What were the Cosmians doing here? Those bastards mostly spent their time higher up in the city, bribing politicians, preaching on street corners, and roughing up anyone who dared criticize them. Riff had moved to this neighborhood to avoid this cult of alien-worshippers. Not to have Grotter himself, the very Cosmian who had dragged his mother to her death, show up on his turf.

I'm going to kill you someday, Grotter, Riff swore, his fingers itching to snatch Ethel, his beloved plasma gun, back from Grotter's belt.

They reached the back of the room. Two life-sized dolls with white whiskers and fedoras, sewn of cloth stuffed with straw, sat here at a chessboard. The two original players had died long ago, halfway through their year-long game, and Old Bat Brown had sewn the dolls himself as a tribute. Behind the frozen game, a staircase rose to the second floor where lived Old Bat Brown, a dog who had once wandered in, and Riff.

As Riff and the Cosmians began climbing upstairs, Bat Brown came hobbling down the staircase, tapping his cane.

"All right, Bat?" Riff said.

The blind old man smiled and nodded. "Bed's all made, Riff."

Riff and the Cosmians walked around the old man, climbing higher upstairs. They reached a hallway and Riff opened the doorway to his humble bedroom.

Most men Riff's age--he was about halfway through his thirties now--lived in nice houses, a pretty wife and pretty children at their side. Riff's only wife now hung across his back: Dora, his beloved guitar, signed by Bootstrap and the Shoeshine Kid themselves. Riff's only children now stood on his shelves: actual vinyl copies--real vinyl like in the stone age!--of the legendary duo's recordings. As for a nice house . . . well, his bedroom was small, and laundry covered the floor, but it was cozy, and it was home.

Riff frowned to see an envelope on his bedside table. The letter "A" was printed upon it in an ancient rune. His father's signature. The old magician never signed his full name, only that fanciful letter. When performing his magic tricks on street corners, he'd even have the "A" embroidered on his robe. Riff hadn't heard from the old man in over a year. Hurriedly, before the Cosmians could see, Riff grabbed the letter and stuffed it into his jeans pocket.

"There's no woman in here." Grotter sneered, entering the room behind Riff. "This displeases me."

Riff nodded. "I speak the exact same words whenever I step in here too."

With a sudden burst of speed, Riff leaped forward, bounded across the room, and jumped onto his bed.

A thousand buzzing metallic bedbugs blasted out from under the blanket, flying toward the Cosmians.

Old Bat Brown always kept a few bedbugs around the Blue Strings. The old man used them as gags--slipping one or two into Riff's bed when he was late on his rent, sometimes tossing a handful at patrons who stiffed him on a bill. In small numbers, they were harmless enough, just little metallic jaws snapping on springs.

A thousand flying at you was a little more intimidating.

The little jaws slammed into the Cosmians and began chomping.

Riff reached forward and yanked Ethel out of Grotter's belt.

The monks roared and began to fire their guns.

Plasma blasted through the room, tearing into the walls, knocking down records. Cosmians screamed as the bedbugs snapped at their robes, their hands, their faces. With a shout, the plasma flying around him, Riff hurled himself through the window.

He tumbled through the air and slammed down onto a pile of garbage bags outside.

He rose to his feet, fear pulsing through him, Ethel in his hand. Had the plasma hit the guitar that still hung across his back? Had the fall damaged it? It was signed by his idols, and--

Grotter appeared at the window, slung his gun over the sill, and began firing.

Riff shot a blast back at him, rolled off the garbage bags, and ran.

His arms pumped as he raced down the alley. Old bottles and cans rolled across the cracked asphalt, and laundry flapped on strings that stretched between the windows overhead. Mandy and Tammy, two young women who spent their nights here smoking cigarettes, screamed as he ran by.

"There's goddamn Cosmians after you, Riff!" cried Mandy, her pink hair standing on end. A blast of plasma flew between them, slamming into a wall.

"I know!" Riff shouted. "Little backup fire?"

The girls reached into their bottomless purses, pulled out guns the size of their arms, and began blasting.

"Now you owe me five bucks *and* your life!" Tammy shouted as he ran by.

Riff kept running, swerving to race down another alley as blasts hit the walls around him. He hooked Ethel over his shoulder and shot blindly while running; the plasma blasted out, searing hot. He leaped onto a garbage bin, vaulted through the air, and crashed through a string of laundry. He hit the ground running, found himself wearing a brassier, and tore it off with a curse. He kept racing, blasts tearing into lamp poles, walls, and fire hydrants around him.

He raced through an old warehouse that stored decommissioned bots, flipped their switches, and sent them racing behind him. He heard the Cosmians curse as they tripped over the metallic critters. Riff kept running and burst out into another alleyway, heading deep into the warren of the dregs.

Riff knew these streets. His mother had died when he'd been only five. His father had rarely been home, either performing his magic tricks on a street corner or, more often than not, traveling the galaxy on some mysterious quest. For thirty years now, Riff had been wandering these narrow streets, finding a home among the gin-soaked blues clubs, the boozehounds, and the old bot shops. Every corner, every doorway, every secret passage--Riff knew them, and soon he vanished into the labyrinth, leaving his pursuers behind.

Finally he barged out into a main boulevard. He leaned against a shop's wall, panting. Skyscrapers soared around him, hundreds of stories tall, their glass walls gleaming. Skyjets flitted among the towers, and a massive airship hovered above, blocking the moon. People rushed back and forth, bustling like they always did in Cog City, this hive of humanity that still lingered on the home planet while the best of the race had long since departed to the stars.

Sweat soaked Riff. The Cosmians were gone. Before checking himself for wounds, he unslung the guitar case off his back. His breath caught when he opened it, and his pulse quickened.

He blew out a shaky sigh of relief.

"You're all right, Dora, my sweetness," he whispered, caressing the guitar within.

It was a red electric guitar, the kind humans had been playing for thousands of years. An ancient, mystical instrument. A bringer of blues. And upon its surface, with black ink, appeared its runes of power: the signatures of Bootstrap and the Shoeshine Kid themselves, legendary heroes of music. Riff closed the guitar case as if sealing a holy relic and slung it across his back.

He stood on the street, head still reeling. A thousand questions raced through his head. Why were the Cosmians, worshippers of aliens, after him? Who was this woman they thought he was hiding? Where was his father?

The immediate question was: Where did Riff go now? He certainly couldn't return to the Blue Strings. With a sinking heart, Riff realized he might never be able to return to that club, the place that had been his only home for years.

His heart sank even deeper when he realized there was only one place he could go now.

"I'll have to go see Nova."

He winced. The Cosmians had scarred his cheek years ago. Nova had scarred his heart. Yet right now, she was the only person who could help him. For the first time in two years, he would have to seek her out . . . and hope that she helped. She was, Riff thought, just as likely to rip out his throat.

He gulped and nodded.

He would seek out Nova, his ex-girlfriend . . . probably the most dangerous person on the planet.

CHAPTER THREE
ALIEN ARENA

Riff walked through the crowd of roaring, pot-bellied drunkards toward the Alien Arena, the most blood-soaked place on the planet.

Some factions on Earth, such as Friends of Aliens, preached tolerance and acceptance of creatures from the stars. Others, like the Cosmians, worshipped them as gods. Not here. People came to the Alien Arena not to befriend, worship, or study aliens . . . but to watch them bash one another's brains out.

Riff sighed. "And Nova calls the Blue Strings a pit."

The arena rose ahead of him, looking like some giant, steel bird's nest which had fallen from the sky. It was all rusty beams, spikes, leaking water spouts, and blinding spotlights. Neon lights blinked above the main doors, spelling out "Alien Are a", missing the *n*.

Thousands of people clogged the streets, heading toward the arena. Almost all were men, a sort so rough they made even the Blue Strings' patrons seem gentlemanly. Riff had never seen so many hairy shoulders, scruffy beards, and beer can hats in one place. The smoke of cigarettes and cigars stung his eyes. The smell of cheap booze infiltrated Riff's nostrils; at least half the men here were drinking home brew from paper bags. There wasn't even any decent blues playing. The arena's speakers were blasting out old rock 'n' roll, the sound so distorted Riff couldn't make out the tune.

A few people had set up soapboxes in the crowd. One woman lifted a "Friends of Aliens" banner, shouting that aliens were to be loved and accepted, not gawked at. An old man stood on another soapbox, crying out that "illegal aliens" were an abomination, that only humans belonged on Earth. On a third box stood a Cosmian monk, preaching about the "skelkrin masters." Riff grimaced and made sure to steer clear of that last soapbox.

A voice roared out from the arena's speakers, rising louder than the music and street preachers: "Tonight only--Nova, the fiery Ashai Assassin, vs. Brog, the Behemoth of Belethor! The battle of the ages at the Alien Arena! Only fifteen bucks a ticket!"

Riff reached into his jeans pocket, rummaging for money. His hand brushed against the rumpled envelope he had found in his room, the one from his father. Riff decided to keep it unopened for now. It was too dark here to read, and besides, Riff wanted to be alone when reading the first communication from his father in a year. Somehow, that moment seemed too important to share with ten thousand roaring, overweight drunkards in sweat-soaked wifebeaters. Riff pushed his hand deeper into his pocket and fished out the last money he had in the world: a crumpled twenty-credit note.

Riff approached a scalper--a ratty little man with metal legs--and bought a ticket and a hot dog. The meat tasted like it probably came from the arena's last loser, but Riff was hungry enough that he ate the whole thing, ignoring his stomach's churning protests. He walked with the crowd, entering the arena.

A few years ago, Riff had owned an old car with a grungy engine that belched out smoke and constantly leaked oil. He imagined that if he shrank in size and stepped into that engine, he'd find a place that looked like the Alien Arena. The arena's insides made the exterior look downright classy. Tiers of iron bleachers rose in a circle, the metal stained with years of spit, gum, cigarette ash, and spat-up hot dogs. Thousands of people filled the place, their shirts just as stained--at least those who wore shirts.

Disk-shaped drones buzzed over the bleachers, tasked with both selling refreshments and providing security. On their flat tops, they carried bottles of beer, bags of popcorn, and dripping cheeseburgers. From their bottom sides, like legs under crabs, stretched out machine guns. One drunkard waved at a scuttling drone.

"You, drone!" the fat man shouted, reached into his pocket, and pelted the flying machine with spare change. "Cheeseburger!"

The flying drone spun toward the drunkard, spilling popcorn off its top. "Attack detected! Attack detected!"

The drone's machine guns unfurled and sprayed bullets. The drunkard wailed and dived for cover. The bullets slammed into the bleachers, blasting holes into the metal.

"Attacker destroyed," the drone announced, then dived down to sell a lollipop to a squealing little girl.

Riff walked along the bleachers, looking for a seat. It was a busy night. Even a few aliens sat in the crowd. A family of green, tentacled creatures with many eyestalks sat nearby, drinking from buckets of *glag*--a thick brew made from the fermented intestinal juices of Velurian rock spiders. Farther back sat a hulking, translucent blob, the contents of its stomach--a few burgers, a whole turkey, and a pair of sneakers--visible to all. Most humans seemed to give the alien visitors a wide berth. People didn't come here to socialize with aliens but to watch them fight on stage.

A round metal grill surrounded that stage like glass around a snow globe, forming a great cage. A little man stood within the enclosure, his hair bright yellow, his suit a garish monstrosity of green and orange stripes. He spoke into his microphone, and speakers blared across the arena.

"Ladies and gentlemen, welcome to tonight's match! We bring you another battle of the ages between two of the galaxy's most ruthless alien killers!"

Riff wasn't sure any ladies *or* gentlemen filled the place, but nobody seemed to mind. The crowd roared, and Riff found a seat and sat down. The emcee continued.

"Now, in the blue corner--he comes to us from the pits of Planet Belethor in the Vega constellation. The Consumer of Worlds. The Crusher of Souls. The Behemoth of Bloodshed. Raise your voices for Brog the Bonecruncher!"

The crowd roared as doors opened, and the first alien trundled toward the stage.

"It's huge." Riff gulped. "It's bloody huge. It's a mountain with eyes."

The living mountain trundled forward on thick, clawed legs that made elephant feet seem dainty. Warty gray hide covered its body, making rhinoceros armor seem as thin as the transparent skin of a baby fish. The creature was so tall it would make giraffes seem short, and it was just as wide. Its massive fists dragged along the floor, each larger than a curled-up man. When the beast reached the stage, it opened its mouth wide, revealing fangs longer than human arms. It roared, strings of saliva quivering between its teeth.

"It's going to crush her." Riff grimaced. "It's going to crumple Nova into a ball."

As the behemoth roared to the sound of applause, the emcee spoke again into his microphone. "And now, in the red corner! She comes to us from Planet Ashmar, the daughter of a warrior king. The Princess of Pain. The Mistress of Mayhem. The Beauty of Bloodletting. Welcome Nova the Ashai Assassin!"

Hard rock music blared out of the speakers, deafeningly loud. Engines roared. The crowd roared just as loudly. With a shower of sparks and smoke, a golden motorcycle, shaped as a scorpion, raced up a ramp and onto the stage.

Nova straddled the bike. The young woman wore a golden catsuit sewn from *kaijia*, an alien fabric that was thin as silk but strong as armor. A black scorpion sigil raised its stinger upon her chest. Her green eyes shone, and pointy ears thrust out from her long blond hair like antennae. Her lips peeled back in a snarl, and she cracked a golden whip that shot out sparks of electricity. She let out a roar that shook the arena, and even the great behemoth, many times her size, took a step back.

"That's my girlfriend," Riff said to the man beside him, a slob sipping from two cans of beer attached to his hat. The drunkard nodded appreciatively.

At least, she used to be my girlfriend before I took my brother's side in their feud. Riff sighed.

Nova pushed down on the throttles, and her bike roared and raced right up the rounded wire mesh that surrounded the stage. She did a full loop, for an instant riding upside down along the cage ceiling, then halted her bike before the behemoth. She cracked her whip again. Sparks showered.

"I am Nova of Ashmar!" she cried to the crowd. "I will tame this beast! For fire and venom!"

Thousands of years ago, Riff knew from the books, humanity had spread to the stars. Most of those starships had been full of scientists, engineers, philosophers--peaceful colonists. But one starship had been full of soldiers, and on the fiery planet of Ashmar, they had formed a new nation. Since then, living in the harsh conditions of Ashmar, they had evolved into a subspecies of humanity. The books now catalogued them as *homo sapiens ashai*. They weren't technically aliens, but not quite human either, not anymore--which was good enough for the Alien Arena. Across the galaxy, the ashais were famous. Warriors of legend. Fighters of pride and bloodlust.

Just the type you'd want on your side when chased by a maniacal cyborg monk and his henchmen.

As the crowd roared, the behemoth swung one of its massive fists; the thing was nearly as large as Nova's entire motorbike. The ashai gladiator pushed down on the throttle, and her bike roared forward and raced up the cage wall. As she drove overhead, upside down, she lashed her whip. The thong slammed against the behemoth's head, and blood sprayed. The beast wailed. Nova drove her bike back down onto the stage, swung her whip again, and blasted out sparks that slammed into the towering alien.

The beast wailed.

"Down!" Nova shouted and cracked her whip. "Down, behemoth!"

Her whip shot out more sparks, slamming again into the alien, knocking it back against the cage wall.

Riff turned to the man at his other side. "Did you hear? That's my girlfriend."

The fight didn't last long. The behemoth kept swinging its fists, but Nova kept riding her bike within the cage, driving up walls, along the ceiling, crisscrossing the floor. Her whip lashed in a frenzy, its sparks slamming against the alien, cutting into its skin. Finally, as her bike roared forward, Nova leaped right from her seat. She soared a dozen feet into the air, cried out, and drove her whip down hard.

The lash slammed into the behemoth's forehead.

The alien groaned and tilted forward.

Nova landed back on her motorcycle's seat and spun around in time to see her opponent crash down, unconscious.

The crowd grumbled, disappointed that the fight was so short. A few grumbled louder than others, handing over sweaty wads of cash to gloaters. Another pair of aliens approached the stage to fight--a slime devil with many eyestalks and a clattering isopod with a bright purple exoskeleton. Ignoring this fight, Riff left his seat and elbowed his way through the crowd, moving down the bleachers.

As the slimer and isopod faced off, Riff walked down a ramp toward Nova's dressing room.

Her bodyguard stood outside the door, a hulking alien who looked like a living granite boulder. Riff could not begin to imagine what star system this creature came from. He was not a short man, yet this stony brute dwarfed him.

"I'm here to see Nova." Riff cleared his throat. "I'm her boyfriend. If you'll step aside, good man--I mean, good . . . rock?-- I shall much appreciate it."

The living boulder grabbed Riff and yanked him off the ground. A crack in the stony countenance opened, and words rumbled out. "Go away."

Riff coughed. "Lovely breath. I detect mint, a hint of cherry wine, and possum carcass. Now please, put me down, and--"

The bodyguard tossed Riff a good ten feet, slamming him into several onlookers. Riff winced and struggled back to his feet.

"Watch it, buddy! Carrying a signed guitar here." Riff stepped back toward the rocky brute and leaned around the creature. "Nova! Nova, you in there? It's Riff. Call down your pet rock and talk to me."

The bodyguard turned toward the door. Riff waited expectantly.

Nova's voice rose from behind the door. "Voora, crush his skull."

The living boulder grinned and took a step toward Riff, reaching out paws the size of dinner plates.

Riff gulped. "Nova, this is important! I'm in trouble, all right? I need your help."

Her voice rose again from behind the door. "Voora, after crushing his skull, tear off a limb or two. You deserve a treat."

Riff scurried back as Voora advanced. "Nova, this is serious! It's about the man who killed my mother, all right? He's after me now, and--God!"

The massive, living boulder lifted Riff right over its head. The stony fingers dug into him. The brute was about to crush Riff, but Nova's door swung open.

"Voora, wait." Nova stood in the doorway, eyes narrowed. "Put the bastard down. Let him in. I'll crush his skull myself."

With a grumble like rolling stones, the living boulder lowered Riff to the floor. Before Riff could regain his balance, Nova grabbed his collar, yanked him into her chamber, and closed the door.

Her dressing room could put most armories to shame, Riff thought. Dozens of weapons hung on the walls: electric rods, laser blasters, plasma spears, mechanical axes. A hundred guns or more rose upon racks. The skulls of defeated enemies gazed from shelves. Her motorbike stood in the center of the room, a great golden scorpion, its stinger raised as if ready to strike.

Some women collected decorative plates. Others collected cats. Nova collected pain and death.

"Mind if I borrow a couple of these?" Riff grabbed two plasma chargers from a shelf. "My Ethel's low on ammo, and--"

Her whip lashed out and wrapped around his wrist. She glared at him. "What do you want, Riff? I told you never to speak to me again."

He winced and pulled the whip off his wrist. It left an ugly mark, but luckily Nova hadn't turned on its electricity. If she pressed the button on the handle, that whip would be more than a lash; it would conduct enough electricity to knock out an elephant.

"Nova, I'm sorry. All right?" He stuffed the plasma packs into his pocket, then held out his open palms. "What else can I say?"

Riff had once read a very old book of mythology titled *The Lord of the Rings*. The ashais reminded him a little of the elves, at least in appearance: slender and beautiful with almond eyes, flowing golden hair, and big pointy ears. But the resemblance ran skin deep. Tolkien's elves had been creatures of grace, wisdom, and nobility, while Nova was . . . well, about as graceful as an enraged wolverine with a thorn in its backside. Facing him, Nova spat right on his face. She grabbed his collar and sneered, a wild animal.

"No!" she shouted. "No, you cannot do this to me, Riff. Gods damn you! After the shit you pulled, you do not come back into my life like this, broke, thugs on your tail, smelling of cheap booze."

"It's not my booze!" Riff objected. "Some drunkard spilled it on me. Guy was drinking beer out of his hat."

Nova growled and shoved him against the wall. "It's always somebody else's fault with you, isn't it? Always somebody else to blame." Suddenly tears filled her eyes, and her voice rose louder. "I left my planet for you, Riff! I disobeyed my father--the damn king of Ashmar. I disobeyed him to come to this stinking planet with you. With a man whom I thought loved me."

"I do love you," Riff said, voice soft now. "I never stopped. I--"

She slapped him. Hard.

"I don't need to hear your shit. Lies. Always lies with you. When are you going to grow up, Riff? When are you going to take some responsibility for yourself? I haven't seen you in two years." The tears were now flowing down her cheeks. "And this is how you show up. When you need me. That's all you ever care about-- what others can do for you. Never what I want. Never what's important to me." She laughed mirthlessly and turned away. "Same old Riff."

He stood, his back to the wall, and lowered his head. The guilt filled him, and suddenly he felt about as worthwhile as a sack of alien slime.

She's right, he realized.

He stepped closer to her and placed a hand on her shoulder. He didn't know if she could feel him through her armor. The golden *kaijia* fabric was thin, clinging to her body, but Riff knew it could stop bullets and plasma blasts. Even with his hand on her shoulder, he felt as distant from her as if she wore armor of thick metal plates.

"I'm sorry, Nova." His voice was soft. "I feel like shit."

She spun around to face him. "That's how you made me feel these whole past two years."

Ouch. That one hurt.

"Nova, the Cosmians are after me. I think my dad's involved. And . . ." Riff's throat tightened. "One of them killed my mother, Nov. You know that. And now the same guy, some bastard cyborg named Grotter, is trying to kill me. He knows where I live. I need a place to crash, at least until I can figure things out. I didn't know where else to go. I haven't seen my dad for a year, and all my friends just live at the Blue Strings or the alleys around them."

He was careful not to mention his brother, Steel. Riff's last big fight with Nova--the one that had finally shattered their fragile relationship--had been over Steel. If he mentioned his brother now, Riff was likely to toss Nova into another rage.

He sighed. As angry as Nova was, a meeting with Steel would be even worse. Best not to even think about his brother now.

Nova sighed too. "I'll let you crash on my couch for tonight. Just tonight! Tomorrow morning, I want you gone."

He nodded. "Deal." It was as good a deal as he was going to get, he knew.

She opened the back door, revealing a tunnel, and tossed Riff a ring of keys. "You drive the bike. You still remember where I live?"

He nodded. Of course he did. He climbed onto the bike and let his guitar rest against his hip. Nova climbed onto the seat behind him and wrapped her arms around his waist. And by the stars above, it felt good. Just at the touch of her body against him, memories flooded Riff: him and her flying across the galaxy, heading back from her planet to a new life on Earth; long days riding this very bike down highways, trees rustling at their sides; and long nights making love in his bed at the Blue Strings.

Riff sighed. *But I could never give her the life she needs.*

Nova was a princess of Ashmar, and he was just a bluesman who lived in a run-down club. Their confrontation over Steel had been only the last straw. Was it any wonder Nova had found a better life, a life without him? She lived in a fancy building now, and she performed for crowds of thousands, while he was still stuck living in the same dump, playing the same old tunes to the same old drunkards.

Her talking pet rock would probably make a better boyfriend than I ever was, Riff thought.

He turned the keys, and the motorbike roared to life. The golden scorpion shot forward, blasting out of the dressing room and into the tunnel. Nova's arms tightened around Riff's waist.

The tunnel took them straight to the 707, a highway outside the arena. Most folk flew their small, slick aerocars above, but Nova had always preferred driving on the road. There were fewer people down here, a chance to move faster, to feel the tarmac against the tires, the jostle of every bump on the road. It was an old way to travel. It was freedom.

They streamed down the highway, skyscrapers rising alongside, aerocars zipping back and forth above. The engine roared louder than any guitar Riff had ever played. The wind whipped his face. The 707 was massive, twenty lanes wide, rising above Cog City like a great concrete ribbon. Beneath the road, thousands of poor folk lived in hovels of scrap metal and tarpaulin, a sub-city lurking in the shadows like barnacles clinging to the bottom of ships. Alongside the road, electric billboards cast out blinding lights, advertising *Android Girlfriends for You!*, *Happy Cow's Shawarma*, and *Cheap Bail Bonds, No Credit Checks!* One billboard made Riff shudder; it showed the Cosmian sigil over the silhouette of a skelkrin, urging motorists to "Donate Now for a Skelkrin Earth." Riff quickly looked away, breathing a sigh of relief as they rode past the sign.

He took the exit off to Dune Plaza, one of the city's wealthiest neighborhoods. No shantytowns lurked under the roads here, and the billboards advertised perfumes, jewelry, and pricey cyborg implants guaranteed to enhance, invigorate, and tantalize. Here was a place where rich businessmen, entertainers, and leaders lived in splendor. A place of green parks, glass towers, statues, fountains. A far cry from the dregs where Riff lived.

Finally he saw Serenity Tower ahead, a great structure of white steel and glass that soared skyward, its balconies topped with lush gardens. Nova's new home.

Sure beats the dump I made her live in, Riff thought.

He slowed down the bike. He was heading toward the parking lot when he saw the black starjets idling out front.

Riff sucked in air. Most people on Earth rode in aerocars, small flying vessels that couldn't breach the atmosphere. But here were starjets--small, two-seater vessels that could fly in both air and space. A dark planet with three moons, symbol of the Cosmians, was emblazoned onto their hulls. Inside one of the starjet's cockpits, a red eye blazed.

Grotter.

CHAPTER FOUR
HOLES ON THE HIGHWAY

"Oh shenanigans!" Riff said, spinning the motorbike around.

Before he could complete the turn, the black starjets came blasting forward.

"What the frag?" Nova shouted, clinging to him.

"Cosmians!" Riff shouted, pushing down on the throttle. The golden scorpion roared down the street, heading back to the highway. "Damn Grotter tracked us here."

"Riff, you son of a bitch!" Nova clutched her whip. "I live here!"

"I know! They knew I'd come here for you." They blasted down the road, swerving between cars. "They're tenacious bastards. I--"

A blast of plasma roared and slammed into the road beside them. Another blast shot overhead, nearly searing Riff's hair.

"Fragging aardvarks!" Nova twisted around in the seat and lashed her whip. When Riff looked in the mirror, he saw the thong blast out electricity. The bolts slammed into one of the black starjets chasing them, cracking its cockpit. Three other starjets roared down the road in pursuit, hovering a foot above the tarmac, and three more flew above, raining down their plasma.

One blast slammed down onto the road ahead of Riff. With a curse, he swerved, nearly fell over, and kept riding. Behind him in the seat, Nova swung her whip again. Lightning bolts flashed out and slammed into a Cosmian starjet above. The vessel, several times the size of the Golden Scorpion, crashed down onto the road before them. Riff screamed, swerved madly, and managed to drive right onto the downed aircraft's wing. He shot up the ramp, soared above the hull, and slammed back down onto the road.

"Riff, some firepower would be nice!" Nova shouted, swinging her whip again and again.

He cursed. Struggling to control the motorbike with one hand, he drew Ethel from its holster. A starjet streamed overhead, dipped in the sky, and came charging toward them. Riff dodged a charge of plasma, fired his gun, and blasted a hole into the starjet.

He roared up a ramp and onto the 707. All around him, the Cosmian starjets still screamed. Plasma rained, shattering the road. Riff swerved around another hole, nearly tipped over, and managed to keep charging forward. He fired his gun again, aiming at the starjets' engines. Nova lashed her whip. Plasma, gunfire, and lightning bolts lit the night. A few police cars raced forward, seemed to notice the Cosmian sigils on the starjets, and quickly turned away; Grotter and his gang owned too many politicians and police brass.

The bastards are so well connected, Riff thought, *they could nuke half of Cog City without the police even clucking their tongues.*

"Where'd you learn how to fire that gun?" Nova demanded. "Aim, frag it!"

He spat and fired again, missing another starjet. "I'm trying to drive your damn scorpion at the same time!"

A starjet screeched overhead, swerved ahead of them, and landed on the road. It came charging toward them.

"Press the golden button!" Nova screamed.

"What?"

"Do it!"

Riff noticed a golden button on the bike's controls; he had thought it just a decoration. Now he pressed down with all his might.

In the mirror, he saw the scorpion's golden tail rise.

It blasted out a sphere of yellow energy.

The beam slammed into the starjet ahead, splitting it in two. Riff screamed as the motorbike raced through the wreckage. They drove through flame, flew into the air, and slammed back down onto the highway.

"I need to get a bike like this," Riff muttered, sweat dripping into his eyes.

Two more starjets still flew behind them. Nova swung her whip, blasting out electricity, knocking one jet down. It crashed onto the highway, veered offside, and slammed into a building. A blast from Riff's gun sent the other crashing down.

The Golden Scorpion drove on, its engine rattling. A scrap of loose metal scraped along the highway, raising sparks. The Cosmians were gone.

"Nova, is my guitar all right?" Riff said, twisting around to see. "Can you check?"

"Your *guitar*?" Her face twisted with rage. "They blasted my bike full of holes, you idiot! They were waiting outside my home. My home, Riff! What kind of trouble did you get me into?"

I wish I knew, Riff thought, driving onward down the highway.

He kept driving through the night. The 707 led them past several more kilometers of skyscrapers, then finally out of Cog City and into open country. Soon corn, wheat, and meat factories rose at their sides--towering metal buildings where grains, steaks, and burgers grew in boxes. The stars shone above. Riff looked skyward, wondering which star was Skelkra, home of the skelkrins, that cursed place the Cosmians worshipped. He wondered too which star Planet Ashmar orbited around--the place he had visited years ago, the place where he had met Nova . . . the place they had left together in better days. Yet driving here, all the stars seemed the same to him, distant specks, out of reach.

When dawn began to rise, Riff could no longer see the city behind him. He pulled over onto a dirt side road. Grass and shrubs rose around them, rustling in the wind, as morning's light spread across the sky.

Nova climbed off the bike too. She stood for a long time, staring into the distance, silent.

Finally she spoke in a strained voice, not turning to face Riff. "Why are they after you?"

"I don't know." He took a deep breath. "Grotter--he's the gang leader--showed up at my club. Was asking questions about a woman. What woman, I have no idea. Somebody he's after, somebody he thinks I'm sheltering." He reached into his pocket and felt the letter from his father, the letter he hadn't had a chance to open yet, the letter he felt he should be alone to read. "Grotter's the bastard who murdered my mother."

Was Grotter dead now? Had he burned in the wreckage of a crashed starjet? Riff didn't know, but until he saw a body, he would nurse his hatred, and he would stay on his toes.

Nova turned toward him. Soot stained her golden, form-fitting armor and her long blond hair. She narrowed her eyes. "Why? What happened back then?"

Riff sighed, the old pain digging through him. The scar on his cheek suddenly hurt again. "You know what the Cosmians believe, don't you?"

Nova spat. "Skelkrin worshippers. My people fought the skelkrins once, years ago. They're nasty buggers. As warlike as us ashais but without honor. Cruel. Murderous."

"And Grotter and his gang worship them as gods. Call them superior beings. The Cosmians have a guy leading them--they call him the Seer--who preaches that the skelkrins will bring salvation to Earth. My mother spoke against them. She held rallies protesting the Cosmians and their plan to bring the skelkrins here. One day, when I was only five years old, Grotter showed up at our house. The Seer leads the Cosmians from a hideout; Grotter leads the brutes on the street. He grabbed my mother. When I tried to stop him, he gave me this." Riff touched the scar on his cheek. "He dragged my mother off to a prison his goons run. She came back to us a year later in a body bag."

Nova lowered her green eyes, and her face softened. She stepped closer, embraced Riff, and laid her head against his shoulder. "I'm sorry, Riff. You never told me."

He nodded. "And now Grotter's back. Looking for somebody. And somehow I'm involved, and now you're involved, and . . ."

He hesitated. He knew that what he had to say would toss Nova right back into her rage. He rather liked her embracing him. It was definitely nicer than the yelling, hitting Nova.

But his words, even if they enraged her, had to be spoken.

He took a deep breath and braced himself.

"Nova, they might be after my brother too. We have to go see Steel. Now."

As expected, Nova stepped back from him, and rage suffused her face. Her long, pointy ears reddened.

"No." She spat onto the roadside and squared her shoulders. "Just no. Not Steel."

Riff took a deep breath. Two years ago, Steel--always the man of stiff honor--had spent long moments lecturing Nova, telling her that a proper lady wore gowns, never cussed, and certainly did not spit. It had tossed Nova into a rage such as Riff had never seen. The ashai had nearly torn out Steel's throat, cursing and spitting all over his "antiquated" code of morality.

"Look." Riff reached out to Nova as the grass rustled around them. "I know Steel is a bit old-fashioned, but--"

"Old-fashioned!" Nova shouted, scaring crows out of a nearby oak. "My motorbike is old-fashioned. Grandfather clocks are old-fashioned. Your brother is a fragging dinosaur!" She laughed bitterly. "Who does he think he is, calling himself a knight? Knights died off thousands of years ago. The code of honor he speaks of was obsolete in the Stone Age. I'm not setting foot anywhere near that old relic with his righteous, sanctimonious rubbish."

The words shot pain through Riff's chest. He himself had often clashed with his brother. Many times, Steel had lectured Riff too, railing against the blues and booze that filled Riff's life. But damn it, Riff still loved the guy. Steel was his younger brother. Only a year younger, but a baby brother nonetheless.

"Nova, he's still family." He stepped closer to her. "And he might be in danger."

Nova raised her fist. "The only danger he's in is of me pounding his brains out."

"Nova! Please listen. If the Cosmians are going after the people close to me, they'll go after Steel too. He might need our help. If the Cosmians fly to his castle, he's likely to challenge them to a duel and die in their plasma fire. We drive up there. We check on him. We figure out what's next from there. Will you go with me?"

She tugged her hair, tossed back her head, and let out a roar. "Fine!" She glared at him. "But if he lectures me again, I'm still pounding his brains out."

They climbed back onto the scorpion motorbike. They roared down the highway through the dawn. As they drove closer and closer toward Steel's home, the fear only grew inside Riff.

Where was his father? Who was the woman the Cosmians wanted? And once he reached Steel's castle . . . would he find his brother alive and well, or would he find a corpse?

CHAPTER FIVE

STEEL AND RUST

Riding through the countryside, Riff and Nova could see the castle from kilometers away. Like a Rigelian howler beetle in a bowl of soup, it was hard to miss.

Growing up, Riff had heard of castles. He had seen models of them in museums alongside spears, mammoth tusks, dinosaur bones, and other relics of the ancient days. As far as he knew, Steel Starfire, his little brother, was the only person left in the cosmos who still lived in one.

Granted, this hilltop castle looked a little different from the models Riff had seen. First of all, it wasn't much larger than a typical city apartment, barely large enough to house one person, let alone the army that most castles would contain. Secondly, the old castles Riff had seen had been built of stone. This one was half metal, a mishmash of bricks, iron plates, and spikes all bolted together. Steel had built it himself a few years back, spending an entire summer on the task.

Sir Steel Starfire was many things, but an architect he was not. The castle looked like it could barely withstand a herd of charging sheep, let alone a charging army.

Or charging Cosmians, Riff thought, stomach curdling.

The scorpion motorbike rattled along the dirt road--there were no paved roads out here--leaving the factory farms and heading up the grassy hill. Scattered elms and oaks rustled around them. Birds flittered overhead and white clouds floated in a blue sky. If not for the men out there trying to kill him, Riff might have almost felt at peace.

When he crested the hilltop, his brief moment of serenity shattered.

A large Cosmian starjet, several times the size of city jets, hovered outside the castle of iron and stone. Several of the cult's goons, clad in black hoods and robes, stood outside in the grass, guns raised.

Before them, protecting his castle, stood Steel Starfire.

Steel was a year younger than Riff, but he looked a decade older. His long years of solitude, of pain over the corruption of his order, had left him with a lined face, with graying temples, with sad-yet-hardened eyes. His long brown mustache, his pride and joy, drooped all the way down to his chin.

Though banished from the Knights of Sol for daring to speak against its lords, Steel still wore his old armor: thick, bright plates of ancient steel. In his gloved hands, he still held his old weapon, a massive antique sword named Solflare. Since his banishment, Steel could no longer wear the sigil of the Knights of Sol upon his breastplate, and he could no longer call himself "sir." But standing outside his castle, facing his enemies with calm determination, he seemed a knight through and through.

"Who the frag still uses a sword these days?" Nova muttered as their motorbike screeched to a halt outside the castle. "Swords are for crusty old dinosaurs."

The Cosmians noticed the new arrivals. They spun back and forth between Steel, Riff, and Nova, guns raised, as if uncertain who posed the greater threat.

If Steel noticed his brother and the ashai gladiator arrive, he gave no sign of it. The gaunt knight raised his sword, and he spoke in a deep voice, a voice yearning for days of old.

"By my honor as a Starfire, by my honor as a Knight of Sol, I challenge you to battle. For Sol!"

Shouting out those last words as a battle cry, Steel raced toward the enemy.

The Cosmian monks all spun toward him, forgetting about Riff and Nova, and fired their guns.

Steel swung his massive sword, deflecting one blast of plasma. Another blast slammed into the knight's chest, dispersing across his armor like waves around a tor.

Steel thrust his sword forward. Light streamed across the blade and blasted out in a great beam. The ray slammed into one monk, tearing a hole through his body.

Nova stared with wide eyes. "I want a sword."

Riff raised his gun and aimed at a monk. "For now use your whip!"

He fired. His blast slammed into a monk, knocking the man down. At his side, Nova cracked her whip. A lightning bolt flew from the tip, slamming into a second monk.

Three monks knelt, turned toward Riff and Nova, and began blasting.

Riff cursed, ducked behind the scorpion bike, and leaned over the seat. He fired his gun, his blasts leaving trails of rippling air. He hit one monk. Another Cosmian fired his gun, and the blast slammed into the motorbike, shoving it against Riff. Sparks showered. Riff fired again and hit the man.

Nova meanwhile stood in the open, flailing her whip. A bolt of plasma flew toward her, and she ducked backward, letting it stream above her chest and head. Another blast flew toward her feet, and she rolled sideways, leaped back up, and swung her whip. Lightning flew from the golden lash, streamed through the air, and slammed into another monk. The man cried out as his robes burst into flame.

Closer to the castle, Steel was swinging Solflare in wide arcs. The blade deflected one plasma blast. Another slammed into Steel's armor and ricocheted, tearing a hole into the grass. The knight refused to dodge for cover but advanced, taking the monks head-on. He thrust his sword forward again, casting another beam of white energy. The light slammed into a monk, tearing through him. The body thumped onto the grass. Another monk, out of ammunition, charged forward, screaming. A swing of Steel's sword cut him down.

The last two monks cursed and leaped into their black, oversized starjet.

The vessel began to rise into the air.

Its guns began to glow red, aimed right at Steel and his castle.

Riff fired his gun.

His blasts shot out, slamming into the starjet's engines.

Fire roared. The starjet swirled madly in the air. Its guns fired, slamming into the castle. Bricks rained. Metal sheets bent and crashed down.

Riff fired his gun again. Nova swung her whip, casting out lightning.

The projectiles hit the starjet, and it exploded into countless chunks of metal.

A hail of fire and scrap metal pattered against the grass.

The last of the Cosmians was dead.

Riff straightened from behind the bike. The battle had burnt a hole in his jeans, and shrapnel had drawn an ugly red line across his arm, but he was otherwise unharmed. Nova stood among the wreckage, brushing burning scraps off her golden armor; the ashai material showed not a scratch. Steel's armor was blackened and dented, but otherwise the knight seemed no worse for the wear.

"Hello, little brother!" Riff grinned and walked through the wreckage toward him. "Seems like I popped by just in the nick of time."

The tall, gaunt knight regarded him, eyes blank. He passed his fingers through his drooping mustache, brushing out the ash; Steel loved that mustache like Riff loved his guitar and Nova loved her motorbike. The knight turned toward his castle, and his jaw twitched.

A great hole, large enough to ride a horse through, gaped open in the castle wall. Ash rained from its rims. Fire burned inside, spreading across austere furniture.

Steel spoke in a low, haunted voice. "The homestead burns. I have failed to defend my castle." He tossed back his head and cried out in anguish. "What kind of knight am I, a knight who could not even protect his fortress?"

Riff stepped closer and cleared his throat. "Well, not a knight at all, really." He tapped his brother's breastplate where the old symbol of his order, the Knights of Sol, had been scratched off. "They banished you from the brotherhood, remember?"

Steel turned those brown, sad eyes toward him--those eyes that seemed so much older and wiser than his years. The eyes of an old man. "The measure of a knight, my brother, lies not in titles, not in sigils, but in his heart. In honor. In chivalry. In great deeds upon the battlefield. My lords have fallen to corruption, and thus my sigil was stripped away, yet the honor still pumps in my heart, and the pride of nobility still flows through my veins. No man can take those from me."

Nova stepped forward, coiling up her whip. "You're talking shite, Steel." She hawked noisily, spat, and scratched her backside. "Still a bloody loony, you are."

The knight turned his hound dog eyes upon her. "And I see that you are still a refined, delicate lady."

She snorted. "To hell with that. I'm a warrior, Steel." She sneered. "A true warrior of Planet Ashmar, not some relic."

He tilted his head. "And yet, last I heard, Planet Ashmar exiled you, same as my order exiled me. Perhaps we're both relics, my lady."

"I ain't a lady." She glared.

He bowed his head toward her. "Perhaps you spit, curse, and show me no respect, yet my honor demands that I treat you as a lady. For I am a knight. And I'm sworn to defend all damsels in distress."

Nova gasped, rage blazing in her eyes, and cracked her whip. Lightning bolts flared out. "A damsel in distress? Do I look like I'm in distress to you, knight? I'm going to show you who the damsel is. I--"

"Enough, both of you!" Riff roared, stepping between them. "The Cosmians will know we destroyed their starjet. More are probably flying over here as we speak--a hundred starjets all armed with blasters, not just one vessel."

Steel raised his chin and raised his sword. "I am prepared to defend the homestead. I shall fight honorably and die to protect the--"

"Nobody is dying today!" Riff grabbed his brother's arm. "Come on. We're getting out of here." He righted the bike and climbed into the seat. "Steel, you got a ride?"

The knight nodded. "I shall ride my noble steed."

Nova groaned. "He's got a steed. Perfect."

"A *noble* steed," Riff said gently, as if that could make things any better.

A moment later, Riff and Nova were riding their scorpion motorbike down a dirt road. At their side, Steel Starfire, clad in armor and bearing his ancient sword, rode upon his horse.

CHAPTER SIX

GREASE AND GRISTLE

An hour later, they approached The Cracked Pot, a greasy roadside diner shaped like a huge coffeepot. Its metal walls were rusting, and weeds grew in the yard. The only vehicle in the lot was a dented old atmojet with a python coiled up in the back seat; it looked like neither jet nor snake had moved in years.

"Classy joint," Nova said as they rolled their motorbike to a stop.

Riff stepped off the seat and cracked his neck. "No less classy than the Blue Strings or Alien Arena. And they'll serve coffee here. Wonderful, hot, black, heavenly coffee. After fleeing Cosmians all night, I'd welcome a cup of joe more than a harem of Orion hula dancers."

Nova glared at him. "Watch it, big boy. I haven't forgiven you yet."

Steel dismounted his horse and stared at the rusty, pot-shaped building. "An establishment of debauchery."

Riff rolled his eyes. "Steel, I told you. Coffee isn't debauchery."

The knight stiffened. "Caffeine is a drug. It is sinful. It is--"

"Shut it, tin can." Nova slapped Steel's armor, shoved him aside, and made for the diner. "Now come with us and drink water while we guzzle down caffeine."

They stepped inside and found a booth. No living waiter could be seen, but a clunky robot made from scrap metal took their orders. Soon Riff and Nova were downing mugs of piping hot coffee, eating ridiculously greasy eggs and bacon, and sharing a slice of apple pie topped with cheddar cheese. Steel ordered a cup of water and plain white toast. The food tasted like something scraped off a starship's engines, but the coffee was half decent, and the jukebox even had "Moonshine Blues" by Bootstrap and the Shoeshine Kid. As caffeine filled his bloodstream, and as Bootstrap's soulful notes filled the diner, Riff began to almost feel like his old self.

For a long while, Riff spoke, telling the others about everything that had happened since Grotter had stepped into his club.

Steel listened with a stern face, not moving, not speaking. Only when Riff mentioned the letter from their father did the knight's eyes widen.

"What does the letter say?" Steel asked.

Riff pulled the rumpled envelope out of his pocket. "With Cosmians firing at me all night and day, I haven't had a chance to read it yet." He tore the envelope open and pulled out a letter. He read it silently first, then showed it to the others.

Riff, my boy!

I hope this letter finds you well and safe. Yet things are not well and safe in the galaxy, Earth included.

I cannot say much now. Not in a letter that might fall into the wrong hands. When we meet again, much will be clarified.

A friend of mine, a young pirilian named Midnight, needs your help. I've sent her to the Blue Strings, but you must not keep her there. I fear that the Cosmians are gaining strength, that all Earth is in danger. Take my friend off the planet. Find shelter in the outposts. Hide. Wait to hear more from me. I will find you.

Do not let the Cosmians find my friend. If they catch her, a greater danger than you can imagine will befall us all. In the wrong hands, Midnight's power could destroy the very universe.

Sorry for being so grim, my boy. Next time we meet, I'll rustle up your favorite walnut pancakes, and hopefully we can laugh about this all, the danger far behind us.

Love,

Dad

Riff placed the letter back into his pocket. "Well, that didn't tell us much, did it? Aside from the fact that the universe is going to end."

"Midnight . . ." Steel frowned at his toast. "There is a damsel in distress out there, and we failed to find her."

Nova rolled her eyes. "Again with your damsels! The whole *universe* is in danger, and you're worried about your maiden to save."

"Pirilians," Riff muttered. "The skelkrins destroyed their planet a while back. Was all over the news--for a day or two, at least. The Cosmians celebrated it here on Earth. I didn't think any pirilians still lived."

Steel brushed crumbs out of his mustache. "Pirilians?"

Riff nodded. "Unique in the galaxy. Got magic to them, some say. They can teleport themselves within any space, crossing any distance instantly, so long as no walls stand between them." He took a deep, wistful breath. "I used to date a pirilian once. That's how I know. She used to port all over the place, vanishing one instant, appearing the next . . ." He glanced at Nova, saw the fire in her eyes, and quickly swallowed his words. "But I haven't seen one in years. And I'd know. They stick out. Purple skin and yellow eyes. Hard to miss."

"Aliens or humanoids?" Steel asked.

"Both, I think. Might be human settlers mingling with aliens thousands of years ago. But what do we do about this one?"

Steel rose to his feet, pushing back his chair. "We seek her. We scour Cog City for her. A maiden is in need, and we shall protect her."

"Except the city is swarming with Cosmians," Riff said. "And they're after us like they're after her. And they're after Dad too. Grotter knew that Dad's involved somehow. The Blue Strings is too dangerous right now. I say we blast off this rock, head to the space outposts, and check every one of Dad's regular haunts until we find him. He might not even know Grotter's on to him. He might need our help."

Steel's face remained hard. "Flee from battle? Abandon a damsel? A knight does no such things."

"Well, I'm not a knight. I'm a bluesman." Riff stabbed at his eggs. "Look, I'll put the word out on the street. I don't have the network Grotter has, but I have my people. Old Bat Brown will wait for the girl in the Blue Strings. Mandy and Tammy, out in the alley, will keep an eye on comings and goings. I got a dozen other guys and girls all over the dregs. Musicians. Panhandlers. Shopkeeps. Friends. I'll have them looking for a pirilian with purple skin and yellow eyes, and if they find her, they'll shelter her until we get back. But us here? We're no longer safe on Earth, not now. Not with Cosmians tracking us down. We need to blast off this rock, sail to the space colonies, and find Dad. We need answers from him." Riff smiled crookedly. "Hell, maybe leaving the planet will even keep this mysterious girl safe. We can draw some Cosmians after us."

For the past few minutes, Nova had remained silent. The ashai princess stared blankly at the wall, her face hard.

"What do you think, Nova?" Riff asked her, trying to keep his voice gentle.

"I think," she said softly, "that I hear an engine outside." She turned her head toward Riff. "I think I shouldn't have used my credit card in this place."

"Damn!" Riff leaped to his feet. He heard the jets from outside now too. "Yeah, they're tracking your card. God damn it! Come on, out the back door."

Steel rose to his feet and drew his sword. "I will not flee from battle."

Riff groaned, grabbed his brother, and whispered into his ear, "Steel, you have to protect Nova. A damsel! You must lead her to safety."

"I'm not a--" Nova began.

"Now move!" Riff shouted.

Within a minute, they were racing down the road--Riff and Nova on the motorbike, Steel on his horse. When Riff looked over his shoulder, he saw a black atmojet, the Cosmian emblem upon it, blast its guns toward The Cracked Pot. The diner shattered and collapsed. Then the bike drove onto a dirt path in the forest, Steel riding close behind, and they vanished into the cover of trees and brush.

They rode for a long time off road, moving between the trees, until the sound of the atmojet faded in the distance.

Just in time, the Golden Scorpion gave a few coughs and sputtered, then rolled to a stop. The motorbike was out of fuel. Steel's horse seemed to run out of his own fuel; the animal ambled toward a patch of grass and began to feed.

The companions stood in the forest, covered in ash, mud, and bacon grease.

"See my point?" Riff said. "Planet Earth bad. Not safe."

A voice inside him whispered that perhaps no place was safe anymore, not even the most distant planets. His dad was involved in something. Something dangerous. Sometimes that would attract bad company even in the outposts, even in the distant stars. Riff had to find the man. Had to keep him safe. Had to find answers. Were the skelkrins heading closer to Earth? Could Midnight, this pirilian woman, hold a secret to stop an invasion? Riff's head spun.

"Steel," he said, "is that old used starship lot still around here? The one Dad used to take us to when we asked to see real starships?"

The knight nodded. "The town's about three kilometers north from here."

"Good." Riff began to walk, pushing the scorpion bike at his side. "We ain't buying tickets on a commercial starship. Too easy to track down. I bet we can buy our own ship off the record--even if it's an old clunker--for ten grand. We blast off, and we look for Dad."

"And what of the damsel?" Steel walked at his side, leading his horse.

"I told you, I'm not a damsel!" Nova began, raising her whip. Mud stained the gladiator's golden armor.

"He means the pirilian," Riff said. "Oh shenanigans, let me make a few calls."

As they walked through the forest, Riff hit dials on his wristwatch, calling up the Blue Strings. He spoke to Old Bat Brown first, thanking him for the bedbugs. Mindful that the Cosmians might be tracking his calls, he then asked Bat Brown to keep a look out for a "brain-scrambler-faced jumper side-riffer, in trouble with some bass players." In old blues-speak, "jumper" meant "teleporter," "side-riffer" meant friend, and "bass players" meant trouble. Riff just hoped the old man understood that by "brain-scrambler," a deep purple cocktail, he meant "purple."

The old bartender, one of the wisest men Riff knew, seemed to understand. Riff made a few more calls, speaking to Rumple McNally who always sat by the stage, Gristle Scotch who was playing that night, and Mandy and Tammy out in the alley.

"If our pirilian girl so much as sets foot in Cog City," Riff told his companions, "my guys will know. They'll look after her while we're looking for Dad."

Steel nodded. "Good. Because we're here."

The knight pointed between the trees, and Riff found himself staring at a giant, mechanical dragon.

CHAPTER SEVEN

THE HMS DRAGON HUNTRESS

The town of Sprocket would have been forgettable if not for the dragon that rose in its center.

Several kilometers out of Cog City, this was barely a town at all. A couple of greasy spoons. A few barns. An antique shop selling old android parts. And the used starship lot.

The lot took up a good ninety percent of the town, a sprawling field full of all manner of ships. A few were slick, two-seater starjets, capable of flying in city, country, and open space. They looked expensive. Other starships were hulking, rusty boxes of metal, the size of apartment buildings--great cargo transports that had seen better days, meant for long hauls between planets. A couple of ships were even fine luxury vehicles, old models but still decent-looking, built for pleasure cruises to the stars.

And among them rose the dragon.

At least, Riff thought the starship was meant to look like a dragon. It seemed to have been rusting here for ages. It didn't even stand on the lot itself but in a backyard, vines and brush climbing its facades. Riff thought it was a starship--it had wings and engines--but it could just as well have been some giant piece of modern art. It rose about the height of a house, its mouth pointing to the sky.

"What a bunch of junk!" Nova said as they walked toward the lot, leaving the forest behind. "I've seen better collections of starships in landfills."

Steel nodded. "Nova is right. None of these are spaceworthy. They're more rust than metal."

Riff rolled his eyes. "Said the man who lived in a self-made castle. These ships are fine! They just need a coat of paint, some love, and they'll fly. That one isn't too bad." He pointed at a white starjet, only for its wing to tilt and thump into the dirt.

When they entered the lot, a man stepped forward to greet them, arms outstretched. His thinning hair was greased back across his scalp, and he puffed on a cigar. His Hawaiian shirt was unbuttoned, revealing a flabby belly, and many golden chains rested upon his hairy chest. Jeweled rings gleamed upon the man's sausage fingers, and cheap plastic sunglasses hid his eyes.

"Welcome, welcome!" the used starship salesman said. "I'm Leroy, and I'm here to make you a deal."

Nova rolled her eyes. "He's greasier than the bacon we had for breakfast."

Riff walked closer to the short, stubby man. "Leroy, we're here to--"

"Wait, let me guess!" Leroy grinned, revealing a golden tooth. "You're here to buy a starship."

"The man's a mind reader," Nova muttered.

Leroy took the gladiator's hand and kissed it, seemingly oblivious to her disgusted look. "My lady! I would be glad to show you a wide variety of pleasure ships in pink, purple, and baby blue, luxury vehicles that will have you exploring the galaxy of pretty stars."

"Got any with guns on 'em?" she asked.

Leroy's eyes widened. He gulped and dabbed sweat off his brow, then turned toward Riff. "Ah, my friend!" He placed hairy hands on Riff's shoulders. "I can see you have a distinguishing eye for quality starships. A musician too, by the guitar on your back. I can offer you a lovely ship that's as beautiful as any melody. Fine speaker system too."

He led the companions toward a green starjet which lay on the asphalt. It looked just large enough for the three of them, if Nova sat on Riff's lap, which he very much hoped she'd do.

"Is it supposed to have holes in it?" Riff asked.

Leroy cleared his throat. "Those are asteroid-protection holes, my friend! See, when little asteroids fly your way, they get sucked right into those holes, sparing your hull."

"I'll take one without holes," Riff said.

Leroy nodded and barked a rather fake-sounding laugh. "There's no pulling the wool over this one's eyes. Here, my friends." He grew solemn. "The masterpiece of my lot. The finest ship I sell. Behold--the Starship Galactica!"

Riff found himself staring at a large, charcoal starship that didn't look too bad. There were no holes on this one, and only minimal rust. He judged it to be about ten years old. "How much for it?"

"One hundred thousand credits, my friend."

Riff's eyes widened. "Are you mad?"

Nova growled and cracked her whip. "Are you trying to rob us?"

Steel frowned. "Theft is against all codes of honor and chivalry."

Leroy stiffened, staring between bluesman, gladiator, and knight. For an instant anger seemed to twitch across his lips. But then those lips grinned again, revealing his golden tooth. "Very well, very well, my friends! You seek something more affordable, I see. How much can you spend?"

Riff cleared his throat and rummaged through his pockets. He turned toward the others, and they huddled together.

"I'm broke," Riff said. "I had some cash stuffed into my mattress back home, but I ain't going back there now, not with the Cosmians skulking about. Steel, what have you got on you?"

The knight raised his chin. "A knight seeks not monetary compensation."

Riff groaned. "In other words, you're broke too." He turned toward Nova, then winced to see the rage blazing in her green eyes.

"No," she said.

"What?" Riff raised his hands.

"I know what you're going to ask me, and no." Nova squared her shoulders. "First of all, I'm not using my credit card again, not after the last purchase brought the Cosmians down on us. And even if I did have cash on me, I'm not buying you a spaceship. You want a ship? Barter for it."

Riff sighed. His shoulders slumped, and he caressed the golden motorbike. "Very well. As much as I'd hate to sell your bike, I--"

Nova grabbed his collar, twisted it, and sneered at him. "Your guitar, your idiot!"

He bristled. "My Dora?" He pulled the guitar to his chest and hugged it. "My baby? She's signed by Bootstrap and the Shoeshine Kid! Legendary blues duo! You know what this guitar is worth?"

Leroy stepped forth, joining the huddle. "About ten thousand credits, I'd say." The greasy man grinned. "Love me some B and the SK. Saw them play about ten years back. Used to play some licks myself." He reached grubby fingers toward the guitar. "Mind if I take a look?"

"Yes, I do mind!" Riff stepped back, hugging the guitar close. "This . . . this guitar is . . . is like a child to me." He turned toward Nova. "You don't understand, Nova. After my mother died, I was in so much pain. So angry and scared. But I still had blues music. When I was older, when I was drunk, when I was alone and living in that piss-stain of a club . . . I still had music. No matter what happened in my life, I could always listen to Bootstrap and the Shoeshine Kid. No matter how alone I felt, how afraid I was, how dark life seemed, I always had their music. When I finally got them to sign my guitar, well . . . it felt like having a baby. It felt like something that could bring me light and joy forever." He lowered his head. "Selling this guitar would feel like selling a child."

They all stared at him, silent.

Nova stepped forward.

She grabbed his ear, twisted it, and shouted, "Riff, you are going to sell that guitar! Do you understand me?"

"Ow! Let go! God!" Riff pried her fingers loose. "Fine! I'll sell the damn thing. But you owe me one. A big one. A trip to see Bootstrap the next place he plays, and backstage tickets too."

She rolled her eyes. "Deal. Now give the nice greasy man the guitar, and let's choose a spaceship."

Riff closed his eyes. He clenched his jaw. He held out his guitar, eyes screwed shut, unable to even look as Leroy took the precious treasure away.

"I'll . . . I'll give her a good home," Leroy said, voice scratchy. For the first time, the man seemed genuine. "I won't play her or nothing. Maybe someday you can buy her back."

Riff opened his eyes and nodded. It was hard to speak. "What starship can this buy us?"

Leroy cleared his throat and scratched himself. "Well, see there . . . guitar like that, even with those signatures, is worth ten thousand credits maybe. Not enough for most of the larger starships. But that's all right!" The grin returned to his face. "You don't want a ship that's too large anyway. Fuel guzzlers, they are. I offer you: The *HMS Dragon Huntress!*" He pointed at the rusty old dragon that rested in the yard.

Nova raised an eyebrow. "That's a starship?"

Leroy shrugged. "Eh, kind of. Used to be part of those Monster Ship shows up around the moon. You know the ones? The dragon used to grab smaller starjets and roast them with fire. Crowd loved it. A few years ago, some guy souped up her engines, ran a small alien pest control business with her, flying around to catch critters on the colonies. She's a good ship."

Nova growled and unfurled her whip. "If she's a good ship, why are you swapping her for a damn guitar? Why not charge a hundred thousand credits like your other ship?"

Leroy tapped ash off his cigar. "Well, I'll be honest with you. There's some folks that claim the *Dragon Huntress* is, well, possessed."

"*Possessed?*" Nova repeated.

Leroy nodded. "By a demon."

"A *demon?*" Nova groaned and tugged her hair.

Leroy puffed on his cigar. "Well, you know folks. They can be superstitious. Claim they hear clanking in the loft. Probably just a family of possums, but rumors of demon possessions spread, and well . . . nobody wants to buy her. Been sitting here on the lot for a year now. But if you're sensible folks, and if you don't believe in demons, she's a steal. A beauty too. Go on, take a look inside!" Leroy patted his new guitar. "I'll go put this baby in a safe place."

Feeling like a part of him was missing, Riff stepped toward the giant mechanical dragon. Flecks of paint hung off its facades. The words "HMS Dragon Huntress" appeared on its hull, and smaller letters underneath spelled, "Alien Hunters Inc." The bridge seemed to be located in the dragon's head, but the glass panes were too dusty to be sure.

"It's a piece of junk," Nova said.

Riff nodded. "It's a cool piece of junk."

Steel tapped one of the ship's wings. He frowned. "A knight should slay dragons, not fly within them."

Riff found a hatch, yanked a lever, and tugged it open. A staircase unfolded, leading up into the shadowy interior.

"Let's take a look," Riff said. He climbed up the stairs, entering the belly of the beast, little knowing that it would be many days before he emerged.

CHAPTER EIGHT

IN THE BELLY OF THE BEAST

Riff climbed the last metal step, opened a second door, and entered the belly of the *HMS Dragon Huntress*.

He found himself in the strangest ship he'd ever seen.

The main deck was about the size of a typical house's living room. Two couches stood against the walls, topped with a few stuffed animals. A board of counter-squares stood on a table, the pieces arranged in mid-game. A goldfish swam in a bowl, and a dartboard hung on a wall. For a moment, Riff wasn't sure if he'd stepped into a starship or somebody's home.

"It's . . . cozy," he said.

Nova entered the starship and stood beside him. She frowned. "Where are the weapons? Starships need weapons. Where are the racks of guns?"

Steel entered next and looked around. His frown deepened, and he stroked his mustache. "A knight has no use for stuffed animals or dartboards."

Footsteps thumped deep within the ship. A voice rumbled. A hatch opened in the floor beside one of the couches. Riff's eyes widened. One of the strangest creatures he had ever seen climbed through the trapdoor and into the living quarters.

"Hello there!" said the creature, voice deep and raspy. "Welcome, welcome to the *HMS Dragon Huntress*! That's HMS for Humanoid Mercenary Starship, in case you were wondering. We bow to no Her or His Majesty here."

Riff blinked.

"What is it?" Nova whispered, leaning closer toward him.

"A gruffle!" he whispered back from the corner of his mouth. "Don't stare."

Riff thought back to his history lessons. Thousands of years ago, when humans first spread across the stars, a group of miners had built a colony on the massive, rocky planet of Gruffstone, far in the Tauros system. The planet was several times the size of Earth, its gravity immense. Over the generations, the settlers had evolved to match the harsh conditions. They got shorter, the gravity pulling them down, and far more muscular than humans back on Earth. Their low stature, wide girth, and sheer strength let them survive on a giant rock the size of several Earths. Like Nova's people, the ashais, the gruffles evolved into a subspecies of humanity: *Homo sapiens gruffian.*

This particular gruffle stood a couple of inches shy of five feet, and he was almost as wide as tall. His arms and legs were all thick muscle. His chest was like a truck. He wore brown leather studded with iron bolts, and his skin was the same chestnut brown. A massive hammer hung across his back, and a luxurious white beard flowed down to his belt.

The gruffle looked, Riff thought, like a square of muscles with eyes.

"My name is Piston Bergelgruf!" the gruffle said, reaching out a hand that looked able to crush granite. "Just call me Piston. No need for Mr. Bergelgruf here. I'm the engineer on this ship."

Riff took the oversized hand and shook it, then winced as Piston nearly crushed his finger bones in his mighty grip.

"The engineer?" Riff asked after introducing himself and his companions. "You . . . don't work for Leroy?"

Piston's bushy white eyebrows rose. "Work for a used starship lot? Laddie, I work for only one place. Alien Hunters Inc. The little business we got going here on the *HMS Dragon Huntress*. At least until the last owner sold it."

Riff looked around the main deck. "Alien Hunters?"

Piston snorted and flopped down onto a couch with a groan. "Aye, it's a small alien control business. We mostly would handle little cosmic critters. Rigelian tunnel worms. Fuzzy Centaurian rodents. That kind of stuff. You know, the sort of aliens that clog up a ship's engines or a space station's plumbing. We had to trap a Taurian digger once, and that was nasty business." The gruffle grumbled. "Not many people last long in the alien hunting business, I can tell you. The previous owner only lasted a year on this ship. So did the owner before him. And the one before that . . . oh gods of granite, he only lasted about three months before selling it all." Piston grinned. "Glad to have new owners on board! Hope you fare better than the past seven."

"Wait a minute!" Nova said, stepping toward the squat gruffle. "Listen here, Piston. We're not buying any exterminator business here. We're only buying a starship."

Piston raised his eyebrows again. "Lassie, the business comes with the starship. So do its employees."

"Its . . . employees?" Riff asked. His heart sank.

Piston nodded and thumped his foot against the floor. "Twig! Twig, damn you! Come up and say hello to our new owners." His voice rose louder. "Twig! Damn it, get your little butt up here."

A clanking ruckus sounded from the lower deck. A voice cried out in dismay. Footsteps padded.

"Twig!" Piston shouted again.

The voice cried up from below, "Piston, I lost my wrench in the engine again! And there's cobwebs growing in the cooling coils, and--" A head popped out of the hatch in the floor. "Oh! Hello."

A second little person climbed out of the hatch into the main deck.

Twig was even shorter than Piston; she couldn't have stood taller than 3'5". While Piston was wide and muscular, Twig was slender as a sapling. Her skin was pale, her hair long and black, her eyes bright and blue. She wore cargo pants, a white shirt, and a tool belt from which hung wrenches and screwdrivers. She grinned, displaying bright teeth.

She's a halfling, Riff realized. Long ago, her people had immigrated to a small, peaceful planet called Haven. The gravity was weak, the land scarce, and slowly the people of Haven had shrunk to diminutive size. Even fully grown, they were now no larger than human children.

"Twiggle Jauntyfoot, at your service!" The little woman reached out a small hand for Riff and the others to shake. "Chief mechanic of the *HMS Dragon Huntress*."

"Assistant mechanic," Piston corrected her.

Twig placed her hands on her hips. "You're the engineer. I'm the mechanic. And since I'm the only mechanic here, that makes me the chief one. Got it?"

Piston growled. "Chief mechanics don't keep dropping their wrenches into the engines! Now go unclog them! I swear, it's a wonder this ship hasn't fallen apart with you messing about down there."

Twig blew him a raspberry, then hopped back into the hatch and vanished.

Steel stepped toward Piston and spoke for the first time. "The used ship salesman told us the *Dragon Huntress* has been idling on the lot for a year now. Have you and Twig been living here for a year?"

Piston nodded, pulled out a pipe, and began to smoke. "Aye, laddie. Best place to live, this ship. It's comfortable once you get used to Twig dropping and breaking things."

Riff glanced up at the ceiling. He could see another hatch there, leading toward an upper deck. A heavy padlock secured that hatch shut. "Leroy told us the ship's possessed. By a demon in the attic."

Piston snorted. "Oh, you can ignore that one. Problem's under control." He leaped off the couch. "Come on! Let me give you the grand tour."

The gruffle lolloped across the main deck, boots thumping, and opened a doorway. He led them into a corridor lined with other rooms.

"This here's the captain's quarters. Nice bed and desk there, as you can see. Fancy stuff. And here's the crew quarters." He pointed into a room containing three bunk beds. "Bit more crowded but comfortable enough. Here's the washroom--decent enough shower when it works--and here's my favorite room, the kitchen." He laughed and patted his belly.

Walking through the ship, Steel pointed at a doorway. Within lay a round chamber with two seats, its windows gazing out upon the weedy yard. "What's this place?"

"Ah!" Piston grew somber. "That there's the escape pod. If the ship's ever shot out of space, this pod will take you to safety. Can survive a fall through the atmosphere, if you need to make it down to a planet in a pinch. Hope we never have to use it." The gruffle shuddered and closed the door. "Moving right along . . ."

Piston hurried up a staircase--it seemed to run up the dragon's neck--and into another chamber.

"And here, my friends, is the bridge!" Piston announced. "The central hub of command. The brains of the ship. The--" He cleared his throat and tugged down some cobwebs. "Excuse the mess. We haven't been up here much in the past year."

Riff entered the bridge and looked around.

He was standing inside the dragon's head. Panes of glass afforded a very dusty view of the outside world; Riff could make out little more than smudges. Three plush, suede armchairs stood before a plethora of control panels. Buttons, joysticks, monitors, and throttles covered the place, and a hula dancer bobblehead stood on the dashboard.

In the center of the bridge stood a woman.

"Konnichiwa!" she said, pressed her hands together, and bowed.

Riff blinked.

The young woman wore a blue kimono embroidered with cherry blossoms, and her smooth black hair fell down to her chin. Her accent and appearance harkened back to Japan, one of the provinces of United Earth, once an independent empire.

"This here is Giga." Piston stepped toward the young Japanese woman and kicked her. "Useless piece of junk."

"Hey, wait a minute!" Riff said, racing forward. Steel drew his sword. Nova raised her whip. All three growled at Piston, prepared to fight.

"Whoa, whoa, hold your horses, lads!" Piston said, raising his hands. "She ain't real. Can't feel a thing. An android, she is. Rather a useless one too." He kicked Giga again. A metallic twang filled the bridge.

Giga smiled and bowed her head again. "I am Giga. Happy to comply!"

Riff sighed and leaned against the wall. "So the ship comes with an android."

Piston scratched his beard. "Well, technically, Giga here *is* the ship. She's what they call an HI. Human interface. They were a fad back when the *Dragon Huntress* was built. See all these control panels?" Piston gestured at them. "Complicated stuff. Too many buttons and gizmos and doohickeys. So they built Giga. You tell her what the ship needs to do, and she'll make it happen. Think of her as a sort of complicated mouse or keyboard."

Steel stepped closer, his sword still drawn. "You will not refer to this damsel as a piece of hardware."

Giga turned toward the knight, still smiling sweetly. A scent of jasmine rose from her, and her silken kimono rustled softly. "But I am hardware, sir! I am Giga. Happy to comply!"

Riff frowned. "I've heard of human interfaces before." He turned toward Piston. "Most are metallic butlers. Not very realistic looking. Giga, well . . . she looks so human."

Piston nodded. "Aye, laddie. Whoever built this ship thought she'd be a friendlier face than a metal man. Thought she'd help reduce stress. If you ask me, she's as big a source of stress as Twig down in the engine room. Always malfunctioning, our poor Giga is."

Giga tilted her head. "Some orders are . . . hard to compute."

Riff turned back toward the android. "Giga, show me your stuff. Can you play any music?"

The android smiled again and nodded. "Yes, sir! My databases contain a full library of the classics: Mozart, Beethoven, Michael Bolton--"

"Do you have any blues?" Riff asked.

She nodded again. "Yes, sir! All the classic blues masters. Half Full Freddy. The Squeaky Newsboys. Old Gin Jackson. Gristle G--"

"Got any Bootstrap and the Shoeshine Kid?" Riff asked.

Giga frowned and tilted her head. "Cannot compute."

Riff groaned. "Gods. You got a cyberspace connection on this thing? Download some B and SK. Play me something."

"Happy to comply!" Giga closed her eyes and seemed to think for a moment. Metallic sounds rose from within her. When she opened her eyes again, the sweet sounds of Bootstrap's guitar filled the ship, accompanied by the Kid's ivory tickling.

Riff stepped toward one of the suede chairs and slumped down. He closed his eyes.

For a night and day, he had been escaping the Cosmians. He had lost his home, his guitar, his old life. All he wanted to do now was listen to music and sleep.

Just as he began to drift off, the roar of engines sounded from outside.

His eyes snapped open. He leaped up.

"Giga, windshield wipers!" he said.

Giga tilted her head. "Cannot compute 'windshield.' There is no wind in space. Did you mean the front fused silica viewport panes?"

"Yes, damn it, wipe them!"

"Happy to comply!" said the android, and wipers whirred across the panes.

Riff stared outside and his heart sank. "Cosmians," he muttered. Several of their starjets were flying toward the used ship lot.

A voice boomed out of a megaphone. Metallic. Cruel. Grotter's voice.

"We know you're in there, Starfire!" One of the jets flew closer, the barrels of its guns turning toward the *Dragon Huntress*. "Step out of the ship and surrender yourself, or you and everyone inside that box of bolts will die."

CHAPTER NINE

DRAGONFIRE AND HELLFIRE

"Giga, fly this thing!" Riff shouted.

The android tilted her head. "Sir, we are low on fuel, and we haven't flown in a year. I need regular maintenance, an oil change, a thorough inspection, a hull wash, a paint job, a resupply of water and toilet paper, a--"

"Just fly, Giga!" he shouted, gripping the armrests of his chair.

Giga nodded. "Happy to comply!"

Steel and Nova leaped into their own seats. With a curse, Piston raced downstairs, muttering something about priming the engines and Twig's wrenches clogging things up.

The *HMS Dragon Huntress* began to rumble and shake.

A black starjet hovered before them. Within its cockpit blazed Grotter's red eye. The cyborg grinned.

"In the name of the skelkrin masters, shut down your engines, Riff! Or you will die."

"Giga, now!" Riff shouted.

She nodded. "Happy to--"

"Just fly!"

With an ear-splitting roar, the *HMS Dragon Huntress* blasted upward.

Smoke burst out, covering the used ship lot. Fire raged. The ship rattled madly, and screws came loose from panels and rolled across the floor.

"This thing is a death trap!" Steel shouted, digging his fingers into his seat's armrests.

"The whole planet's a death trap!" Riff shouted back. "Giga, get us higher! Out of the atmosphere. Far as you can go!"

"Happy to comply!"

They kept soaring skyward. Riff's seat shook so madly he thought it would collapse. The windshield panes rattled so loudly he thought they'd shatter. Through the glass, he saw the Cosmian starjets follow, slick black sharks chasing a lumbering whale. Blasts of plasma shot out from the enemy ships. One slammed into the *Dragon Huntress*, and the bridge rattled. Sparks flew.

"Giga, you got any weapons on this ship?" Nova shouted, clinging to her seat.

Giga nodded, the smile never leaving her face. "Yes, ma'am! Fully loaded stocks of plasma jets, ma'am."

"Then fire! Down the enemy ships!"

Giga smiled sweetly. "Cannot compute. *HMS Dragon Huntress* cannot fire its weapon while leaving the atmosphere."

More blasts of plasma rose from the enemy ships. Another hit the *Dragon Huntress*, and more sparks flew. Riff cursed. *This might turn out to be the shortest business venture in history,* he thought.

"Giga, do something! Evasive action! Dodge the enemy fire."

She nodded. "Happy to co--"

"Enough with that! Just do it!"

The ship jerked madly in the sky, swerving in another direction. Steel tumbled right out of his seat and slammed against a wall. Nova flew into the air. Riff clutched his seat for dear life. Enemy fire flew all around them, crisscrossing the sky. The enemy jets roared, swarming upward. The ground was distant now; they were flying high above the clouds. The dragon ship jerked again, flying left and right, dodging the enemy plasma.

She's rusty and full of misfits, Riff thought, *but damn she's fast.*

"Keep going higher, Giga," he said. "Get us into space and then engage those weapons of yours."

The android nodded, smiling sweetly. "Happy to co-- I mean, yes, sir."

The *Dragon Huntress* kept soaring and the land grew more and more distant below. And then the sky vanished. Riff saw the stars. They were in space.

And the Cosmians were still following. Their black jets soared up, firing their weapons.

"Giga, that plasma cannon?" Riff said.

"Ready to fire, sir."

"So fire!"

The *Dragon Huntress* soared higher, then swerved in the air, positioning its head down toward the Earth. Riff found himself staring right at the soaring Cosmian jets.

Then the dragon blasted out its fire.

The plasma flowed from beneath Riff's feet; he felt the floor thrumming. The energy flared out like fire from a true dragon's mouth and slammed into an enemy jet.

The Cosmian vessel shattered and rained down toward the Earth in pieces.

Riff gasped and leaped from his seat. "Fire, again!"

Giga nodded. "Happy to comply!"

The *Dragon* blasted out her dragonfire, burning down the jets soaring from below. One by one, the enemy vessels shattered and fell back down to the planet.

The *Dragon Huntress* flew on, rising higher, traveling deeper into space, serene, still in one piece, floating like a leaf on the wind.

For a long moment, they were all silent, staring at the pieces of enemy jets still raining down.

Finally it was Nova who spoke. "I like this ship."

Steel nodded. "So do I."

Riff collapsed back into his seat. "I miss my guitar."

Nova leaned across her seat and punched his shoulder.

"Giga, take us far out into space." Riff's voice was weak. "Out into the emptiness. I . . . I'll . . . I'll wake up later."

He closed his eyes and he slept.

* * * * *

The Earth was but a speck in the distance when Riff, suddenly captain of a starship, called a staff meeting.

They met in the main deck, a motley crew. Riff stared at them one by one.

Nova, warrior-princess from Ashmar, still wore her golden armor, and her whip hung at her side. Her pointy ears thrust out from her blond hair, and her green eyes stared back at Riff, and he saw the rage inside them. He had already taken her off one planet, her homeland, where she could have risen to the throne. Now, after she had struggled and fought to find a new home on Earth, he was yanking her away from that world too, leaving her old life in tatters. The guilt still filled Riff's stomach like a bad meal.

He turned to look at his brother. Steel stared back solemnly, his expression inscrutable. His long brown mustache drooped down to his raised chin. He had polished his armor, and his hand rested on the pommel of his antique sword. He stood in the corner, refusing to sit, forever the knight on his guard.

I shattered his life too, Riff thought, even more guilt piling up.

He turned to look at his new companions next. Piston sat on the couch, smoking a pipe and stroking his long white beard. The gruffle stood shorter than Riff's shoulders but probably weighed more, most of that weight in his muscles. His hammer hung across his back, its head the size of a shoebox. If the battle had perturbed the gruffle, he showed no sign of it. He stared down at the counter-squares board, studying the pieces, seeming as relaxed as a drunken patron at the Blue Strings.

Beside Piston sat little Twiggle Jauntyfoot. The halfling was a fraction of the gruffle's size, not much larger than a toddler. Her legs didn't even reach the edge of the couch, let alone the floor. She too was busy studying the counter-squares board, tapping her cheek with her wrench and mumbling, deep in thought.

Finally, Giga stood behind the couch, smiling and pleasant as ever. Not a wrinkle marred her blue kimono, not a single hair lay out of place on her head. Her scent of jasmine tickled Riff's nose. Riff wondered how much sentience filled Giga, whether she was aware of herself as an android, or whether she was essentially just a clever keyboard.

He cleared his throat. "All right, everyone. Listen up. First staff meeting. Giga's brought us far into the depths of space, and she's cloaking our signals. We're safe from the Cosmians . . . for now. But not for long. There's trouble going on in this corner of the galaxy, and we've got to solve it."

Nova snorted. "Trouble in the galaxy? Riff, more like you got into trouble in *your* life and dragged us into it."

Riff tightened his jaw. "Nova . . . not in front of my staff."

She laughed. "Your staff? Riff, two days ago, you were playing guitar for spare change, too poor to even get drunk. You're not some space captain."

"I am now, Nova. I gave you a chance to buy this ship yourself. You refused. I swapped my guitar for the *Dragon Huntress*, so I'm your captain now."

She growled, leaped to her feet, and unfurled her whip. "Like hell! If you think I'm going to obey your orders like some docile geisha, you've got a reality check coming." She glanced over at Giga. "Sorry, sweetheart. No offense."

Giga only smiled and bowed her head.

A large thump sounded above. Riff stared up. On the ceiling, the padlocked hatch rattled.

"What was that?" Nova whispered, clutching her whip.

"Ignore it." Piston moved a piece on the counter-squares board. "Trust me. Ignore it."

At his side, little Twig glanced up to the ceiling, then back down. "Listen to him."

A loud moan sounded above, then died. Something scraped overhead, then fell silent. Riff frowned up at the ceiling.

A ship possessed by a demon? He shuddered. Utter nonsense. Impossible. No such things as demons existed. Probably just a family of possums, just like Leroy had said.

Riff looked back at the others. "All right, gang. How much fuel and food we got on this ship? How far can we get?"

Twig sighed. "Not far. Romy ate almost all the food and drank almost all the fuel. She--"

"Hush!" Piston said, glaring at the halfling. "Get back to the engine room, you clod. They don't need to know about that." He turned back toward Riff. "We've got enough to reach Mars. Saturn maybe if we tighten our belts. We could have gone farther on hyperdrive, but we're out of hyperfuel. If we coast to the nearest colony, we can stock up on more supplies there."

"And this time keep Romy locked up!" Twig said. "Or she'll just eat it all again."

"Hush you!" Piston pointed at the hatch on the floor. "Get to the engines."

Riff blinked, looking back and forth between gruffle and halfling. "Who's Romy?"

"Nobody!" Piston insisted.

Twig opened her mouth, prepared to speak again, then closed it when Piston glared at her.

The scratching sounded again above. The padlock rattled. A new moan rose from the attic.

Riff frowned. "That does it. What the hell is up there? Piston, you got the key to that padlock?"

The stocky gruffle grumbled and twisted his fingers. "Aye, Captain. But . . . with all due respect, sir. I've been engineer on this ship for years now, and I've learned a thing or two about how the *Dragon* operates. You really do want to keep that hatch locked."

"Especially if you don't want somebody drinking *more* fuel," Twig added.

Riff held out his hand. "Key. Now."

Piston took a deep, shaky breath, and Twig curled up on the couch. Even Giga's smile faltered. With a wince, Piston held out the key, and Riff snatched it.

"Nova, Steel, watch my back." A ladder was attached to the wall, leading to the hatch above, and Riff began to climb. "Whatever's up there, if it tries to bite my head off, kill it."

"Maybe yes, maybe no," said Nova, lazily flicking around her whip.

Steel raised his sword. "By my honor, brother, if any foul demon of the Abyss slays you, I shall avenge your death."

Lovely, Riff thought.

He gulped, placed his key into the padlock, and unlocked it. The hatch swung open.

A voice wailed.

Wings beat and with a squeal, something large and red and squirming fell down onto him.

"Fragging aardvarks!" Nova shouted, leaping back.

Riff thrashed, heart pounding, trying to free himself. Leathern wings beat. Claws flashed and fire crackled. The creature wailed above him, crushing him.

"Oh shenanigans!" Riff finally managed to shove the creature off. He rose to his feet and stared down.

His eyes widened.

"Yep," Nova said, "it's a demon all right."

"My bum hurts," the demon said, sounding miserable. "I fell on my bum." Tears welled in her eyes, and she began to suck her thumb.

Riff rubbed his eyes in disbelief. In storybooks, demons were hideous creatures, all hooves and blazing hatred. The demon who sat before him, sucking her thumb, looked anything but intimidating. She was a young woman, it seemed, perhaps twenty years old. Her skin was red, her fingers sprouted claws, and a long tail flicked behind her. Bat wings grew from her back, and her hair seemed woven of flame, crackling like a torch. She wore pajamas with little teddy bears printed on them, and she held a real teddy bear in one hand.

Piston sighed. "Meet Romy."

The demon pulled her thumb out of her mouth, waved, and grinned. "Oh hai! Got any fuel around? I'm parched."

"No drinking fuel!" Piston roared.

Romy leaped to her feet and wagged her tail. She turned toward Riff, thrust out her chest, and saluted. "Hi there, Captain Riff, sir! I heard your name from up above. They usually keep me locked up there. At least since the time I gnawed through the cooling coils that day we flew by the sun. Bad timing. But I can hear everything!" She grinned, revealing long fangs. "Cadet Romy, reporting to duty!"

"You're not a cadet!" Piston rumbled. "And you're not part of this crew! You're a very bad demon that's possessing this ship." The gruffle sighed and turned toward Riff. "I'm sorry, sir. I did warn you, though. She'll be a right nightmare to lock back up now. Last time she got loose, she hid in the engine room for a week."

Twig nodded. "And she ate three of my wrenches! *Ate* them!"

Romy stuck her tongue out at the little halfling. "Well it's your fault for leaving them in the kitchen."

"They were on my tool belt!"

Romy snorted. "Tool belt, kitchen, same difference." The demon turned back toward Riff. "Ignore the little ones. I'm the most valuable crew member you have. Got any enemies you need clawed to death? I'll claw 'em!" She lashed her claws. "Got any nasty aliens you need bitten to death? I'll bite 'em!" She bared her fangs. "Got any poodles?"

Riff frowned. "Why poodles?"

"I like poodles." Romy wagged her tail. "I was hoping you'd have one around. They're delicious." She smacked her lips.

"Right." Riff turned toward Piston. "Lock her back up."

Romy gasped, let out a wail, and her eyes welled up with tears. "You can't make me go back! I won't go! I won't I won't!" With a wail, the demon leaped forward, barreling between the others. Her hair of flames crackled. Fast as wildfire, she leaped through the trapdoor in the floor, racing down into the engine room.

"Great!" Twig said. "She'll be guzzling down fuel again and eating more wrenches." The halfling grumbled and raced downstairs after the demon. "It can take days to catch this one, and we'd be lucky to have any bolts left without chew marks on them."

Riff sank into a couch and clutched his head.

"Giga?" he whispered.

The android nodded. "Music, sir?"

"Yes please."

Soon the sounds of guitar and keyboards filled the ship again.

Nova flopped down onto the couch beside Riff, leaned against him, and patted his knee. "Not how you imagined your week would go."

He sighed and leaned closer to her. It felt nice. Oh gods, it felt nice. It had been so long since he'd sat like this with Nova, seen her relaxed, felt her touching him.

He looked at her. His ex-girlfriend. The fiery warrior he loved. Even now.

I still love you, Nova, he thought, gazing at her freckled face, green eyes, pointy ears, hair like molten gold.

"Nov, I'm sorry." He held her hand. "Honestly. I'm sorry I dragged you into this mess. I know that . . ." His throat felt tight. "I know that you found a better life without me. Fame in the arena. A fancy motorbike. A luxury apartment at Dune Plaza. A new life on Earth, better than the one I gave you. And I'm sorry." He looked around him at the ship. "You deserve more than to be dragged across the solar system inside a rusty dragon, a crazed cult in pursuit, and a demon guzzling down fuel in the engine room."

Nova nodded. "I do. I was a princess of Ashmar once, you know, until I followed you away from my home down to that rock you call Earth. And I still follow you." Her eyes were suddenly damp. "Damn you, Riff. Damn you."

Riff turned to look at Steel. His brother stood, stiff as always, his hand clutching his sword. "Sit down, Steel."

The knight raised his chin. "A knight does not sit while defending his--"

"*Sit.*"

Steel sat.

"Look, brother," Riff continued. "I want to apologize to you too. I didn't want to drag you into this either. I know you were happy in your castle, with your horse, with--"

"I was not happy," Steel said.

Riff blinked. "But . . . you had it all. A castle, a noble steed, the life of a knight."

Steel sighed and lowered his head. "Brother, I'm a relic of an older time. I know this. A rusty old relic, as Nova has called me. What's a knight without a battle to fight? Without enemies to slay?" He looked around him and nodded. "But now . . . now I'm a knight who found a dragon. Who found a quest." He squeezed Riff's shoulder. "Who fights with a brother he loves. We'll find Father. Our family will reunite, fighting together."

A great, sniveling sound rose below. Romy's head thrust out from the basement, and she blew her nose into a handkerchief. "That . . . that was beautiful." Tears streamed down the demon's red cheeks. "Just beau--ow!" Romy glared down into the engine room. "Stop tugging my tail, Twig!"

The demon vanished back into the basement.

Riff sighed. He rose to his feet and began walking toward the bridge. "Giga, come with me. We're taking this hunk of junk to the nearest colony. We begin our search for my old man there. And if any Cosmians show up on the way? Do that dragonfire thing again."

The android grinned and followed. "Happy to comply!"

The *HMS Dragon Huntress* sailed onward through space. The music played on. Down in the basement, wrenches clattered, Twig cursed, and Romy wailed.

CHAPTER TEN
EMPEROR IN THE ALLEY

Grotter, Field Commander of the Cosmian Order, walked into the alleyway, his metal claw ready to draw blood. With every step, his body clanked and his anger grew.

Starfire almost killed me, he thought, clenching his fist. *He almost blasted my jet from the sky.* If Grotter hadn't swerved his jet around, the dragon's fire would have burned him. Now fire seemed to blaze inside Grotter, an unquenchable rage.

The alley was a narrow, filthy tunnel like the intestine of a Carinian stone-beast. Scraps of newspaper, Styrofoam cups, and empty beer bottles rolled across the ground. Laundry hung between the windows of the apartment towers that rose all around him. A homeless man lay by a trash bin, drinking spirits from a bottle in a paper bag. Muffled blues wafted from ahead, discordant wailing like dying cats.

Sickening, Grotter thought.

Once the skelkrin masters arrived on this planet, he knew, they would clean up the filth. They would burn all the beggars, the musicians, the unwashed masses. They would tear down the hovels and alleyways. They would erect great towers in their stead, massive monuments of black iron. They would turn Earth into a world of might, of ruthless efficiency. A great outpost of the Skelkrin Empire.

And I will rule this planet for them, Grotter thought. His mouth watered with anticipation. *For my masters, I will turn the Earth into the greatest fortress the galaxy has ever seen.*

He sucked in air. Humans were weak. Humans were pathetic. Humans could lose their arms to the fire, lose their faces, lose half their insides. Grotter looked down at his body, a body more machine than flesh now. Skin, muscle, veins, all fused with tubes, metal plates, screws, gears, moving parts. A body both frail and strong. A clockwork worm.

He kicked an alley cat, sending the vermin fleeing, and kept walking closer to the music. Bile filled his mouth.

"But the skelkrins are strong," he hissed into the shadows. "The skelkrins are superior beings. And I, Grotter, am blessed to serve them."

Finally, with the guitar wailing grown to intolerable volume, Grotter reached the backside of the Blue Strings club. The two girls stood there in the alleyway, leaning against a wall and chewing gum.

"Hey, mister!" said one, a scrawny rat of a girl with frizzy yellow hair. "This here's our alleyway. Skedaddle."

"Yeah!" said the other, a lanky girl with garish makeup. "We ain't letting no strangers in here, mister. Get lost!" She popped her bubble gum at him.

Grotter stepped closer. A gust of wind blew back his cloak and hood, revealing his body and face, the flesh fused with the metal. He raised his claws, gears clicked, and the fingers flexed. The girls gasped and took a step back.

"Your names are . . . Mandy and Tammy, yes?" Grotter stepped closer, a smile twisting what remained of his mouth. "Friends to Raphael 'Riff' Starfire."

Mandy, the girl with frizzy yellow hair, flipped him the finger. She was trembling but managed to glare at him. "Who's our friend ain't none of your business, mister. What are you anyway, some kinda freak or somethin'?"

"Yeah!" said Tammy, the girl with garish makeup. "Ain't none of your beeswax who we's friends with." She drew a gun and pointed it at him. "Now amscray!"

Grotter stepped even closer; he now stood only two feet away from the girls. They backed up, pressing against the back wall of the Blue Strings. The wailing of guitars still rose from inside, and now they sounded to Grotter like screams of anguish. He brought his claw closer to the girls, letting the gears click, the blades move up and down. He fixed his red, dilating eye upon them.

"Yes, I remember you two," he whispered. "When my men chased Riff out of this cesspool you call a club, you fired your guns at me. You let Riff escape. I will let you live . . . but only if you tell me where Riff fled to. I know he left the Earth. Where is he heading?"

Mandy snorted. She turned toward her friend. "I've had enough of this bozo. You wanna go play some stickball?"

"Yeah!" said Tammy. "Boring here anyways." She pointed her gun at Riff. "Now get lost, freak! Go suck on a rusty pipe, you piece of scrap metal."

The girls tried to shove past him.

Grotter thrust his claws.

He grabbed Tammy by the throat and squeezed.

The girl screamed and fired her gun. The bullets slammed against the metallic half of Grotter's face and ricocheted. He tightened his claws, and her screams died. Blood sprayed him.

The second waif, that rat named Mandy, screamed and tried to flee. Grotter opened his metal palm wide. Light coalesced and blasted out, slamming into Mandy's back. She pitched forward, hit the ground, and her blood pooled. Weeping, she began to crawl away.

Grotter approached slowly and knelt above the wounded vermin.

"You could have lived," he whispered. "You could have lived to see my skelkrin masters arrive in all their glory, could have gazed upon their holy might . . . at least before they burned you." He shook his head. "The folly of youth."

"Please, mister, I ain't gonna hurt you, I--"

He thrust down his claws.

She gave a last scream, then fell silent.

Grotter flicked blood off his claw, pulled a handkerchief from his pocket, and patted his face dry. Killing was such a dirty job, but somebody had to do it.

Two girls lay dead, but a third girl still evaded him. A girl more important by far. A girl who could change the fate of the Cosmos.

"Where are you, my precious Midnight?" Grotter whispered.

He turned back toward the Blue Strings. The old wizard had sent the pirilian here, yet she dallied. Perhaps she hid in the shadows of a nearby alley. Perhaps she hid in the swamps or forests of a distant world halfway across the galaxy.

"And perhaps . . . perhaps you shelter her, Riff Starfire," Grotter whispered. His metal hand clanked as his finger-blades flexed. "I will find you, Riff, and I will kill you too . . . slowly. Lovingly. Bit by bit."

Deep inside his mechanical head, his communicator beeped.

Grotter's heart seemed to sink down to his pelvis with fear. An instant later, it soared in elation.

Yes. He feared his master. And he loved his master. Grotter's body trembled, and sweat dripped down his forehead.

He knelt in the blood, bowed his head, and answered the call.

Light streamed out from his mechanical eyeball, hit the ground several meters away, then rose into a hologram of his master.

Grotter bowed deeper. "Master!"

Before him, a flickering hologram in black and crimson, stood Emperor Lore himself.

The skelkrin master was a massive, towering figure, eight feet tall and so wide he filled the alleyway. The hologram needed no magnification; this was a life-sized representation of the warrior-god. Spikes, hooks, and blades rose from the emperor's black armor. His eyes, two white smelters, blazed with the fury of supernovas. His claws, long and black and gleaming, made Grotter's own mechanical hand seem no more intimidating than a butter knife.

Emperor Lore opened his massive jaws, revealing rows of daggerlike fangs. He spoke in a deep, rumbling voice that thudded against Grotter's eardrums and seemed to pound against his very bones.

"Have you found the pirilian girl, Grotter?"

Cold sweat dripped down Grotter's back. "Not yet, my lord. Forgive me! Forgive my failure! I am but a human, not a mighty skelkrin as you are." He glanced up, desperate to please. "I will find her, master. I swear it! I will find her and--"

Grotter screamed.

Through their connection, Emperor Lore had access to Grotter's internal mechanisms, the plethora of wires, engines, and moving pieces that filled him. And now Lore twisted those mechanisms like a fist crumpling a can. Metal dented. Electricity sparked out, driving into what remained of Grotter's human flesh. Pain--horrible, white, all-consuming--surged through him.

When finally the pain ended, Grotter fell and shuddered. Smoke rose from his robes.

"You will find the girl and bring her to me," said Emperor Lore. "Without her, my plan to build a skelkrin utopia on Earth cannot commence. Do you not wish to see a Skelkrin Earth?"

Grotter pushed himself to his knees, still shaking. "I wish for it with all my heart, master! With every breath!"

"Then find her. You have one of your Earth weeks. The clock is ticking, Grotter. If you disappoint me, you will not rule this planet as my servant. You will instead scream in my dungeons, my slave to torment."

With that, the hologram vanished.

Grotter remained kneeling for a long time, allowing the pain to subside.

Finally he pushed himself to his feet and began walking again.

His men would remain on this planet, scouring the alleys and bars of Cog City. But he, Grotter, had farther places to search.

"The girl is seeking you, Riff," he whispered. "And so I will seek you too."

His small, fragile starjets had failed to stop Riff's dragon. It was time to soar in a great beast of his own.

CHAPTER ELEVEN
GIGA'S LAMENT

Riff was sitting in the *Dragon*'s kitchen, drinking strong black coffee, when Piston lumbered in holding a sheaf of papers. Shorter than Riff's shoulder but quite a bit wider, Piston lollopped more than walked.

"Captain, I thought you might like to take a look." The burly gruffle placed the papers down on the table and smoothed his long white beard. "What with us being sat on the lot for an Earth year, our projects have piled up."

They were several days from Earth, coasting on thruster engines deeper into the solar system. It was slow progress, and so far quiet progress too. No Cosmian ships. No other ships at all, just the emptiness of space. Within a few days, they would reach the asteroid belt and the human miner colonies. Riff was hoping to hear some news of his father there.

Riff placed down his mug and stared at the pile of papers. Over a hundred sheets rose there. "Projects?"

Piston nodded. "Aye, sir. From our clients, sir. The year we sat on the lot, no captain around, our clients kept calling. We've got a year's worth of work to catch up on. The alien control business is a busy one."

Riff sighed and turned toward the coffeepot, hoping for a refill, only to see Romy holding the pot up with both hands, guzzling down the dark brew. The demon's throat bobbed, her tail wagged, and her wings flapped with every gulp. Her hair of fire crackled, casting its light upon her red skin and claws. Despite being an adult demon--if she were a human, at least, Riff would have guessed her to be about twenty years old--Romy wore dinosaur pajamas, and she held her beloved teddy bear under her arm.

"Mmm, good." Romy lowered the empty pot and licked her fangs. "Not as good as poodle soup. And not as good as fuel. But better than licking the mildew off the cooling pipes. Not that I . . . ever tried that. At all." She glanced around nervously.

Riff turned back toward Piston.

"Piston, I'm a blues player. I'm not in the alien control business."

"You are now, sir." Piston nodded. "With all due respect, sir, you became an alien hunter when you bought the ship. Alien Hunters Inc. is tied to the *Dragon Huntress*, sir. And we're low on cash. Fact is we're dead broke. We need to get to work. We've barely got enough fuel to reach the colonies, let alone leave the solar system."

Romy held the empty coffeepot over her mouth, shaking out the last drops. "I'm thirsty again! Being a demon with fire for hair makes you thirsty. And I love drinking fuel. We need to buy more."

Piston shook his fist at her. "Hush, you, and return to the attic or I'll blast you out into space."

The demon blew him a raspberry, then tugged up her pajama pants and began rummaging through bottles of juice in the cupboard.

Riff moved the papers farther away from the demon; with her flaming hair, he thought she might ignite the pile. He sighed. Perhaps Piston was right. They needed cash, and a short gig couldn't hurt. He began rifling through the papers, looking at their upcoming jobs.

The first sheet showed a request from a Martian colony. A family of Centaurian rodents, little furry critters, had made it into their silos and was eating all the grain. They needed a team to dive into the silos, fish out the pests, and save as much of the grain as possible. The idea of swimming in wheat didn't appeal much to Riff. He flipped to the next page.

This request came from a station orbiting Jupiter. A cloud of nano-biters had infected one of their quarters, little pests that bit into people's skin and laid eggs within. Riff quickly turned to the next page.

This job was even worse. Floating alien ghosts, origin unknown, had possessed the bodies of several astronauts exploring solar flares. It sounded like they needed an exorcist more than alien hunters.

"Is business always this busy?" Riff asked, looking up at Piston.

"Not normally, sir." The gruffle shook his head. "But what with the Skelkrin Empire expanding across the galaxy, loads of cosmic critters are fleeing. Like animals from wildfire, they are. Pushing deep into human territory, sir."

Riff shuddered. The skelkrins. Grotter's favorite killers. Riff didn't want to even think about those predators getting anywhere near the solar system.

He flipped to the next page and gasped. "Bloody hell!"

This work order came from light-years away, a planet called Cirona in the Vega system.

They were having trouble with a pirilian.

"A pirilian." Riff rose to his feet, clutching the paper. "They need a pirilian removed!"

Romy tossed down an empty bottle of orange juice. She scratched her backside. "What's a pirilian? Is that anything like a poodle?" The demon hiccupped. "I want some poodle soup!"

Riff ignored her. He stared at the paper, reading it again and again, getting more and more excited.

"It's her," he whispered. "Midnight. It has to be her! Look at this, Piston. A pirilian girl--purple skin, yellow eyes, able to teleport herself at will and blast *qi* energy from her palms. Says here she showed up on Planet Cirona and has been terrorizing the settlers. Stealing their sheep. Eating their crops. Scaring the children. Says her starjet crash-landed and burned down a farm, and nobody's been able to catch her." He slammed the paper down onto the tabletop. "How many pirilians could be left since the skelkrins destroyed their planet? Not many, I wager. This might be her. The girl the skelkrins are after. The girl Dad tried to send to me."

Both Piston and Romy gaped at him silently, eyes wide, mouths open. Crumbs fell from Romy's mouth, and she dropped the box of cookies she held.

Finally Piston found the ability to speak. "Captain, I don't know much about what sort of trouble you're in, or what pirilian you've been looking for. I'm only an engineer, sir, no more, no less. And what I can tell you is that we can't travel to Cirona."

Riff paced the kitchen. "Why not?"

"Well, sir, Cirona lies light-years away, all the way at the Vega system. We're traveling on thruster power only, sir. Would take us decades to get there at this rate."

"We need to get our hyperdrive engines working." Riff's fingertips tingled. *Maybe Dad is there.*

"Aye, sir. We've got the best damn hyperdrive engines in the galaxy. But no juice to them. Somebody ate all the hyperfuel packs." He gave Romy a dirty look.

The demon pouted. "I was hungry!"

Riff groaned and tugged his hair. "All right. We head to the nearest colony. We buy more hyperfuel."

Piston shifted his weight around. "Sir, as I said, we're dead broke. Even a single hyperfuel coil will cost at least a thousand credits, if we buy the lowest grade and haggle. We need money. We need a gig in the solar system before we can buy enough juice to blast out toward another star."

Riff groaned and paced the kitchen, tugging at his hair. Empty bottles rolled around his feet. It was infuriating. He wanted to fly over to Planet Cirona now, to find the girl, to find answers, damn it. Not go to some blasted outpost to fish out alien pests clogging up somebody's toilet.

Finally he sat down with a sigh. "Fine! We do one gig. For quick cash. Then buy hyperfuel." Riff turned to glare at Romy. "And you're not eating that one! So help me God, I will blast you out into the vacuum of space if you cause any more damage to my ship."

The demon pouted, hugged her teddy bear close, and fled the kitchen.

Riff lifted another sheet of paper from the pile. "This one here. It's from an asteroid nearby. We can get there within a day, even on thruster power. Says here . . ." He squinted. "Says they got a Denebian tardigrade in their pyrite mine." He looked up at Piston. "That doesn't sound too bad. I've heard of tardigrades. Tiny little critters, aren't they?"

"Aye, sir." Piston nodded. "Wee little buggers. Shouldn't be a problem, sir. Probably could fetch a thousand credits for the job too. Not a lot of money, but might just buy enough fuel to get us to Cirona."

Riff nodded. "I'll have Giga set a course." He was surprised to find a grin stretching his cheeks. "We're off to hunt an alien."

* * * * *

Riff sat in the captain's chair, watching the asteroid grow closer. To his left sat Nova, wearing as always her armored golden catsuit, her whip at her side. To his right sat Steel, clad as always in his armor.

"Giga, bring us in slowly," Riff said. He pointed. "See that landing pad? Set us down."

The Human Interface stood at his side. She bowed, her kimono rustling. "Happy to comply, Captain."

The rest of the crew was off the bridge. Piston and Twig were down in the engine room, keeping the *Dragon Huntress* flying. They had given up on trapping Romy back in the attic, instead keeping her busy in the crew quarters with a stack of comics. Riff was finally able to relax, to feel a little bit like an actual captain.

He returned his eyes toward the asteroid outside. It was a massive rock, the size of Cog City back home. The sort of rock that had wiped out the dinosaurs. Only this rock, instead of slamming a hole into Earth, had Earthlings digging holes into it. Mines gaped open on its surface, pockmarks in the stony face. A city had sprung up around the mines, its lights bright and parti-colored.

"Pyrite City," Steel said softly, watching it approach. "A hive of gambling, flesh for hire, and booze that flows like water."

Riff leaned back in his seat. "Sounds like my kind of town." He ignored his brother's frown.

Just the place where a traveling magician might perform, Riff thought. *Dad might have been here. Might be here now.*

They were a hundred kilometers away when a light began to ding on the control panels. Riff leaned toward a monitor and groaned.

"Captain, we have now run out of fuel," Giga said, chipper as always.

Riff groaned. "I can see that. Can you still land this thing?"

Giga tilted her head. She emitted mechanical hums and clinks like an overheated computer struggling to push through its algorithms. "Uncertain."

"Uncertain!" Riff leaped to his feet. "Giga! This is kind of important to know."

She smiled at him and bowed her head. "Captain, I've calculated an accurate course to the landing pad. But we need some fuel to slow our descent and engage our landing gear."

"God damn hunk of junk," Nova muttered. Riff wasn't sure if she was referring to the ship, to Giga, or both.

The asteroid was getting a lot closer now. Riff could no longer see space around it, just a massive city on a massive rock, getting closer and closer.

He cursed and hit the communicator he kept strapped across his wrist. "Piston! You hear me down there?"

The gruffle's voice rose through the speakers. "Aye, Captain. We're out of fuel, Captain!"

"I know!" Riff winced seeing the asteroid approach. "Can you slow our flight and get out our landing gear?"

"Aye, Captain," Piston said. "I can reroute battery power to the side thrusters, and I can hack through to the landing gear. Shouldn't take more than an hour, sir."

Riff cursed and turned to Giga. "Get us out of here! Fly away from this damn rock. Give Piston time to work."

The android smiled sweetly. "Cannot compute. No fuel left to change course."

Riff let out an enraged groan and spoke back into his communicator. "Piston, you have thirty seconds." He hung up and turned toward Steel and Nova. "Put your seatbelts on."

"There are none!" Steel said, gripping his armrests.

Nova leaped right onto the knight's lap. She began to tie her whip around them.

"What! Nova!" The knight blustered. "Stop that, this is not the place nor the time for--"

"Shut up!" she shouted. "I'm saving your life!"

"What about me?" Riff cried as the asteroid zoomed up toward them.

"You can fly through the windshield!" Nova shouted back. "Maybe it'll knock some sense into your head."

"Cannot compute 'windshield.'" Giga tilted her head. "There is no wind in space. Did you mean front fused silica viewport panes?"

"I meant windshields!" Nova shouted. "That's what I call them. I--whoa!"

The ship jerked madly. Steam blasted out into space. They veered through the vacuum. The lights of Pyrite City streamed below upon the rock.

"Captain!" rose Piston's voice from the communicator. "Captain, I had to blast air out from the attic! Might want to avoid stepping up there, unless you enjoy time in a vacuum. I have a clever way to bring out the landing gear too, sir. I just got to divert the cooling vapor into--"

"Stop explaining, just do it!" Riff shouted.

He could see the landing field ahead. A hundred other starships stood there, clinging to the asteroid's microgravity. Riff gritted his teeth and clung to his seat. At his side, Steel tightened his arms around Nova, who sat in his lap; her whip wrapped around them both. Only Giga seem unperturbed, standing in the open. Riff reached out and grabbed the android's hand.

"Hold onto me, Gig," he said. "This might get bumpy."

"Happy to comply!" Her hand tightened around his.

For another two seconds, they streamed through space.

Then the universe seemed to shatter.

Sparks flew in a great shower, covering the windshield.

The impact bolted Riff out of his seat. He clung to Giga with one hand, to his chair with the other. From deep in the ship, he could hear Romy cry out in terror. Smoke blasted out. Bolts rattled. The hula dancer bobblehead fell off the dashboard. The ship jerked again, pushing Riff deep into his seat. Giga fell right onto his lap, and he clung to her.

With a great screech, the *HMS Dragon Huntress* ground to a halt on the landing pad.

"Yeah!" Nova shouted, a huge grin on her face. "That was fun. I like this ship."

Steel's face looked green. "I miss my horse."

Romy's voice rose from deep within the ship, sounding miserable. "I fell on my bum again."

Riff had to sit for long, quiet moments, holding Giga on his lap. He spat out a strand of her hair.

"Are we landed?" he whispered.

Giga nodded. "Aye, sir."

"Good. Good." Riff gulped. "Giga, do we carry any spare underwear on the ship?"

"Aye, sir."

"Fantastic." He wiped his brow. "Wonderful thing to keep stocked, fresh underwear. Useful when you have a bunch of morons flying your ship."

He groaned and rose to his feet. His head spun. Outside the windshield, he saw the runway, several other parked ships, and beyond them the bright glass buildings of the city. No sirens. No enraged police. If anyone in Pyrite City had noticed the near-crash, it seemed they had shrugged it off.

The door to the bridge opened. Piston and Twig entered, badges with the words "Alien Hunters" pinned to their chests. Piston held out several more badges in his massive palms.

"We have to wear badges?" Steel asked, frowning. He placed his hand over his heart. His breastplate was still scratched there; it was the place that had once displayed the sigil of the Knights of Sol, a sigil he had been forced to efface.

"Aye, laddie." Piston nodded. "It'll snap right onto your armor. Got to be professional when dealing with the clients, you know."

"Is that why there's mustard on your clothes?" little Twig asked, poking a stain on Piston's leather-clad gut.

The gruffle raised his hammer; its metal head was nearly larger than Twig. "Hush you!"

Twig thrust out her chin at him and smoothed her own clothes--cargo pants and a white shirt--obviously rather proud of how clean they were. Her collection of wrenches, her pride and joy, hung from her tool belt.

Riff was still wearing the jeans and T-shirt he had worn in the Blue Strings. He chose an Alien Hunters badge from the pile and pinned it to his chest. At his side, Nova snapped a badge onto her catsuit. Steel snapped a badge onto his breastplate, hiding the old sigil that had once shone there.

"Great," Riff said. "Ready to hunt a tardigrade and make some bucks?"

And look for Dad, he added silently.

They all nodded.

Before they could leave the bridge, Romy darted in through the doorway. She had finally changed out of her pajamas. She now wore jeans shorts and a T-shirt with a purple dinosaur on the chest. Holes were cut into the clothes for her tail and wings. An

Alien Hunters badge proudly shone upon her breast. She held a red pitchfork in one hand, her teddy bear in the other.

"Oh hai, everyone!" The demon wagged her tail. "I'm ready."

Piston glared at her. "Not you! You stay on the ship, you clod."

Romy's tail hung low between her legs. Her hair of living fire drooped. "I thought you wanted me off the ship."

"I do!" Piston said. "Oh gods of stone and metal, I do. But I don't want you roaming loose in Pyrite City neither. You're likely to blast the whole asteroid to bits. Get into your attic!"

"I can't!" Romy stamped her feet. "You took all the air out, and it's a vacuum in there now, and my hair needs air to live." She pointed at the fire on her head. "If you haven't noticed, it's made of fire. And fire needs oxygen." She raised her nose. "So I have to come with you. I have to or I'll *die*."

"No." Piston crossed his arms.

Romy pouted. She turned toward Riff. "Please, Captain! Oh please. I'll be ever so good. Piston never lets me go anywhere. He keeps me cooped up in this ship all day long, and I never get to hunt aliens. Please let me come along! I promise I'll catch the tardigrade for you. I'm good at hunting tardigrades. Back in Hell, when I was only a little demon, I always used to hunt them."

"There's no such thing as Hell," Riff said. "That's just a myth."

She snorted. "Well, how do you explain a demon? I ain't no alien. I hunt aliens!" She growled and brandished her pitchfork.

Riff rolled his eyes. "Fine! If I leave you here, you're likely to eat the furniture." He turned toward Giga next; the android had not pinned a badge to her kimono. Riff's voice softened. "Aren't you coming with us, Giga?"

Romy snorted. "She can't!"

Riff frowned and stepped closer to the android. He held her hands. "You can't come with us, Giga?"

For the first time since he'd known her, the android did not smile. She lowered her head, her eyes sad. "I am a Human Interface, Captain. I'm part of this ship. I cannot ever leave it, no more than a brain can leave a body." The android turned to stare out the windshield, her expression almost wistful. "For many years, I've dreamed of stepping out there, of seeing the wondrous worlds of the galaxy. Yet should I leave this ship, my positronic network will lose its connection. I would die."

Riff squeezed her hand. "I'm sorry, Giga. I didn't know. How about I buy you a gift out there--bring a bit of that outside world inside the ship? What would you like?"

The android's face brightened. "A bobblehead." She pointed at the hula dancer who swayed on the dashboard. "Our old captain bought me that once, when I was only a new android, still fresh from my packaging. I would quite like another one."

"If I can find one, I'll buy one." Riff nodded. "That's a promise." He turned to the others. "Now let's go! While the cosmos is young."

Leaving Giga on the bridge, the others stepped through the main deck, opened the airlock, and climbed outside to hunt an alien.

CHAPTER TWELVE
FOOL'S GOLD

Six Alien Hunters walked into Pyrite City, their badges on their chests, hefting their weapons.

Riff Starfire, his gun in his holster, his jeans torn but his head held high. Steel Starfire, clad in armor, a massive mustache covering his lip and a massive sword at his waist. Nova the ashai gladiator, swaying in her golden uniform, her electric whip crackling in her hand. Piston, gruff and burly, a hunk of muscle with a beard and a hammer large enough to shatter worlds. Twiggle Jauntyfoot, small and quick, a deadly electric wrench in her hand, the pockets of her cargo pants jangling with screws and bolts. Finally, struggling to keep up, Romy the demon, her hair a living torch, her fangs gleaming, her wings wide, a pitchfork and teddy bear in her hands.

Their badges all gleamed, displaying their name: Alien Hunters.

Has anyone in the galaxy, Riff wondered as they entered the city's main boulevard, *ever seen a more useless bunch of misfits?*

Pyrite City, true to its name, glittered like fool's gold. Halls of glass and metal rose upon the asteroid, clutching the great rock in a garish embrace. Within shone a thousand bars, clubs, brothels, and casinos. The miners who had first drilled here had grown rich. They had brought their families. They had attracted thousands of other businesses like a carcass attracts flies. Where money flowed from the rock, places to spend that money grew in a forest of light.

Riff and his crew now walked down the main boulevard which led from the spaceport deeper into the city. Above, through a glass ceiling, Riff could barely see the stars. Too much light shone from the buildings at his sides. Tourists played slot machines within glittering dens. Animatronic animals roared and reared as children squealed on their backs. Miner's wives shopped for jewels and gowns. Teenagers laughed as they played minigolf in a field of robotic dinosaurs.

As they walked deeper into the city, Steel's frown deepened too.

"What has happened to humanity?" the knight muttered. "We've replaced honor with idols of gold."

"Of pyrite," Riff said. "We no longer live in the dark ages, brother. Gold is useless. Pyrite holds the universe together. Can't enter hyperspace without it."

The knight snorted. "In the old days, they called it fool's gold. Fools are what I still see."

While the knight glowered, Romy looked around with huge eyes. Her jaw hung loose.

"Riff, Riff!" The demon ran up to him, tail wagging. "Can I go play minigolf? Please please please."

"No, Romy."

She whined and hopped around. "Can I go ride the elephant?" She pointed at a pink animatronic elephant with a top hat and swan wings. "Oh please!"

"Romy, no!" Riff grabbed her hand and dragged her along. "We've got no time or money for games. We have to catch a tardigrade."

The demon pouted. "But I want to ride the elephant!" Her voice rose almost as loud as an elephant's trumpeting. "I want to, I want to, I--"

"Romy, if you misbehave, I'm going to lock you up in the spaceship again."

She groaned and stamped her feet, but she shut her mouth and walked along with him. Her tail dragged between her legs.

As they walked deeper into the city, Riff moved to walk closer to Steel. He leaned over and spoke softly for only his brother's ears.

"Steel, keep both eyes open. I don't trust that Grotter's not still skulking about, or that he can't reach us even here. See any sign of something off? Anything you suspect?"

The knight looked around, eyes narrow. "I've seen evil here, but not the evil of the Cosmians." He met Riff's eyes. "If they arrive here, you have my sword. We fought them on Earth. We will fight them here if we must. I've got your back, brother. Always."

Riff turned to his left and saw Nova walking there. She moved closer to him. She held her whip with one hand, and she placed her other hand on his shoulder.

"And you have my whip, Riff." Her green eyes stared at him steadily.

He nodded. His throat suddenly felt too tight for words. The past week had turned his life upside down and shaken it more wildly than a crashing starship. He had killed men. He had lost his home, lost all that was dear to him. And now he was here, so far from Earth, poor, afraid, Cosmians behind him and an empire of predators ahead of him.

But I have Steel and Nova, he thought. *I have my brother. I have the woman whom I love.*

In a cosmos torn apart, they were his anchors. Forever at his sides.

A high-pitched voice rose from ahead. "Alien Hunters! Are you the Alien Hunters?"

Riff looked forward to see a little, balding starling in a gray polyester suit rush toward them. Starlings were what most folk called "mostly human." Over thousands of years in the galaxy, a few humans had picked up some alien genes. Often the babes died, horribly deformed. Sometimes they survived and passed on the starling genes to future generations. The starling before Riff reminded him of a mole. The man had long whiskers, buck teeth, and very large, very dark eyes that made sucking sounds as they blinked.

"Alien Hunters, at your service," Riff said. It still felt strange to think of himself as having an actual job. Aside from his three days at age sixteen working at an egg whisk factory, this would be his first day doing real work.

I never had a real job, real money, a real life when I brought Nova to Earth. I'll show her that I can be the man she has always needed me to be.

Riff reached out his hand, and the starling shook it in his paw. The man had fingers that ended with small, hard claws like halved coins. Sweat dripped down his forehead.

"Thank goodness you're here. You're three months late!" The starling wiped his hand on a handkerchief. "I am Myron, chief of logistics here at Pyrite Mines, and it's been a disaster, an absolute disaster."

Riff nodded sympathetically. "I heard you have a tardigrade infestation. Cute little critters. Shouldn't be too hard to remove. Lead the way. We'll take care of it."

I'll step on the little bugger, then collect our thousand bucks and get off this rock, he thought. He wanted to leave quickly. The casinos, pubs, rides--none of it appealed to him. He needed to be back out in space. To blast off to Vega and find the pirilian woman . . . and maybe his father.

Myron led them through the city, his gait shuffling and nervous. The starling kept rubbing his hands together, mumbling of lost revenue, of pyrite shipments late to deliver, and of the ruin that would befall his little kingdom. He led them away from the bars and neon lights and to a platform overlooking a track. A tunnel drove deep into darkness.

"I'll take you to see the mines." Myron wrung his hands. "Oh, by the golden gods . . . it's tearing them apart."

The starling pressed a button, and lights flared in the tunnel. A yellow train emerged from the shadows, shrieking across the tracks, looking like a great caterpillar that moved on many legs. When Riff looked closer, he saw that it *was* a caterpillar--a massive, train-sized caterpillar that scuttled across the tracks. The great beast skidded to a stop at the platform.

"It's . . . a living train." Riff rubbed his eyes.

Myron frowned. "Well, we wouldn't kill it!" He gestured. "Come on, come on. Hurry up now."

He swung open a door on the caterpillar's body, revealing a hollowed out interior. Riff glanced at his fellow Alien Hunters. They seemed as shocked as he was.

"While we're young!" Myron said, stepping into the cabin.

Riff shrugged and stepped into the giant caterpillar. Clutching their weapons and glancing around, his companions followed. On the inside, the caterpillar was smooth and hard. Framed advertisements for lingerie, casinos, and Happy Cow's Shawarma hung on the walls. Once the door was closed, the great caterpillar burst into a run. Through windows, Riff saw the walls of the tunnel stream by.

Romy leaned closer to Riff and whispered, "This is even better than an elephant ride!"

The caterpillar kept scuttling down the tunnel, sloping downward into the asteroid. Lights streamed alongside. Smooth jazz played within the cabin from hidden speakers, officially known as the worst music in the universe. It made Riff more queasy than the swaying floor did.

Finally, blessedly, the living train slowed to a halt and the doors swung open. Myron led the way, and the Alien Hunters stepped outside to find themselves gazing upon the mines of Pyrite.

"Wow," Riff whispered.

"Wow," Nova agreed.

Piston *tsk*ed his tongue. "Amateurs, you humans are. Amateurs. Back on my planet, dogs dig better holes than this."

Riff had never been to Piston's planet, the great mining world of Gruffstone, but he was hard-pressed to imagine any mines more impressive than these.

Below the platform, a shaft sank deep into the asteroid. It seemed to plunge down for kilometers, lined with blinking lights. Hundreds of smaller tunnels branched off from it, leading in every direction. Metal tracks rose along the walls, and wagons moved up and down like elevators. When Riff tilted over the edge, he could see pyrite glistening below; flecks of the precious metal covered the walls. The shaft rose even higher than the platform, leading for another kilometer upward. Far above, Riff could see the stars; a shimmering force field kept the air inside.

"Where are all the miners?" Riff asked.

Myron wrung his hands. "Striking! Most are at the casinos and bars. Some flew home to their planets. It's awful, awful!"

Piston nodded. "I'd strike too in a mine like this. Look at that! No symmetry to the side tunnels. No system to the carts.

Give me a platoon of gruffles, and I'd dig up all the pyrite in this mine within a month, leaving a network of beautiful tunnels for the ages to admire."

Myron gulped. "Sir Gruffle, they don't strike because of the size or shape of tunnels. They strike because . . ." A roar sounded below, and Myron squeaked. "Because of that!"

The mines shook.

Dust rained.

The bellow grew louder, and a creature moved below.

"Fragging aardvarks!" Nova cursed, unfurling her whip.

"Worse," said Myron. "A Denebian tardigrade."

Riff stared down into the shaft, queasy. The creature was climbing like a worm through a vein. It was massive. It was bloody massive. It made the caterpillar train seem puny. Its sluggish body undulated as it chomped on rocks flecked with fool's gold. Its six legs, each larger than a man, stretched out, tipped with claws. It drove higher and higher, snapping its jaws.

Steel drew his sword. "By my honor, I shall slay this beast."

Piston hefted his hammer. "I'm slaying it right with you, laddie."

Twig trembled, the smallest of the bunch, but managed to raise her wrench. An electric charge crackled between its prongs. "And I'm helping."

Romy, meanwhile, rubbed her eyes and gaped down, nearly tilting over. "A giant elephant!" she breathed. "Can I ride it? Can I, Riff, please?"

The beast in the mine rose higher, increasing speed, and suddenly burst up toward the platform, jaws opened wide enough to swallow them all.

Romy squealed and hid behind Riff, dropping her pitchfork. The others leaped back too--even Steel. Towering teeth snapped before them, and then the creature sank back into the mine, grumbling.

Riff gasped for breath. He reeled toward Piston. "You told me tardigrades are tiny! Wee little buggers, you called them."

"They are!" Piston insisted. "But this here is a *Denebian* tardigrade. Totally different variety, sir. I thought you were asking about the kind you have back on Earth."

Riff groaned and tugged his hair. "Right. We blast the bastard to death. That force field up there?" He pointed up the shaft to where a shield blocked the vacuum of space. "We lower it. We fly the *Dragon Huntress* over the mine. And we blast this place full of plasma. Dead tardigrade. Job's done."

"You can't!" Myron said. "You'll destroy the mine."

Riff patted the starling's shoulder. "We'll set the weapons to roast flesh, not rock. We won't damage the mine much. But our friend here will roast."

"You don't understand!" Myron wrung his hands so madly he seemed close to tearing them off. "We're still governed by Earth laws out here. Laws protecting endemic wildlife. If we kill this tardigrade, we'd be fined for millions. With the losses we've had over these past few months, we can't take any more. We'd have to close down." Tears filled the little man's eyes. "You have to remove it peacefully. To draw it out of the mine and send it on its way."

Riff's eyes opened wide. "And where do you expect us to take it?"

Twig approached him. The halfling tugged at his pant leg. "Captain, sir!"

Riff turned to look down at the diminutive mechanic. "Yes, Twig?"

She gulped. "We used to get Denebian tardigrades back in Haven. The planet I'm from. Where all halflings are from." She shuddered. "Horrible creatures! They used to sometimes land on our planet and eat us. They love to eat halflings. We're their favorite dish. A tardigrade once ate my uncle. It's all right. He passed through alive. Wasn't too happy on the other end, though." She gulped. "Point being, tardigrades are space farers. They travel through the sky like whales in the ocean. They can survive in vacuum. That's how they get from planet to planet. Probably how it got here--swam through space. We just need to do what we did back in Haven. Fish it out!"

Piston nodded thoughtfully, stroking his beard. "Aye, the lassie's right. Got a good idea or two in that noggin of hers sometimes. We can fly the *Dragon* up there." The gruffle pointed at the sky. "I can attach the iron cables we picked up a couple of years back. Just like a fishing rod. We just need to find proper bait."

Twig nodded and bounced around, excited. "It'll work! We'll attach a nice meal for the tardigrade to eat, something really delicious. What bait can we use?" She grinned, turning from one Alien Hunter to another. "Any ideas?"

Riff tapped his foot. "You did say they love eating halflings."

Twig nodded. "They do! They love us! They . . ." She gasped. "Wait. No!"

Riff knelt before her and held her shoulders. "It'll be safe. We'll give you helmet."

Twig wailed. "No! I won't do it!" She pointed at Romy. "Let the demon be bait."

Romy snorted. "My hair's made of fire. It would never eat me. Animals are scared of fire."

"And I'm too large a meal," Piston said, patting his barrel chest. "It would just see me as a choking hazard." He turned to look at Riff, Nova, and Steel. "And surely you won't ask the new owners of our ship to do the dirty work."

Twig groaned and flopped down onto her backside. She crossed her arms. "I always have to do the dirty work! Whenever you clog up the toilet, Piston, it's me who has to fix it."

"That's because you drop wrenches into the pipes!" the gruffle roared.

The halfling ignored him. "And that time we cornered the snot-monster on Rigel Six, who had to climb into his nostril to retrieve the diamonds? Me!"

Piston raised his hands defensively. "You know I'm allergic to snot-monsters!"

Twig looked from one person to another, seeking some support. They were all silent . . . other than Steel.

The knight stepped forth and raised his chin. "I'll do it. Strap me up like a worm onto a hook. I'll be your bait. Even if I die, it's for the good of our cause."

Twig rose to her feet and groaned. "It's no use. Tardigrades won't even touch humans. Hate the stuff." She heaved a long, deep sigh. "Fine! Fine, fine, fine! But I want a bonus, mister." She poked Riff. "Fifty extra credits."

Riff nodded. "Done. Thank you, Twig." He turned toward the others. "We came here for a hunt. Turns out it's a fishing trip."

CHAPTER THIRTEEN
GONE FISHING

The *HMS Dragon Huntress* hovered above the asteroid, a spool of cable attached to the dragon's head.

"Easy now," Riff muttered. He stood on the bridge, fiddling with controls. "Just got to release a little . . . bit of . . . cable. Oh shenanigans."

Outside the windshield, the spool spun madly. A great length of cable, a good twenty meters long, rolled out. Attached to one end, Twig shouted. Her voice rose through the communicator strapped to Riff's wrist.

"Captain! Slow down!"

Riff nodded. "Sorry, sorry! Hang in there."

She groaned. "Do I have a choice?"

Riff leaned toward the windshield and looked down. About five hundred meters below shone the surface of the asteroid. The mine gaped open like an eye socket leading deep into a stony skull. All around the pit spread Pyrite City, its glittering halls and neon signs bright. Twig dangled over the colony like a worm on a hook, dressed in a space suit. Inside her helmet, her eyes nearly bugged out with fear. In her gloved hand she held her precious electric wrench.

"Captain?" Twig's voice rose again through the communicator. She gulped. "Captain, I'm scared."

"You're all right, Twig." Riff returned to the controls. "I've got you. I'm going to release just a little bit more cable. Much slower this time. Stay cool, little buddy. All right?"

Her voice shook. "All right."

The others crowded around Riff, silent and staring. Nova clutched her whip nervously, and her long, pointy ears cocked toward the windshield. Steel stood sternly, chin raised, sword in hand; only the knight's eyes showed the pain he felt over seeing a damsel in distress. Piston anxiously tugged his beard, and even Giga seemed a little concerned. Only Romy seemed delighted with the proceedings; the demon bounced around and chewed her tail.

Riff pressed down lightly on the controls. The cable continued to spool out, meter by meter. Twig descended closer and closer to the mine.

Riff still saw no tardigrade below. Only the shadowy pit leading into the depths of the asteroid.

"Twig, you see anything down there?"

The halfling spun around on her cable, turning to face the asteroid. She gazed down into the mine.

"Nothing, sir. Just shadows and . . ." She gulped. "Oh, stars. I told you that a tardigrade once ate my uncle, didn't I? I don't want to be eaten."

"You're not going to be eaten, Twig." Riff tried to keep his voice calm and comforting. "We'll pull you right back up as the tardigrade emerges. We just need to lure him out, not actually let him bite you. Once he's out of the mine, we can ram into him. Send him hurtling out into space."

He lowered Twig another few meters.

"Captain?" Her voice trembled over the communicator, staticky. "Captain, I can see movement. I . . ."

"Twig, your heart rate is elevated. Stay calm, buddy. You're in good hands."

The sound of her gulping filled the bridge. "Yes, sir. I . . . if something happens to me, tell Piston that he can have my wrench collection."

The gruffle snorted. "Useless bunch of junk! You better survive, Twig, because half of your wrenches are still clogging up our engines, and I'm not reaching in there myself to pull them out."

Riff kept loosening the cable, lowering Twig closer and closer to the mine. Soon the halfling had reached the shaft and was now descending into the darkness. Her heart rate increased further.

"Stay calm, Twig," Riff said. "Tell me about something relaxing. Tell me about a beautiful place on your home planet."

Twig suddenly sounded like she was crying. "Haven is so beautiful, Captain. I haven't been there since I was a girl. It's all rolling, grassy hills. Rustling trees. Beautiful farmlands of wheat and barley. In autumn, all the leaves turn red, and the wheat and corn turn gold, and we sit around the hearths, eating pumpkin pie, and . . ." She whimpered. "Captain! Captain, I can see it!"

"All right, Twig. Wave your arms around a bit. Lure it up."

Riff leaned toward the windshield again. Several hundred meters of cable now stretched out from the *HMS Dragon Huntress*--nearly its full length. Twig dangled about a hundred meters deep in the pit, waving her little limbs about.

Below her, rising from the mine like water gushing from a geyser, came the Denebian tardigrade.

"Reel me up, reel me up!" Twig shouted.

Riff pressed down on the controls, trying to tug Twig back up.

Instead, the spool released its last few meters of cable.

Twig fell deeper into the pit. The tardigrade leaped toward her, jaws snapping.

"Captain!" the halfling screamed.

"Damn it," Riff muttered. "What's wrong with this thing?" He hit controls madly. "Spool's loose!"

"Fragging aardvarks, Riff!" Nova shouted, banging against the windshield.

"Captain!" Twig cried.

The tardigrade soared and opened its jaws wide, and Twig fell down into its gullet.

"Giga, get us out of here!" Riff shouted, turning toward the android. "Reverse, reverse!"

The android smiled sweetly. "Happy to comply!"

The *Dragon Huntress* engaged its front-thrusters. Blasting out gas, the ship pulled back, moving away from the asteroid.

The tardigrade's jaws snapped shut, sealing Twig inside its mouth.

The *Dragon Huntress* kept reversing. The steel cable pulled taut like a fishing line, running from the tardigrade's mouth to the starship's spool.

Twig was nowhere to be seen.

"Twig!" Riff shouted into his communicator. "Twig, can you hear me?"

Her voice sounded muffled. "Captain, it's eating me! Get me out, get me out!"

Riff wiped sweat off his brow. "Hang in there, buddy. We won't let him swallow you." He turned toward Giga. "Keep reversing. Tug that giant slug out of its hole."

"Captain, it's swallowing me!" Twig cried.

"Hang in there! Giga, damn it, more thruster power."

The android bowed, smiling. "Increasing front thruster power, sir."

The *Dragon Huntress* continued reversing. The engines groaned in protest. Metal parts creaked. Down below, the tardigrade thrashed. The massive alien slug began retreating into its burrow, Twig still in its mouth.

The *Dragon Huntress* jerked forward, tugged toward the asteroid.

"The fragging thing is fishing *us*!" Nova shouted.

"Giga, more power!" Riff said.

"Cannot compute." The android tilted her head. "Forward thrusters at maximum power, Captain."

"Then turn us around and engage the back engines." Riff cursed as the *Dragon Huntress* was yanked down again. The starship was now only three hundred meters from the asteroid, and the tardigrade kept tugging. Twig's screams rose from Riff's communicator.

"Cannot compute," said Giga. "Cannot turn the *Dragon Huntress* around while cable attached to spool. Cable would tangle in our wing and snap it, sir."

Riff cursed. "You have to reverse somehow, Gig. Come on!" He clenched his fists, and suddenly his eyes widened. "Blow our fire! Blow down dragonfire onto the asteroid! Newtonian laws. It'll shove us back into space."

"And you'll burn Twig and the tardigrade!" Piston shouted, running toward Riff. The gruffle's eyes dampened. "The damn fool will burn, and . . . her wrenches, and . . ." He wiped tears from his eyes and grabbed Riff. "We've got to save the little clod, Captain."

Riff ignored the gruffle and leaned against the windshield. The tardigrade kept tugging them down; in seconds they would crash against the asteroid.

"Giga, can you turn us around just a few degrees? Point our weapons there." He pointed a hill of excavated rock. "Blast those rocks with dragonfire."

"Happy to comply!"

The ship tilted. The steel cable creaked. The tardigrade gave a massive tug, and the *Dragon Huntress* sank another hundred meters, nearly hitting the asteroid.

Its dragonfire blazed.

The blasts of plasma shot out in a fury, slamming against the rocks just outside the mine. Stones cascaded and melted. Twig screamed.

The force shoved the *Dragon Huntress* backward.

They blasted away from the asteroid, yanking the tardigrade clear out from its hole.

"Fragging hell," Nova whispered, pressing herself against the windshield. "It's huge."

Romy's eyes were so wide they almost popped out. "It's even bigger than an elephant!"

Riff stared down. The tardigrade kept rising from the tunnel until finally its tail emerged. The full length of the beast flapped in space, a great wriggling blob. Its pudgy six legs thrashed, and its jaws were still snapped shut, sealing Twig within. The line of cable ran from its lips to the ship. The *Dragon Huntress* kept retreating, pulling the creature farther away from the asteroid.

"Twig!" Piston tugged Riff's wrist toward him and shouted into the communicator. "Twig, can you hear me, you clod?" Tears streamed down the burly gruffle's brown cheeks and dampened his white beard. "Talk to me, Twig! I'll never yell at you again, I promise. I'll never make you climb into the septic tank, burrow into snot-monster nostrils, or even sweep the engine room floor again. Please, Twig, just talk to me." Piston was trembling now. "Please. I can't run this ship without you. You're the best damn mechanic I know. You're . . ." He sank to his knees. "You're my best friend."

Silence filled the bridge.

Outside the ship, the tardigrade wiggled on the line, floating through space.

Only static came through the communicator.

Piston lowered his head, tears falling, and Riff placed his hand on the gruffle's broad shoulder. Everyone else stared in silence.

The communicator crackled with static.

Twig's voice rose from the speaker. "Well, go on, Piston! Tell me more about how wonderful I am."

Piston's eyes widened. The gruffle leaped to his feet. For an instant, pure joy suffused his face. Then rage overflowed it, and he shook his fist. "Why you little clod! How dare you fool me! I'm going to . . . I'm going to . . ." He fell back to his knees. "Aw, you wee lassie, I'm going to give you the world's biggest hug once you're back."

Riff sighed with relief and sank back into his chair. The ship moved farther and farther away from the asteroid, pulling the tardigrade along.

"Giga, can you blast some thruster power against it? Spray its head. Let's see if we can get it to sneeze Twig out."

"Happy to comply!"

The forward thrusters, normally used to steady and turn the ship, blasted out gas like smoke from a dragon's nostrils. The streams hit the tardigrade's head. The giant alien thrashed and mewled.

Its mouth, however, remained closed.

"Twig, you hear me?" Riff said. "You still have your electric wrench handy? Give the creature a little shock. We just need it to open its mouth."

"It'll swallow me!"

Riff shook his head. "Not with us holding you on the line. Go on. Give it a little bolt."

Through the communicator, they heard electricity crackle as Twig turned on her electric wrench. "Shocking it right on the gums, sir. I--whoa!"

Below the ship, the tardigrade whimpered and twitched. Its nostrils flared. Its body wrinkled up.

Then, with the might of a shattering star, the tardigrade sneezed.

"Captain!" Twig shouted.

A blast of green mucus flew through space and splattered against the *Dragon Huntress*'s windshield.

"Gross!" Romy said, wagging her tail in delight.

"Captain . . ." Twig whimpered. The little, mucus-covered halfling clung to the outside of the windshield, painted green. "Captain, I hate this job."

Riff wiped sweat off his brow. "Twig, make for the airlock. Piston, go pull her into the ship." He turned toward Giga. "On my signal, Gig, prepare to thrust the ship forward."

Piston lolloped off the bridge. Out in space, the tardigrade-- the bait and line free from its mouth--began to fly back toward the asteroid.

"Piston, you got her?" Riff shouted over his shoulder.

The gruffle's voice rose from the main deck below. "Got the little slimeball."

Riff clutched his armrests. "Giga, now fly! Ram that thing! Knock it out into open space."

"Happy to comply!" Giga smiled sweetly, and the sounds of processing CPUs rose from inside her.

The *Dragon Huntress* changed course . . . and charged forward, engines roaring.

The tardigrade bellowed and tried to escape, but it was too slow. The *Dragon Huntress* rammed into the massive creature's soft body. The tardigrade wailed and thrashed . . . and went tumbling deep into the darkness, flying far from the asteroid.

"Give it a warning shot, Gig." Riff pointed. "Just enough fire to scare it away."

Plasma fire blasted out from the *Dragon Huntress*. The flames reflected against the tardigrade. The creature turned tail and began flying away, fleeing the asteroid until it vanished into the distance.

Riff exhaled. It felt like he'd been holding his breath for the past hour. Air had never tasted sweeter.

Actually, the air here stinks. He sniffed and grimaced.

The stench came from behind him. He turned around to see a tiny, slimy green monster pointing at him.

"You owe me, Captain!" Twig said, dripping ooze. "Big time. I want a big, big bonus."

Romy covered her nose. "You stink."

Twig's fists shook. She roared out in fury, then spun around and marched off.

Hopefully to the shower, Riff thought.

He nodded with satisfaction and looked at the others.

"Friends? The Alien Hunters are back in business."

CHAPTER FOURTEEN
THE HUNT

An iridescent beetle, green and purple and mottled in gold, scurried across the grassy forest floor, one of Planet Cirona's most beautiful and treasured forms of native life.

A massive boot, tipped with iron claws, slammed down and crushed it.

The beetle died with a squeak.

Skrum, warrior of the Skelkrin Empire, wiped the sole of his boot against a mossy boulder. He spat.

"This damn planet is swarming with vermin." He looked around at the trees, ferns, and flying birds of many colors. Bile rose in his throat. "Disgusting backwater. Just the sort of planet the humans would settle. Just the sort of planet a filthy pirilian would hide on."

Skrum did not know who he hated more--the pathetic, sniveling humans, mere apes who dared venture to the stars, or the pirilians with their purple skin, glowing yellow eyes, and magic. It was like deciding what you hated more: bugs infesting your home or a wild wolf pawing at your door. Luckily, like most skelkrins, Skrum had enough hatred in him for more than one species.

"We should burn down the forest." Hotak, a soldier with matted white hair, sneered and hefted her flamethrower. "Burn down every damn tree and fern."

Skrum turned to stare at the female. He didn't care much for females, especially not on field missions. Yet even he had to admire Hotak's sheer strength. Muscles coiled across her long, crimson limbs. Her white eyes blazed like molten stars. Her tongue reached out from her jaws to lick her fangs. She stood eight feet tall, almost as tall as Skrum. Like him, she wore a black breastplate studded with spikes. Like him, she served Emperor Lore, the greatest of the skelkrin warriors.

But unlike me, she's a fool.

He gripped her wrist, forcing her flamethrower down. "Use that rotted piece of meat inside your skull!" He huffed. "Midnight is hiding here. If you burn down the forest, you'll burn her too."

Hotak snorted. Her drool dripped down her chin and sizzled against the floor. "Good! Pirilians are pathetic little wretches. I'll enjoy feasting on her charred flesh."

Skrum backhanded her. "You fool! We need her alive. Emperor Lore demands it."

At the thought of his emperor, Skrum felt a trickle of fear. The Emperor thought that Midnight was still on her way to Earth, perhaps on Earth already. Skrum had dared not reveal that he had captured the pirilian above Planet Cirona, only to let her slip from his grasp.

If Emperor Lore learns that we had her in our hangar, that she escaped us . . . Skrum clenched his fists. He did not want to think about the torture he would endure. He would not feel safe hailing Emperor Lore again until he had the pirilian back in his grasp.

Skrum turned toward the other skelkrin warriors he led. Twenty stood in the forest, beings of crimson skin, bulging muscles, gleaming claws and fangs, cruel white eyes, black armor. Beings of strength. Apex predators. All they needed was one girl, one more conquest . . . and the galaxy would be theirs.

"We will find her alive," Skrum said. "Every day that she's gone, I will kill one of you. The first skelkrin to find her will become my second-in-command! Now follow. We hunt."

Their nostrils flared, sniffing the forest. They continued moving, trampling over the ferns and the small animals that scurried underfoot. The air stank so badly of life that Skrum could not smell the pirilian. But he knew she was here. He had seen her starjet crash down. He would find her, bring her back to his emperor.

And then I will command more than just a single warship. He licked the drool that dripped down his chin. *Then I will rise to command a great armada for my master, an armada to conquer the Earth.*

The skelkrins kept tramping through the forest. The trees grew tall here, their leaves deep green, their blossoms white. Blue and purple flowers spread across the floor in a carpet. A bird of red, green, and yellow plumage flew overhead, cawing. Hotak sneered and raised her blowtorch, but Skrum shoved her weapon down.

"No burning."

They traveled on, sniffing, leaving a wake of trampled plants, wilted flowers, and sizzling drool.

As they moved through the forest, Skrum thought back to his time as a hunter on Planet Skelkra. Again in his mind, he was but a youth, thirsty for blood, hungry for raw meat. Again he was hunting through the black, barren plains of Skelkra, climbing over jagged boulders and the walls of canyons, howling at the black moon that hid the stars. Again his pack moved with him, a hundred predators, their skin crimson like the blood they drank, their fangs bright, sharp, ready to tear into flesh. Again they raced across the wilderness, leaping onto the trundling beasts that roamed in the darkness, ripping them apart, guzzling blood, chomping bones, sucking marrow.

We were savages, Skrum thought. *Nothing but barbarians. But that is where I learned the ways of the hunt.*

It was on the black, rocky plains of Skelkra that Skrum met his master.

The emperor had descended in his warship, a jagged chunk of iron like a mountain ripped out of the earth. Lore had come to the wild plains to seek warriors, to seek savages who had not gone soft in the great cities of metal. Skrum had spat upon this lord, had swung his claws at the towering warrior . . . only for the emperor to beat him down. To shatter his crude armor with his mighty weapons. To break his body. To crush him into obedience.

"Rise," Emperor Lore had hissed that night. "Rise before me."

Skrum had only lain on the ground. "My legs are shattered."

"Rise!" Emperor Lore roared. "Rise and become a great warrior. Or lie down in the dust and die as a worm."

Skrum had screamed, coughed up blood . . . and risen.

Since then, he had always obeyed his master. Emperor Lore had asked Skrum to slay his own parents to prove his loyalty. And Skrum had obeyed, slashing his parents' throats. Emperor Lore had asked Skrum to thrust a blade into his own belly, to prove his strength. And Skrum had obeyed, wounding himself, nearly dying, screaming for days before finally healing.

And now Emperor Lore, the greatest warrior in the galaxy, had asked Skrum to find a girl. An escaped prisoner. A pirilian who could win the war, who could bring the galaxy to its knees before the Skelkrin Empire.

And I will not let you down, my lord, Skrum swore. *As always, I obey.*

"Foul worm!" Hotak said. Her screechy voice drew Skrum's attention back to the forest of Cirona. He turned to see the burly warrior raising her flamethrower toward a caterpillar that was climbing a tree trunk.

He grabbed the flamethrower from her and hissed. "No burning!"

Hotak bared her fangs and growled at him. Her eyes burned like stars, white, horrible. "Return my weapon."

He howled and spat. She snapped her teeth. The two circled each other as the other skelkrins leaned in, staring, smiling, eager for blood.

"I will not." Skrum slung the flamethrower across his back. "You disobeyed me for the last time. You--"

She lunged toward him, claws outstretched, screeching.

Skrum stepped back, dodging her claws, and leaned in to bite. His fangs clanged against her armor. She roared and grabbed his head, squeezing, trying to crush his skull. Around them, the other skelkrins howled and thumped their chests.

"Kneel before me," he demanded.

She squealed, clawing at him. "I will not!"

He grabbed a fistful of her white hair and tugged her head down, banging it against a rock. "Kneel!"

She snapped her teeth again, trying to bite off his face. "No!"

He punched her crimson cheek again and again. "You will serve me. You will not disobey me again. You will call me master."

She grinned as he beat her. She laughed, gurgling on blood. She relaxed and reached out to stroke his cheek with her claws.

"You would make a good mate," she said.

He grunted and stepped back from her. "Kneel now."

She knelt. Her blood dripped. "Master."

Skrum snorted. "Any other day, I'd have slain you for your disobedience. Today I grant you mercy. I grant you the mercy Emperor Lore granted me. Today I let you live, Hotak. And you will serve me well. Forever."

She bowed before him, bringing her bleeding face to the ground. "Forever, Master."

The other skelkrins grumbled under their breath. They had hoped for death, Skrum knew. They had hoped to feast upon Hotak's corpse. He would give them corpses, but not yet. Not here, not now. Not while Midnight the pirilian still hid from him.

They walked on, predators on the prowl.

The sun was low in the sky when they reached the field.

Planet Skelkra had no use for farming; not a single plant grew on that rocky planet, and the very idea of feeding on plants disgusted Skrum. His people were predators, feasting upon the flesh of weaker animals. The humans were weaker animals, and here on Cirona, they plowed fields, grew crops, spread like a disease.

"They think this is a farm for grains," Skrum said. "They are wrong. This is a farm for human flesh. The farmers will be our meal."

Leaving the forest behind, the twenty skelkrins walked through the field. The stalks rose high, but skelkrins were towering predators, and they trampled over the crops like over the corpses of so many enemies. A barn rose ahead, built of wood and painted red. Several human farmers stood outside in a garden. The weaklings didn't even wear any armor, so confident they were, so foolish, so weak.

"Skelkrins!" shouted one of the farmers, a female pup. The vermin turned to flee.

"Skelkrins! Men, skelkrins attack!" shouted another farmer.

Skrum kept approaching, amused, as several of the human males rushed forth, holding their puny weapons--humble guns that could barely kill a bug, let alone apex predators like the skelkrins.

"Stand back, strangers!" cried one of the farmers, a man with a brown beard and straw hat. "This planet belongs to the Sol Federation. This is human territory."

Skrum looked aside at his fellow hunters, then back at the farmers. The skelkrins burst out laughing, a sound of shattering boulders, of cracking bones. As the predators kept approaching, Skrum raised his gun and fired a single shot.

The blast slammed into the bearded farmer, tearing a hole right through him. The human was dead before he hit the ground.

The other farmers fired their guns. Bullets flew toward the skelkrins, harmlessly ricocheting off their armor. Skrum fired his gun again, hitting another farmer.

"Lower your guns and live!" Skrum cried. He shot down another farmer, then kept walking through the hailstorm of bullets. "Kneel! Kneel before your new overlords!"

A few of the farmers dropped their guns and turned to flee. Others knelt outside their barn. From inside a farmhouse rose the wail of women and children, an appetizing sound that made Skrum's mouth water. He shot his gun again and again, knocking down those humans who fled, and kept walking until he stood above the kneelers.

The twenty skelkrins came to stand around the humans, forming a ring of claws and fangs and sizzling drool. The farmers were trembling.

"Please, sir," one young man begged, his face tanned bronze, his eyes full of tears. "Please, sir, spare us."

Skrum reached down his claws to caress the young man's cheek. "I will spare you . . . if you hand over the girl."

The farmer gulped. "The girl? What girl?"

Skrum clutched the young man's head and tore it off.

The other farmers screamed.

"I want the girl!" Skrum howled. "A pirilian girl with purple skin, yellow eyes, a dark cloak. I found her crashed starjet only kilometers away. Hand her to me."

The kneeling farmers tried to flee, but it was too late. The skelkrins surrounded them, a wall of muscle and iron. The humans fell back to their knees, begging.

"There's no pirilian here!" said a woman.

"You lie!" Skrum grabbed her throat. "Pirilians are weak. They feed on grains and fruit like worms. She would have fled here. She would have sought sanctuary with humans, another weak species. Hand her over now and I will spare your lives."

"Please, sir! No pirilian is here. This is a human planet. A hu--"

He thrust his claws. The farmer fell silent.

"These ones know nothing," said Hotak, her face still smeared with blood. The skelkrin grinned. "Let me burn them. I like my meat burnt."

Skrum raised his head and howled at the setting sun.

Where are you, Midnight? Where do you hide, my precious prize?

"Burn them." He spoke through gritted teeth. He handed back her flamethrower. "Burn them all and we will feast. Our search continues in darkness."

Hotak wailed with joy, and her fire blasted out, and they fed. They were skelkrins. They were predators. They would find their quarry, and they would spread across the stars.

They continued walking in darkness, bellies full. The hunt continued.

CHAPTER FIFTEEN

HYPERSPACE

The *HMS Dragon Huntress* stood back in Pyrite City, its mission completed, its payment collected.

Riff stood in the hangar, staring up at his starship. A deep, satisfied sigh ran through him.

"She's looking good, Captain." Nova came to stand beside him, her golden armor silent as she moved. She gave him a crooked smile. "Proud of your new home?"

He nodded and slipped his hand into hers. They stood together, watching as robots bustled across the ship, scrubbing off the rust and applying a fresh coat of paint. At the engines, Piston and Twig stood on ladders, installing new hyperfuel cubes.

"She's beautiful," Riff said softly.

With the tardigrade gone, Myron had paid them the promised one thousand credits, even adding a three hundred credit tip. Since then, Riff had been *spending*.

"A thousand credits for hyperfuel," he said, watching as Twig dropped a wrench, incurring a stream of curses from Piston. "A fifty credit bonus to Twig. Two hundred credits for a wash and paint job." He hefted the little bobblehead bulldog in his hand. "And ten credits for this, a little gift to our dear Giga."

And yet along with his pride, a sense of deep disappointment filled him. Nova saw and leaned against him.

"I'm sorry we heard no word of your dad here." She stroked his hair, and her green eyes were soft. "Wherever the pirilian girl hides, I have a feeling we'll find him."

Riff nodded, a lump in his throat. For long hours, he and Steel had walked through the bars and clubs of Pyrite City, asking about a traveling magician with a long white beard and wooden staff. None had seen Aminor Starfire here in years.

Riff stared at the ship, watching the robots paint the hull. The ship, once a bucket of rusty bolts, suddenly looked almost presentable.

I wish you were here with me, Dad, Riff thought.

"Come on, Nov." He squeezed her hand. "Looks like Piston's done installing the hyperfuel. It's time to fly on. To Cirona. To find Midnight . . . and maybe answers."

The robot painters applied the last few strokes, then bustled off to another ship in the hangar. Piston and Twig climbed off their ladder and brushed their hands against their pants.

"Just hope Romy doesn't drink this fuel," Piston said. "Expensive stuff, hyperfuel. Made with pyrite, you know."

Twig nodded. "I like how it smells." The halfling's nostrils flared. "Hyperfuel. Best smell in the world."

They climbed back into the ship together. Piston and Twig both climbed down into to the engine room. Romy was pacing up in the attic; Steel had managed to draw the demon up there using

some chocolate milk as bait, and the knight now stood in u.
deck, sword in hand, guarding the loft's hatch.

"If the beast tries to escape again," Steel said, "I shall slay
her."

Riff patted his brother's shoulder. "No slaying necessary.
Just keep her locked up and away from the fuel."

Steel nodded grimly. "By my honor, I swear it shall be
done."

Riff continued walking through the ship. He climbed the
stairs inside the dragon's neck, Nova walking behind him, and
they stepped back onto the bridge. Through the glass panels, he
could see several other starjets in the hangar; robots bustled
across them, painting, refueling, and scrubbing off space-
barnacles.

Giga bowed to him, smiling sweetly. She wore a new
kimono today, he saw, one embroidered with stars and moons.

"Welcome back to the bridge, Captain! Hyperfuel is
installed and we are ready for takeoff."

Riff approached the android and held out his palm. The
plastic bulldog sat there, bobbing its head. "For you, Giga. A new
dashboard toy. The gift I promised you."

He didn't know if androids had feelings, but if not, Giga
certainly gave a convincing show of joy. Her eyes widened and she
grinned. She took the toy gingerly, and her eyes even dampened.
She leaped onto Riff and embraced him.

"Arigato!" she whispered. "I love it."

Her scent of jasmine tickled his nostrils, and suddenly she seemed so human that Riff was sure Piston had lied to him, that Giga was not an android after all. With a smile, she darted toward the dashboard and placed the bulldog beside her second bobblehead, the swaying hula dancer.

"They are friends," she said.

Riff glanced over to Nova. The ashai gladiator stood at his side, clutching the handle of her whip. All the softness was gone from her face, and her eyes narrowed, green and burning, as they scrutinized Giga.

Was there something about Giga they didn't know? Something Piston hid, something Nova suspected? Riff looked at the android; she was leaning forward, tapping the bulldog's head, and bobbing her own head with it.

Instead of a bob, Riff shook his head to banish the thought. He had bigger things to worry about now. He sat in his captain's seat, sinking into the plush suede.

"Giga," he said, "take us off this rock."

The android turned toward him and tilted her head. "Rock? Does not compute."

"Off this asteroid. Back into space."

She nodded and a smile spread across her face. "Happy to comply!"

Nova sat in another seat, and Giga took the third chair. The android closed her eyes, and clicking sounds rose from inside her. The *HMS Dragon Huntress* began to move.

The starship rolled across the hangar, navigating between the other ships, heading toward the doors. Beyond spread the stars. As Giga hummed and clicked, the *Dragon Huntress* rolled out of the hangar, through a towering airlock, and out into the vacuum of space.

"Take us a hundred kilometers away from the asteroid," Riff said. "We'll make the jump to hyperspace from there."

Giga nodded and Riff leaned forward in his seat, watching the asteroid grow smaller in the distance. Soon all Pyrite City was only a glimmer in the darkness.

"Ready to engage hyperdrive, sir," said Giga.

Riff gulped. He had only flown in hyperdrive twice before-- once when heading to Planet Ashmar for his first interplanetary blues show, then again when traveling back to Earth with Nova. He had hated both trips.

Normal engines were too slow to reach the stars, of course. They were good for traveling within the solar system, but not for crossing the great distances between the stars. At least, not unless you wanted to grow old on the journey. Traveling with normal engine power, Riff would be an old geezer by the time they reached Planet Cirona in the Vega system.

Hyperdrive worked a bit differently. Its engines warped spacetime itself, forming a bubble of strange physics around the ship, allowing you to travel far faster than the speed of light. Riff didn't pretend to understand half of how it worked. He only knew that the two times he had traveled through hyperspace, he had felt as queasy as the time he'd eaten Old Bat Brown's clam stew.

But I need to reach Cirona. I need to find answers. The Cosmians, the skelkrins, my dad . . . all want Midnight. A woman who can destroy the universe. I have to find her.

He took a deep breath. "Giga, we're ready. Engage hyperdrive engines."

Her smile and chipper "Happy to comply!" denoted that androids, at least, did not get nauseous when bending the laws of physics.

The *Dragon Huntress* began to rumble.

New engines roared to life.

The hula dancer swayed, and the bulldog vigorously bobbed his head.

With a flash of light and a *whoosh*, the starship shot into hyperdrive.

The stars stretched out into long, gleaming strands like the tails of comets. They streamed by across the dashboard in a dizzying pattern of light. Globs of purple, pink, and deep blue floated between the strands. A hum rose from outside, and the walls of the ship rattled. The whole thing felt *wrong* somehow, as if Riff were somewhere between wakefulness and a dream. He needed a drink, even one of Bat Brown's concoctions.

"We are now fully in hyperspace, sir." Giga smiled from her seat. "Estimated time of arrival at the Vega system: four days, thirteen hours, and thirty-two seconds. Would you like me to run a countdown?"

He shook his head. "Just let me know a day before we get there so I can wash my hair."

Nova rose from her seat and leaned against the windshield, staring outside at the lightshow. The lights gleamed against her armor, pale skin, and bright hair, turning her into a statue of gold. The ashai princess turned toward the android.

"Giga, do you ever sleep?"

Giga nodded. "Yes, ma'am. I'm programmed to go into sleep mode when all is functioning properly."

Nova nodded. "Then take a nap."

"Happy to comply!" Giga's eyes closed and she slumped back in her seat.

Riff raised an eyebrow. "She's an android, Nova. She was doing android stuff. You didn't have to put her to sleep."

The ashai glowered at him, hands on her hips. "An android who hugged you after you gave her a gift. An android who has feelings for you."

Riff rolled his eyes. "Nova! For pity's sake. She's a piece of hardware. She doesn't have feelings." He tilted his head. "Wait a minute . . . are you jealous of a robot, Nova?"

She groaned. "First of all, I'm not jealous. Second of all, being jealous would imply that I still have feelings for you. The only thing I feel toward you is contempt." She stepped toward him and jabbed a finger against his chest. "First you drag me off Ashmar, my home planet. Then you drag me off Earth, the planet where you dumped me."

"Hey, wait a moment!" He rose from his seat. "You dumped *me*. I was happy living with you on Earth."

She snorted. Suddenly her eyes were damp. "Living in a dump. Living in a tiny bedroom above a blues bar. Watching you squander your money on booze--the little money you did earn, which wasn't much." She shoved him back into his seat. "I was a princess of a planet! I could have ruled an entire world. And I left it, Riff. I left all that for you. But you fooled me. You told me you were a famous musician."

He bristled. "I am!"

"Don't make me slap you." Her voice shook with rage, and tears flowed down her cheeks. "You lied to me. You promised me a good life on Earth. And look what happened." She turned around and covered her eyes. "Frag this."

Riff sat in his chair, watching her. Obviously, this had been boiling inside her for years.

He rose to his feet and approached her. "I thought we did have a good life." He placed a hand on her shoulder. "It was the perfect life for me, Nova. Playing my music. Living with you. I was happy."

She spun back toward him. A tear dangled off the tip of her nose. "You were happy. A perfect life for you. But what about what I wanted? You never cared about that."

"I cared," he whispered. "I just didn't know how to make you happy."

"That much is obvious."

A loose strand of her hair fell across her face. Riff tucked it back behind one of those long, pointy ears he used to love kissing. "I'm sorry, Nova. What else can I say? I messed up. I know it. For two years since you left me, I was sorry, and I missed you, and I prayed that we'd somehow get back together. I never stopped loving you. Even now, after all this time, I love you."

She lowered her head, but she did not push him away. "And I hate you," she whispered. "I hate you so much. For what you did to my life. For what you still do to me." She looked up at him, and her lips trembled. "For making me love you even now."

He kissed her. The lights of hyperspace streamed around them, and she kissed him back. Their bodies pressed together, and he placed his arms around her waist. She slung her arms around his shoulders. They kissed deeply, and it felt like old times. Like their first kiss long ago on a distant world. And Riff had never loved her more.

He reached his hands down and began to unbuckle her armor. Nova moaned into his kiss, and her hands reached down to his belt.

"Cannot compute! Cannot compute!"

Riff jumped and tore away from Nova's kiss. He turned to see Giga standing beside him, staring at them.

"Damn it, Giga!" Nova said. "I told you to go to sleep."

Giga bobbed her head. "Captain, Captain! Cannot compute fridge cooling system. Fridge door open. Romy eating supplies."

From across the ship, Riff could just make out the sound of Romy feasting while Steel demanded that the evil beast return to her lair.

Nova groaned and tugged her hair. "I'll go take care of this." She blew out her breath, spun around, and marched off the bridge. She slammed the door behind her.

Riff remained on the bridge, alone with Giga.

The android smiled in relief. "Fridge closed. Situation under control." She placed a hand on Riff's shoulder, leaned forward, and kissed his cheek.

As the android returned to her seat and closed her eyes, a small smile played on her lips. If Riff didn't know any better, he could have sworn two things: Nova was jealous of the android . . . and the android was jealous of Nova.

He really, really hated hyperspace.

CHAPTER SIXTEEN

METAL AND FIRE

Sir Steel Starfire stood in the main deck of the *HMS Dragon Huntress*, staring out the porthole at the streaming lights of hyperspace, and it seemed like the weight of the cosmos hung across his shoulders.

I am farther from my home than I've ever been, he thought as the lights flowed. *A lone knight on a quest to save a damsel. A lone man without a castle. Without a brotherhood.* He lowered his head and placed a hand on his breastplate. *Without a coat of arms.*

He wanted to go lie down. He was tired. He had hardly slept for days. The rest of the crew members were all sleeping in their quarters. But how could Steel sleep while the others needed him? He had vowed to defend this ship from the evil infesting it. He stared up at the locked hatch in the ceiling. Beyond lay the demon of Hell, the creature he had vowed to keep at bay.

"Why are you so sad, sir knight?"

The voice rose from behind him.

Steel spun around and gasped. The demon stood there!

He drew Soflare, his ancient blade. "Stand back, foul creature!"

Romy waved at him, and her tail wagged. Her pitchfork gleamed. Her fangs and claws shone in the lights from the window. Her hair was a pyre of hellfire. Her wings stretched out, curtains of the abyss.

"I'm bored," she said. "Do you want to play counter-squares? Do you want to wrestle? Do you want to look for poodles? Do--"

He pointed his sword at her. "Do not speak, evil one!" He glanced up at the hatch; it was still locked. He returned his eyes to the demon. "How do you keep escaping?"

Romy grinned. "It's easy! The ship is full of heating vents, cooling vents, pipes, shafts, sneaky passageways. I can sometimes squeeze in them, when I haven't eaten too much." She glanced over her shoulder at her backside. "It's getting a bit harder to fit through. All that fatty fuel goes right into my bum. I really would prefer to eat poodles, if Piston ever agreed to buy any."

Steel blinked. His voice dropped to a shocked whisper. "Do not speak of such things!"

"What, of bums? Or of eating poodles?" Her eyes softened. "Is that why you're sad? Because there are no poodles here to eat?"

Steel spun away from her and faced the porthole again. "I do not understand all these things of which you speak."

Romy nodded thoughtfully. She came to stand beside him and gazed out the window with him. "People say that to me all the time." She leaned against the glass. "It's pretty out there. I like how the lights get all flowy in hyperspace. They remind me of fire, only softer."

Steel found himself agreeing. His voice softened. "They are pretty."

Romy turned toward him. "You didn't answer me, sir knight. Why are you so sad? Your eyes, they . . . they're like a hound dog's eyes. Why?"

Steel turned away from her. He stepped away from the window. "I would not share these things with a creature of evil such as yourself."

Romy reached around him, holding up her teddy bear. "You can tell Mister Floofie!" She moved the puppet around, mimicking its voice. "Hello, sir knight! Tell me why--whoa!"

Steel shoved the doll aside. "I am no child!"

"Neither am I." Romy raised her chin. "I'm over five thousand years old, you know. I'm a big girl!" She wagged her tail proudly.

"Yet you have the mind of a child, it would seem."

Romy flopped down onto the couch. "Fine, don't tell me. I know the answer anyway. I can see it on your heart." She pointed at his breastplate. "There was a symbol there once. It's all scratched out. You were part of a brotherhood once. A knighthood! And . . . now you're not. Your coat of arms was scratched off." She lowered her head. "They banished you. Why?"

Her words cut deep. Truly, this was a creature of evil. A demon and mind reader. He wanted to slay her. He knew it was his duty to slay demons.

Yet it's also my duty to slay dragons, and now I fly within one's belly.

He sighed and sat down on the couch beside her.

"Not all knights are honorable," he said, staring at the wall.

"You are." Romy reached out to touch his shoulder. "I can tell. I know these things."

He nodded. "I have dedicated my life to honor, to chivalry, to righteousness. Thus, when I saw the corruption within my order, I had to speak up. My honor demanded it. I confronted the head of my order, Lord of the Knights of Sol. I told him that I knew. That I knew of his dealings with the Cosmians, a band of skelkrin worshippers who would see Earth destroyed." Steel squared his jaw, and his eyes stung. "I gave him a chance to redeem himself. He repaid me with banishment." He clenched his fist. "I don't know why I'm telling you this, demon."

Romy shrugged. "Maybe because I'm the first person who's not afraid to ask." She lowered her eyes. "I'm sorry you were banished, Steel. I was banished too once. Long ago. From Hell. I was a torturer. Really! It was my job to torture the dead souls of sinners. So I tortured them. I told them bad puns. I made them smell my stinky socks. I even gave them wet willies." She sighed. "They thought I was a horrible torturer, so they banished me from Hell, and I ended up here."

Steel groaned. "You tell fibs."

"Uh-uh!" She shook her head wildly, spraying sparks. "The truth, the whole truth, and nothing but the truth." She patted his knee. "We're two outcasts. Two relics of an older time."

Romy reached across the table and picked up one of the ship's badges. The words "Alien Hunters" appeared there, written in gold. She placed the badge upon Steel's chest; it snapped onto the armor.

"You have new friends now, Steel Starfire." Romy nodded. "A new group of heroes. The Alien Hunters."

Steel smiled wanly. "A group of heroes? More like a group of misfits."

Romy grinned. "Good. I like misfits. Sometimes they're the most fun."

"Fun," Steel whispered.

She tilted her head. "Haven't you ever had fun?"

He stiffened. "A knight cares for honor, for chivalry, for--"

Romy groaned. "Yeah, yeah. But you need fun too!" She reached toward the table and pulled over the counter-squares board. "Let's play a game. Look, there's even a knight piece." She pointed. "You can play with that one. And there's a dragon piece too, like our ship. Here, let me show you how they all move."

She spent long moments speaking, moving pieces about, grinning and laughing at her jokes. Her tail wagged. Steel understood little of it, but he found himself enjoying her company, the light in her eyes, the brightness of her smile.

They began to play. Romy kept laughing as she won round after round. And for the first time in many years, Steel felt some of his old pain melt. For the first time in many years, he had fun.

Finally Romy fell asleep on the couch. She leaned against Steel, snoring, and drool dripped down her chin. Her hair of fire crackled near Steel's head, but he found that it was only slightly warm. When he dared reach his fingers toward the flames, they did not burn him. He found himself stroking her hair as she slept against him.

"But mom!" Romy mumbled in her sleep, leg twitching. "All the other kids have ponies. Can't I eat one too?"

Steel sighed. A blanket lay crumpled up at the corner of the couch. Gently, careful not to rouse her, Steel pulled the blanket over Romy. He sat beside her as she slept, letting her lean against him, letting her feel safe.

He was, after all, a knight. And Romy was a damsel to protect.

CHAPTER SEVENTEEN
BARRACUDA

The *SS Barracuda* charged through space like its namesake--a beast of teeth, scales, eternal hunger.

Inside the silvery starship, Grotter sat alone at the bridge, gazing out into the darkness.

"You're out there, Starfire." The cyborg's bionic eye narrowed, scanning the vastness of space. "You are like me. A fighter. A man on a quest. But you will learn, Starfire, that this is a game you cannot win."

Grotter had left his small, weak starjets back on Earth. On his own, Riff--a slovenly ne'er-do-well--had posed no threat. But now the sluggard flew with an ashai gladiator, with a trained Knight of Sol, and with a horde of other unwashed mercenaries. Now Riff Starfire flew in a dragon warship that could blast plasma like dragonfire. And so Grotter too had upped his game. His *Barracuda* was massive, the largest warship in the Cosmian fleet. The great fish charged across the solar system, its metal teeth stretching out, its scales shimmering silver. It was a ship to dwarf the *Dragon Huntress*, to crush Starfire, to crush anyone in Grotter's way.

"I will find you, Starfire. And then you will know true pain."

Grotter looked away from the stars that shone outside the window. He turned toward the framed photograph that stood at his side between the control panels. He took this picture frame with him on every flight. He would take it to his grave. He reached out his bionic hand, the clattering claw of metal, and caressed the picture frame's glass.

"You are always with me, Kira," he whispered.

She smiled back at him from the photograph. A beautiful woman, yet sad. Her smile full of light, yet wistful. The only woman Grotter had ever loved. The woman who had married another man. The woman who had spoken against him, had picketed against the Cosmian Order.

The woman he had killed.

"You chose to wed that fool of a magician instead of me," Grotter whispered, caressing her framed face. "You chose to fight me. But I will always love you, Kira. Even though your blood stains my hands, I will forever love you." He turned back to look into space. "And I will kill your sons. I will kill Riff and Steel Starfire."

A smile stretched across what remained of Grotter's mouth, twitching. How sweet it would be! Killing Kira had not been enough, had not filled his cravings for vengeance, had not punished her enough for spurning his love. But to kill her sons! To kill that fool of a bluesman and that relic of a knight! And in the name of Emperor Lore of Skelkra, no less!

A day of great victory approached. A day of vengeance. A day of glory.

Finally Grotter saw it ahead. The asteroid floated before him through space, a hundred kilometers across. As the *Barracuda* flew closer, Grotter saw the glittering colony clinging to the great rock--Pyrite City.

Grotter snorted. A city of sin. A city of sleaze. Once he caught the pirilian girl, it was a city he and his skelkrin masters would destroy.

He flew his starship closer to the mining colony. The halls of Pyrite City clung to the asteroid like luminous barnacles: brothels, opium dens, casinos, bars, a thousand hives of debauchery. Grotter directed his ship toward a port, and the great *Barracuda* landed, dwarfing the other starships that anchored here.

Grotter left the control bridge, walked through the gleaming halls of the *Barracuda*, and exited the warship. A hundred of his warriors exited the ship with him, Cosmians in black robes and black hoods, their guns larger than human arms. Across the starship lot, several robots saw the militia and fled, squeaking and clattering.

One Pyrite denizen, however, was more brazen. A little man in a gray polyester suit rushed forth. He had a timid, ratty look to him, his fingers tipped with small claws no larger than coins, his nose sprouting whiskers.

Probably a starling, Grotter thought. A human mixed with alien genes. A badge on his suit named him "Myron."

"You cannot land here!" Myron was whining, his voice high-pitched. "Your starship is too large, too large!"

Grotter raised an eyebrow, amused. He turned to stare at the *Barracuda* behind him. The massive warship filled most of the lot. The crushed remains of several starjets lay beneath it, flattened and showering sparks. His fellow Cosmians smirked, turning between the wreckage and the wailing little bureaucrat in the gray suit.

"You must leave, must leave!" Myron cried, waving his arms about, seemingly undaunted by the sight of a hundred Cosmian warriors.

Grotter snickered, stepped toward the little man, and reached out his metal claw. He grabbed Myron's throat and lifted the thrashing creature off the floor.

"I'm looking for Riff Starfire." Grotter's bionic eye narrowed. "A piece of space scum, traveling in a dragon-shaped ship with a crew of miscreants. He was here. Do not deny it. Where is Starfire now?"

Myron thrashed, gurgling, pawing at the metal claw that squeezed his throat. The little creature was trying to speak but only wheezing.

"Speak louder!" Grotter demanded, squeezing his claws tighter. "I can't hear you."

"Starfire . . . gone!" Myron managed. "Flew off! Release . . . me!"

Grotter tossed the sniveling rat to the floor. Myron fell with a thud and tried to scurry away. Before he could flee, Grotter slammed down his boot, pinning the starling to the floor. He reached down his claws, pointing the sharp metal fingers at Myron's whiskered face.

"Tell me everything," Grotter said. "When did Starfire leave? Where was he heading?"

"I don't know, sir!" Myron said. "I--"

Grotter lashed his claws, slicing off one of Myron's earlobes.

The starling screamed. Blood spurted onto his polyester suit, only to slide off the shimmering fabric.

"You'll have to do better than that," Grotter said, "unless you want to lose more body parts."

Myron wept. "I don't know, sir! He . . . he bought hyperfuel. Just one pack. Just enough for twenty or thirty light-years, sir. Flew off only yesterday."

Grotter pressed his claws against Myron's other ear. "Where was he heading?"

"I don't know, sir! I saw him heading . . ." Myron gulped and pointed. "That way. To that star. The bright one in the Lyra constellation."

Grotter snarled and looked up. Above, through a transparent force field, shone the stars. Myron was pointing toward Vega, one of the brightest stars in the sky.

Yes, Grotter thought. Vega was close, only twenty-five light-years away. Just close enough for a single pack of hyperfuel. Humanity's newest colony lay there on a planet called Cirona, a frontier backwater.

Daniel Arenson

Grotter pulled his foot off Myron and turned toward his men. "We go to Vega!"

The Cosmians bowed their hooded heads and began filing back into the *Barracuda*.

Myron rose to his feet, clutched his wounded ear, and began fleeing the starship lot.

"Myron!" Grotter said.

The starling turned toward him. Grotter raised his claw, opened his palm, and blasted out a ball of plasma.

The red projectile slammed into Myron. The starling screamed, fell, burned, twitched . . . then fell still.

"You tried to hide information from me," Grotter said to the corpse. He snorted. "Also, your whining was annoying."

Grotter stepped back into his shimmering, silver warship. With a blast of engine fire that roasted the other starships on the lot, the *SS Barracuda* rose back into space, leaving the asteroid behind.

As the ship blazed into hyperspace, Grotter sat on the bridge, smiling thinly, and clutched the framed photograph of his beloved.

CHAPTER EIGHTEEN
THE ENGINE GRINDERS

Piston paced across the engine room, his nerves refusing to unwind.

"The coils are overheating," he muttered, tapping them. "The hyperfuel is burning too hot." He peered at the gauges. "Too much steam building up." He twisted a valve, releasing a blast of heat. "Damn ship's falling to pieces, and you keep getting underfoot."

Twig sat on a pipe. She glared at him. "Me? I'm just sitting here."

"Sitting here being useless!" Piston shook his fist at her. "We're flying far, Twig. Farther than we've ever flown. Deep to the most distant of human outposts. Near . . ." He gulped. "Near the Skelkrin Empire. And you're just sitting there!"

The diminutive mechanic tossed her long, black hair and rolled her eyes. "Well, what do you want me to do? Summon the armada? Lead an army to war?"

"You could help me with the damn tension coils." Piston knelt. His old knees ached whenever he knelt. "Damn it, Twig, I'm too old for this. I need you."

She groaned, leaped off the pipe, and knelt beside him. She reached under the panels and twisted at the coils, setting them aright. "There. Better?"

He nodded and grumbled. "Better."

Twig playfully punched his shoulder. "And I know you need me. You'd be so lonely without me. You love me and I'm your best friend." She grinned and hopped away as he tried to slap her. "I heard you say it! Back when I was inside the tardigrade. You said it all, and you were *crying*. And--all right, all right!"

She scurried away as he roared and tried to grab her. The damn little clod was so fast. He was a lumbering hunk of muscle, slow and sturdy. He was built for the rocky, giant planet of Gruffstone, a place of immense gravity. There his stocky body thrived. But this ship here was set to Earth gravity, always leaving him feeling slow, cumbersome, a brute. He couldn't catch Twig. He could barely catch a cold on this ship.

Finally he sat down on a box and sighed. "I'm not meant for this business no more."

Twig was halfway across the engine room. She peered around a bar. "What, fixing tension coils?"

He glowered at her. "I'm fine at fixing coils! I mean traipsing across the galaxy like this. This is a young gruffle's game." He tugged at his long white beard with his knobby brown hands. "I'm old, Twig."

She rolled her eyes. "No you're not."

"I am!" he insisted. "I'm very old. Ancient. I'm far, far older than you."

"Well, I'm only nineteen. You have crumbs in your beard older than that."

He glared, brushing that beard. "Well, I'm far older even than this ship."

Twig raised an eyebrow. "The *Dragon Huntress* is only sixteen. Even *I'm* older than it."

"Well, I'm very old! Leave it at that. So old I've forgotten how old. So many years out here in space, far from home. Far from Gruffstone."

There were no proper windows down here in the engine room, only a small porthole. Piston stepped toward it and stared outside at the streaming lights of hyperspace. He wondered if Planet Gruffstone, home to the gruffles, was somewhere out there in his field of vision, stretched into a streak of color as the hyperdrive engines bent spacetime around them.

Twig came to stand beside him. She stood on her tiptoes, hopped up and down, but still couldn't reach the porthole. Standing more than a foot shorter than him, she could never reach a damn thing.

"Here." He knelt, grumbling. "Hop on my shoulders if you want a look outside. You'll just keep hopping around otherwise and probably break something."

She climbed onto his back, a fraction of his weight, and onto his shoulders. She gazed out the porthole. "It's pretty out there."

Piston nodded. "And it was pretty back home. On Gruffstone. Oh, the stars you could see from there! The sky's not as murky as on Earth, you know. As a wee lad, I used to climb the mountains and gaze up at the stars. They shone like diamonds. Have I ever told you about the diamond mines we had back on Gruffstone?"

Of course he had. He knew that he had told her. A million times or more.

"No," Twig said softly. "Tell me."

He inhaled deeply, seeing them again. "So many diamonds shone there, Twig! And rubies. And emeralds. And sapphires. And topaz and amethyst and tiger's eyes and a thousand other gemstones. That's why we first moved to Gruffstone, you know. To mine for precious jewels." He caressed his ring and the ruby that shone there. Suddenly he felt older than ever. Suddenly the ache inside him seemed too great. "She's still buried there, you know. My wife."

Twig hopped off his shoulders and stood before him. Her brow furrowed. "You were married?"

"Aye, lassie. To a beautiful woman, a living jewel. The greatest beauty in Gruffstone." He sighed wistfully. "Her skin was smooth as a chestnut. Her eyes were large and deep like the night sky. Her beard was long and flowing, and--"

"She had a *beard?*" Twig's eyes widened.

He frowned. "All gruffle women have beards! And they're proud of it, lassie."

Twig rubbed her very smooth chin. "Hmm. I don't think I'd want one."

"That's because you're a knuckle-brained little halfling! But gruffle women are proud of their beards and weave them into many elaborate braids that shine with jewels. And I brought my love many jewels." He lowered his head. "She fell ill. She was still young. Still so beautiful, still so happy. Even until the end, she was happy." He placed his hand against the porthole. "I miss her. After she died, I couldn't stay. I left Gruffstone. Found myself in this floating hunk of junk."

"You never told me," Twig whispered.

"You never asked!" He shook his fist, then lowered his arm and lowered his head. "And I never wanted to speak of it." He snorted. "Funny thing. You're the closest thing I've come to a soul mate since she died. Never thought I'd end up being friends with a knuckle-headed halfling."

Twig stuck out her tongue. "Well, when I left home, I never thought I'd be stuck in an engine room with a grumpy old gruffle. A gruffle who has crumbs in his beard, might I add." She twirled her wrench. "You know, Piston old boy, maybe you like mines and gemstones and pretty rocks. But not me. Not us halflings. I come from a planet of grassy hills, swaying fields, rustling trees, sunlight, flowers. So many flowers. There was true beauty there."

He snorted. "Flowers! Hah. Allergy monsters. Why'd you ever leave if you love them so much?"

She shrugged. "Well, everyone in my family has been a farmer. Farmer after farmer, going back for generations. While they were all growing carrots and mushrooms, I was in the shed with my tools, fiddling around and building robots. Junkbots, my old gaffer would call them. They were simple things, just made from tin cans, springs, gears, old batteries and wires and little motors. But they worked. They really did!" She sighed. "I never had any friends back on Haven. I'm small, even for a halfling, and weak, and . . . for a long time, I was very sad. Melancholy, our village doctor called it."

Melancholy suddenly filled Piston's own heart. "You suffered from depression, even among the flowers?"

Twig looked down at her feet and shrugged. "Some call it depression, others anxiety, and . . . well, I don't know. Even though it's beautiful in Haven, with flowers and forests, I always felt like there was a gray cloud above me. For many years--Haven years are short, but they seem long to us halflings. I didn't eat much as a youngling. Maybe I was afraid of growing too big. Maybe I felt safer being so small, able to hide, to disappear, to stay a child." Her eyes dampened. "But when I worked in the shed with my tools, building robots, that cloud went away. The robots I built became my friends. While everyone else talked about turnips, mushrooms, and pumpkins, I talked about gears, bolts, screws. I knew I wasn't meant to be a farmer. I knew I was meant to work on great machines like starships. To work with huge, massive hyperdrive engines, not just little motors I took out of lawnmowers. So I left Haven. Hitched a ride to Earth. Saw a dragon starship and knew it was my home." She rubbed the tears out of her eyes and grinned. "It's tough to beat life on a dragon starship. Especially when there's a grumpy old gruffle inside."

Piston mussed her hair, and suddenly he felt sadder than he had in many days, but also more joyous, a sort of sweet sadness.

"Aye, lassie." He patted her hand. "There's worse lots in life than this. There's worse than flying through space in a dragon with a good friend."

She hopped back onto his shoulder, and they stared out together at the stars.

CHAPTER NINETEEN

THE PRINCESS OF ASHMAR

Nova lay in her bed in the crew quarters, feeling like a maestro trapped in a room with tone-deaf, accordion-playing monkeys. The noise was driving her crazy.

How could one sleep like this? There were three bunk beds in the room, and from each bed rose a symphony. Piston was the loudest, snoring like an engine; Nova was surprised the sound wasn't knocking down the walls, exposing them to hyperspace. Steel's snoring wasn't as gruff or grainy; the knight emitted a high-pitched wheeze that billowed his mustache with every breath. Twig, barely larger than a toddler, kept kicking her feet in her sleep like a dreaming dog, thumping the wall.

Romy was the worst of the bunch. Riff had allowed the demon to sleep here tonight instead of in the attic, and the demon now lay sprawled out across her bed, drooling and talking in her sleep.

"Please, mommy, can I have a puppy? I don't like my vegetables. I want a puppy!"

Nova rolled over toward the wall, wrapped a pillow around her head, and tried to sleep. But it was impossible.

She sighed. She missed her home. Back on Earth, she had lived in one of Cog City's finest buildings. Her penthouse had gazed out onto the cityscape--a dazzling view of towers, parks, and countless starjets. Inside her apartment, her bed had been large and soft and topped with satin sheets, not a hard bunk like this. After leaving that useless scoundrel Riff, she had worked hard for her money, had become a famous gladiator, then a rich gladiator. She had found wealth again, the wealth she had lost leaving her planet.

"You're breaking my heart!" Romy cried out in her sleep. "Put it back in the jar."

Nova screwed her eyes shut and thought of that lost planet. Of Ashmar. The great, red, fiery world she came from, the homeland of all ashais. She had been born there, had lived there for five Ashmari years--nineteen years as the planet Earth turns. The daughter of Ashmar's king, Nova had grown up in a palace overlooking a lake of fire. She had grown up a warrior, training with blades, with whips, with guns, learning all the ways there were to kill a man. She had grown up a princess, an heiress, destined to rule a world.

And then, six Earth years ago . . . he showed up.

A scruffy human, ten years her senior. He wore no armor like her people, only jeans and a T-shirt. He carried no crackling whip, only a gun and a guitar. Scruff covered his face, and he played for her people, played on stage, a human come to Ashmar to share his music. He had met her eyes in the crowd, had winked at her, and Nova--young, stupid Nova, only a youth--had fallen for him. For somebody who didn't care that she was a princess. For somebody who wasn't just a grim, gruff warrior, but somebody who could play music for her. Who could make her laugh.

So I loved you, Riff Starfire, she thought. *I told my father I would marry you.* She winced. *And he cast me out.*

She grabbed her blanket in her fists.

I gave up two worlds for you. Ashmar. Earth. And now I end up here, in a bunk bed, surrounded by an orchestra from hell. She opened her eyes and looked at Romy. *Literally, in this one's case.*

Finally Nova could take it no longer. She climbed out of her bed, stepped between the others, and left the crew quarters.

She walked down the dark hallway, wearing a long T-shirt that draped over her underpants. Her feet were bare and the floor was cold. Up a flight of stairs, she could see the doorway to the bridge. The door was open, and Giga stood beyond, staring out into hyperspace. Nova wondered if the android slept like humans did, if she too dreamed, if she too was full of fears, regrets, old pain.

Nova looked away and kept walking down the corridor until she reached the captain's quarters. She opened the door and tiptoed inside.

Whoever had built the *Dragon Huntress* had obviously believed the captain first among equals. This chamber was almost as large as the crew quarters, but built for just one. That one--Captain Riff Starfire--lay sleeping in his bed.

Nova rolled her eyes. Captain! He was only captain because of that damn guitar of his. Nova should have just swapped her motorcycle for the *Dragon Huntress* and now she would be the captain. Riff was no hero, just the man who had ruined her life.

She tiptoed closer and looked down at him. During the past six years, they had both grown. Both changed. She wondered if she even still knew him. She saw that a white hair grew from his temple now, that new lines of worries appeared on his brow, and she realized that he wasn't young anymore. He was already a man halfway through his thirties, a man who had never wanted to grow up, who now found himself forced to.

But he's still the same man I fell in love with.

Cursing everything in the cosmos, including herself, Nova climbed into bed with him.

He moaned, his eyes opened, and he looked at her. "Nova?"

"Hush. I'm not here for anything that will make you happy, so calm down. Everyone else is snoring, so I'm here."

He closed his eyes again. "There's a couch in the main deck."

She growled. "And you'll be sleeping there if you don't shut up."

Thankfully, he shut up. Nova lay down beside him, her back to him, and closed her eyes. Then she wriggled a little closer. Then closer. Then she pulled his arm around her, and she held his hand to her breast. His breath tickled the back of her neck, and finally Nova slept.

CHAPTER TWENTY
MIDNIGHT

Midnight huddled in the dark forest, shivering and cold, as the bluewolves howled around her.

"Please, gods of my forebears," she whispered. "Please protect me."

The trees rustled around her, their leaves hiding the moon and stars. Insects buzzed, yellow eyes glowed between the leaves, and the howls grew closer. The bluewolves had picked up her scent, and they were drawing near. And they were thirsty for her blood.

Midnight let a small ball of *qi* form in her hand. It glowed there like a lantern, woven of many dots of light flowing together.

The bluewolves saw at once. They yipped. They scuttled forward through the brush. In the light of her *qi*, their fangs shone. Their eyes blazed. One leaped toward her, twice her size, ready to feast.

Midnight tossed her light.

The ball of *qi* slammed into the slick, blue creature, knocking it back. It thumped onto the forest floor with a wail.

Another bluewolf leaped from behind her; she heard it howl.

Midnight sucked in a breath and ported.

In the forest, it was dangerous to port. She could only move in open space. Here in the dark, she could accidentally port through a tree trunk; she would reappear inside the wood, crushed, dying.

But she ported still, blinking out of existence, then back into reality behind the leaping bluewolf. She tossed more *qi*. The animal yelped and fell down dead, the light coiling across it.

A dozen other bluewolves surrounded her, snarling among the trees. Midnight snarled back at them. She raised both palms, displaying two balls of *qi*. She made to toss them.

The bluewolves whimpered, turned their tails, and fled. The brush settled behind them.

Midnight shuddered and let her *qi* fade away. Using this much energy drained her. She had not eaten in a day and night. Not since stealing food at the last farm. Her head spun and she wanted to lie down, to rest, to sleep. But she could not.

The skelkrins might have heard the howls, she thought. *They might have seen the light.*

Midnight swallowed a lump in her throat. She could still beat bluewolves, native predators of Cirona. But skelkrins were far crueler, stronger predators, and she had seen their tracks on this planet. Twenty or more had landed here, and they were hunting her. And if they found her, she could not defeat them.

She had to move.

Leaving the dead bluewolves behind, she pushed through the forest, traveling in the darkness, daring not even summon any *qi* for light. She was too weak, and using more *qi* would further drain her. She walked in blackness.

A root snagged her foot. She stumbled and fell, banging her elbow against a rock. She pushed herself up. She walked onward, more slowly this time, hands held before her. Her palms kept hitting tree trunks she couldn't see, and tears stung her eyes.

I miss home, she thought. *I miss my family.*

Her tears flowed. She thought of Per, her home world--the forests that glowed with fireflies, the crystal caves, the cities of glass and marble. She thought of her family, her kind mother, her wise father. She remembered the song of her people, the taste of sweet summer wine, the lights that glowed in the temple chandeliers.

Home. Peace. Beauty.

She lowered her head, her body shaking.

Until they burned it.

It had been a night of fire. A night of screams. Of death from the sky. As with so many other worlds, the skelkrins had come to Per.

They had come to kill.

"I tried to fight," Midnight whispered. "I tried to stop them."

So had armies. So had millions of her people, firing their *qi*, flying their fleets up to face the great warships from the depth of space. And they had died. Their ships had rained down like dying fireflies.

Only I survived.

Even worse memories now filled her. Memories of the skelkrin masters strapping her down. Poking her with needles. Cutting her with scalpels. Speaking of carving out her magic, of using her in their ships, of cloning a million Midnights to break and torture and harvest.

How she had screamed. How she had begged to die.

Until he arrived. The traveler.

"Aminor," Midnight whispered in the darkness.

The old human with the long white beard had saved her. Placed her in a blue starjet. Sent her off into space, to find Earth, to find his son. To find Riff Starfire and safety.

"But I never made it to Earth." Midnight sobbed. "I fell from the sky to a strange planet, and I'm scared and alone now, Aminor. I'm so scared. They're hunting me and I don't know what to do."

She fell to her knees in the dark forest. The trees creaked around her and more wolves howled, or perhaps they were the howls of the skelkrins hunting her.

You will live, spoke a voice in her mind.

She raised her head, and her heart thrashed. Who had spoken?

You will live, Midnight. You will survive. I'm with you, my child.

It was his voice! The old traveler! Aminor! Midnight whipped her head from side to side, seeking him, but she saw only darkness. The voice had spoken inside her.

"You still watch over me, traveler," she whispered.

A warmth filled her even in the cold night, and she imagined that she saw his kindly old face again. For him she would survive. She would keep moving. She would find shelter, find food, find hope.

She pushed herself back to her feet. She raised her chin. She kept walking.

And there she saw it ahead: a field out in the moonlight. A barn. Shelter from the cold.

Midnight stumbled across the moonlit field, and she crawled into the barn. Horses slept around her, flicking their tails. Warm. Comforting. A basket of apples stood on a shelf, and she ate. She curled up on the straw. She hugged herself.

"I'm alive," she whispered. "I might be the last pirilian in the cosmos, but I'm alive. I will stay alive."

At dawn she would move again. For now, Midnight pulled her knees up to her chin and thought of home.

CHAPTER TWENTY-ONE
OUT OF THE BAG

Riff was lying in bed, dreaming of the Blue Strings, when the lights turned on and Giga stepped into his chamber.

"Captain!" The android smiled and bowed. "We're nearing our destination, Captain."

He blinked, his dreams still tugging at him. For a moment, he thought he was still back home in the Blue Strings, that Giga was a fan approaching the stage. He looked around him and groaned. Of course. He was on the *HMS Dragon Huntress*, trundling through hyperspace. Specifically, he lay in the captain's quarters, a cozy room containing his bed, a desk, and his holstered gun hanging on the wall.

"Thank you, Giga." He rubbed his eyes and sat up in bed, only to realize he was naked. The cooling coils were on the fritz again--though Romy had sworn she hadn't eaten them this time--and Riff remembered kicking off his clothes before falling asleep. His jeans, boxer shorts, and T-shirt now lay on the floor several feet away. He clutched his blanket over his lap.

"You're welcome, Captain." Giga smiled at him sweetly.

"Uhm . . . mind turning around as I get dressed?"

Giga's smile didn't falter. "I'm a Human Interface android, Captain. It's no different than getting dressed in front of a keyboard or mouse." She didn't look away.

"Yes, well, I've seen a lot of shifty keyboards in my day. Hand me over my clothes, will you?"

"Happy to comply." She didn't sound very happy, but she handed the clothes over.

He pulled on the important bits under the blanket, then stood up and tugged on the rest. Giga smiled at him sweetly.

"Would you like me to brush your hair, sir?"

"No!" He stared into the mirror, saw his hair standing on end, and ran his fingers through it. "Gods no. Giga, you just worry about keeping this boat in the sky. Come on. Let's hit the bridge."

On their way, they stepped into the main deck. Steel sat on the couch, clad as always in his armor. The knight stared down at the table, where a game of counter-squares was in progress. Steel's brow was furrowed, and he seemed so engrossed in the board game he didn't even notice Riff and Giga entering the room. Across the table, Romy lay on the floor, rolling around, flicking her tail, and moaning.

"Come on, Steel!" The demon rolled her eyes. "You've been thinking for so long. Make a move!"

"Silent, foul beast of the Abyss." Steel didn't even raise his eyes. "I'm planning a brilliant strategy."

Romy snorted. "Is your brilliant strategy to bore me to death? Because it's working. If you don't make a move, I'm going

to torture you. I learned how to torture people in Hell, and-- Oh!"
She leaped up and her tail wagged. "Hi, Riff. Hi, Giga. Want to
play counter-squares too?"

Riff walked past her, heading toward the bridge. "We're
nearing Cirona. We're about to leap out of hyperspace. Steel, join
me at the bridge?"

The knight rose to his feet, leaving the game. His face
darkened. Romy too made to follow.

"I'll help too!" The demon wagged her tail.

Riff shook his head. "Romy, I need you to help by staying
here and guarding the counter-squares board. I heard there are
evil aliens who like to rearrange the pieces when nobody's
looking."

Romy gasped and covered her mouth. She moved to stand
by the game, eyes darting and lips peeled back in a snarl.

Riff climbed the stairs to the bridge, where he found Nova
sitting in one of the suede seats. The ashai was nervously flicking
her whip against the floor. Outside the windshield, the lights of
hyperspace were still streaming in a dizzying pattern of blue,
lavender, and white.

Riff sank into his captain's chair. The suede creaked. "All
right, Giga. Let us know when we're there."

The android nodded. "Approaching Planet Cirona in thirty
seconds . . . twenty-nine . . . twenty-eight . . ."

While Giga continued the countdown, Riff felt a chill run
down his spine. Out there on Cirona, light-years away from Earth,
was a pirilian girl--an alien with powerful magic. She might be the

same pirilian his father had tried to send him. The same pirilian the Cosmians were after. The same pirilian the skelkrin masters wanted.

The same pirilian who just might hold the fate of the universe itself in her hands.

". . . seventeen . . . sixteen . . ."

Riff caressed Ethel, his old gun. Who was he to try to save such a creature? Who was he to get involved in the games of planets and empires? He was only a failed musician. That was all. A scruffy refugee. Not a hero.

He looked to his right. Steel sat there. His brother. A knight. A man Riff trusted with his life. A man Riff knew would forever fight for his honor and his family.

He looked to his left. Nova sat there, the woman he loved. The strongest woman he knew. He could feel her kiss again, and he knew that, somewhere deep inside her, she loved him too.

I might not be a hero, Riff thought. *But for the people I love, I will become one.*

"Three . . ." said Giga. "Two . . . one . . . turning off hyperdrive engines."

Across the ship, a rumble rose, then faded. The streams of light outside shortened, rolled up, and formed fixed stars. The dancing splotches of color faded. Riff's temples squeezed inward as if trying to meet. He shook his head wildly and blinked a few times.

Giga spoke in a calm, pleasant voice. "Spacetime curves straightened. We are back in normal three-dimensional space, Captain."

Riff nodded. "Thank you, Giga."

"Happy to comply, Captain."

Rubbing his temples, Riff leaned forward in his seat. He found himself staring down at the green planet of Cirona.

Twenty-five light-years away from Earth, Cirona was one of several planets orbiting the star Vega. Riff remembered hearing about it as a kid--one of the new planets humanity had only just begun to settle, expanding Earth's sphere of influence deeper into the Milky Way. Here was the frontier of the human empire. The planet reminded him a lot of Earth--white clouds, green landscapes, and thousands of pale blue lakes. The planet's star, the luminous Vega, was rising above Cirona's horizon, twice the size of the sun back home and casting out white beams of light.

Riff had been to space before, but no matter how many times he saw another planet, it still filled him with wonder.

Here is a whole other world, he thought. *A world a hundred trillion kilometers from home.*

A glint in the distance caught his attention. He narrowed his eyes, rose from his seat, and stepped closer to the windshield. The glint vanished, then rose again in the sunlight. Whatever it was, it seemed to be orbiting the planet.

"Giga, see that glint?" He pointed. "Magnify that. Put it on the HUD."

"Happy to comply!"

One pane of glass on the windshield acted as a head-up display, able to magnify, shrink, or analyze the view. Right now, an image of the glinting object appeared there, zooming closer, taking form.

Riff inhaled sharply.

"What," he whispered, "is that?"

At his side, Steel and Nova stiffened. Both spat our curses.

Riff leaned closer to the HUD. It was some kind of starship, he thought, but unlike anything he'd ever seen. This was no human starship. Not even a ship built by humanoids such as gruffles, halflings, ashais, or other subspecies that had evolved from humanity. Whatever this was, aliens had built it.

The vessel was charcoal and jagged. Iron spikes rose across its hull, and two great claws thrust out from its flanks. The starship looked like some mutated crab, dipped in tar, that had grown to monstrous size.

"How large is that thing?" he asked Giga. "What's the scale on that zoom?"

"The object is one thousand and fifteen meters long, Captain," said the android.

Riff's heart sank. "Are you telling me that ship is a *kilometer* long?"

"No, Captain." Giga shook her head. "One kilometer and fifteen meters, sir. Counting the claws."

"Counting the claws," he muttered. "Lovely. Always count the claws." He gulped. "And each one of those claws is large enough to grab the *Dragon Huntress* and crush it like a grape."

"This vessel is not human in origin," Steel muttered.

"Thank you, Sir Obvious," said Riff. He paced the bridge. "Gig, run a scan of all alien starship designs you have in your memory banks. See if you can find a match."

"Already complied, Captain," she said. "Enemy vessel matches description of skelkrin warship, sir."

Riff felt faint. He had to sit back down.

"Skelkrins," he whispered.

Giga nodded. "If my translation of the letters on her hull is correct, sir, she's called *The Crab*."

Steel and Nova exchanged dark glances. Riff gripped his gun. As bad as Cosmians were, they were only servants. The masters were the skelkrins, these deep space killers who had been swarming across the galaxy. This was still human territory. What were the bastards doing here?

"Wait a minute, Giga," Nova said. She frowned at the android. "You call this an enemy vessel. Why?"

The android tilted her head. "This is a skelkrin ship, ma'am. All skelkrin ships are enemies. They have only one mission: destroy all in their path." Giga smiled sweetly. "Would you like me to engage them in battle, ma'am? Or should I prepare the escape pod?"

"Wait. Wait!" Riff rose back to his feet. "Before we flee or fight, let's think. If they're skelkrins, and they're an enemy, why aren't they attacking? If we can see them, they can see us." He frowned. "Why are they just idling? Why aren't they blasting us out of the sky?"

Giga tilted her head. "Cannot compute. Answer unknown." Her face brightened. "Would you like me to hail them and ask, Captain?"

"No." Riff shook his head. "No, we stay silent. We stay distant. We've stumbled upon a sleeping wolf, and I don't think we should wake it." He licked his dry lips. "Giga, there should be a town of settlers below. Are you still picking up their signals?"

She nodded. "Yes, Captain. Colony still showing up in scans, sir. Would you like me to hail them?"

"No. I want full communications silence." He frowned and pointed at the distant vessel. "This might not be a warship after all. This might be a spy ship. They might be monitoring the planet . . . or monitoring us. Giga, plot a landing course. Take us down to the colony. Let's see what the skelkrins do."

"Happy to comply, Captain."

The *Dragon Huntress* veered and began to descend toward the planet.

The skelkrin ship hovered in the distance, silent, still, dead.

Riff sat back in his seat as they shot through space toward the atmosphere. Soon the *Dragon Huntress* was rattling madly, and the first layer of ozone flared around them. Fire blazed outside the windshields. The hula dancer swayed so madly her hips almost dislocated, and the bulldog bobbed his head like a headbanger at a metal concert.

"We really need seat belts on this thing!" Riff shouted as the air roared around them.

Steel and Nova sank into their seats, gripping the arm rests, not even able to reply. Giga swayed madly across the deck until Riff caught her, pulled her into his lap, and held her close.

The fire blazed.

The ship roared.

From the main deck, the sound of clattering counter-squares pieces rose along with Romy' screams.

Then, with streams of vapor, blue sky opened up below them. The fire died. They flew within the atmosphere of Cirona, gazing down at forests, mountains, and lakes.

Sunlight, soft and golden, fell upon them.

Riff realized he was holding his breath and exhaled in relief. He also realized he was clinging to Giga, nearly crushing her, and released her. The android walked toward the windshield and pointed down.

"The colony of Cirona City lies below us, Captain. Taking us down."

He nodded, still shaken. "Good. Any sign of the skelkrin ship?"

"My systems show them still in orbit, sir. They haven't moved."

"Keep an eye on them."

Giga frowned. "An eye, sir?" She blinked. "Cannot compute."

"Your radar, Giga."

She grinned. "Happy to comply, Captain." She turned back toward the windshield. "Cirona City coming into view, sir."

Riff stepped forward and stared down. He whistled softly. "Quite a bit nicer than Cog City back home."

Steel and Nova rose from their seats too, and they all stared down below. Cirona City was in fact barely more than a town. A hundred or so buildings of stone rose here along several streets. Back on Earth, most buildings were metal, glass, concrete, or plastic. Here the colonists used actual bricks of real stone, and smaller homes were built of wood. It reminded Riff of the old, historic pictures of Earth from thousands of years ago.

Beyond the town spread fields of crops--real fields, not just towering metal grain factories. Red barns and farmhouses rose along dirt roads. And beyond them spread the virgin forests of a new, untamed world.

Suddenly Riff understood the appeal of settling distant worlds. Gone was the smog, squalor, and soot of Earth. Here was a place of pristine beauty, of majestic wilderness, of wondrous vistas still untouched by man, of--

"It looks *boring*," Romy said.

Riff spun around to see the demon standing behind him. He groaned. "I thought I told you to stay in the main deck and guard your board game!"

Romy frowned, hands on hips. "I did! I guarded it while we flew in space. Then I guarded it as we crashed through the atmosphere and the pieces fell over." She gasped and pressed her face against the windshield. "Ooh, look, they have birds!" She bit her lip. "Do you think they have poodles here? I'm starving."

Nova growled and cracked her whip. "Off the bridge!"

Romy pouted, stuck out her tongue, and marched away in a huff.

The town grew closer beneath them. A gravelly lot spread between several stone buildings. A handful of starjets, smaller than the *Dragon Huntress*, parked there.

"Giga, bring us down. Right there." Riff pointed.

The *Dragon Huntress* thrummed and shook as its thruster engines belched out smoke. The dragon's wings spread wide, and it slowed its descent, gliding down toward the field. With a puff of smoke and a cloud of dust, they thumped down onto Planet Cirona.

The bobblehead bulldog finally had enough. It tilted over and rolled down to the floor.

"Good," Riff said. "Good, we didn't crash. Always nice. Still in one piece." He wiped sweat off his brow. "Main deck, everyone." He spoke into his communicator. "Piston, Twig! Main deck."

They all gathered there, careful not to step on the fallen counter-squares pieces. Twig walked back and forth, handing out "Alien Hunters" badges. Vega's golden sunlight fell through the windows.

Riff pinned his badge to his shirt and addressed the others. "All right, boys and girls. Here's the situation. We're going to be working with the colonists to find a missing pirilian woman named Midnight. For those who don't know, pirilians can be extremely dangerous. Some call them magical. They can teleport at will, reappearing behind you to stab you in the back. They can blast out energy from their hands, tearing a hole right through your flesh. We don't know if the woman we're seeking will be friendly or hostile. I want you all to be on your guard--constantly. Understood?"

They all nodded.

Riff nodded back. "Good. And . . . we might be facing a threat even worse than a pirilian. As some of you already know, we spotted a skelkrin warship in orbit around the planet. The ship was idling and did not react to us. The skelkrins themselves might be on the surface, hunting the same pirilian."

Twig gasped and covered her mouth. Piston shuddered and his eyes widened.

"Captain!" the gruffle blurted out. "Hunting a tardigrade or even a pirilian is one thing." Sweat beaded on Piston's brow. "But skelkrins, sir . . . we've got no business facing enemies like that. They're far beyond what we can handle, sir."

Despite his humble height, Piston was the heaviest among them. His mighty hands easily held a hammer that Riff could never lift. Yet now the burly gruffle was trembling. At his side, tiny Twig was shaking like a leaf. She scurried to hide behind her gruffle companion. The bolts and screws in the halfling's pockets jangled.

"My friends!" Riff said to the pair. "I've never seen you like this. You don't need to be frightened. You're Alien Hunters! I mean . . . all those aliens you hunted before I bought the ship. The snot-monster you tamed. The Carinian stone-beast you crushed. The Altairian fire-hopper you blasted out of space. All those aliens you told me about." Riff placed a hand on Piston's shaking shoulder. "If you defeated all of them, you can defeat some skelkrins with me."

Piston licked his lips and glanced around nervously. "Well, Captain, you see . . . the thing is . . ." The gruffle sighed. "Well, Captain, I suppose with skelkrins outside, you need to know the truth." He pulled Twig out from behind his legs. "Tell him, Twig."

The little mechanic was pale and shaking. "Those were just stories!" she blurted out.

Riff's eyes widened. Nova gasped. Steel took a step back, face darkening.

"Stories?" Riff whispered.

Piston lowered his head, and his hammer drooped. "Aye, Captain. Stories. Truth is . . ." The gruffle gulped. "Truth is, we were never really Alien Hunters."

Riff took a step back. "But Piston! What do you mean? The ship. The 'Alien Hunters Inc.' letters on the hull. The badges!"

Twig burst into tears. "All fake, Captain! All pretend." She flopped down onto the floor, crying bitterly. "Piston and I made it all up, sir."

Piston dared not raise his eyes; he could only stare at his feet. "Aye, Captain, that's the truth. See, Twig and I are no warriors. We're just two outcasts. Two souls who ended up on Earth, far from our home planets. We were homeless before we found a giant, metal dragon in a yard of weeds, and we sneaked inside. Truth be told, sir, we didn't even know the *Dragon Huntress* could fly." He sighed. "For a year, we lived in the used starship lot, and well, sir, we pretended. To pass the time, you know. We painted "Alien Hunters" on the hull. We made ourselves badges. We even built ourselves a cybersite. We just pretended to be heroes. We never thought we'd actually blast into space and hunt real aliens."

Riff stared in silence. For a long moment, he could only stare, breathing, too shocked for words. Finally he whispered, "But . . . the work orders that came in. All those requests from clients."

"See, that's the funny thing, sir," Piston said. "You know that cybersite Twig and I uploaded? Completely fake, but people started sending us work orders. They wanted us to really fight aliens. So we'd print out their requests, and we'd make believe, running around the old lot, pretending to fight aliens. And well, sir, now this is no game. Now we're really on a distant planet, and now there are real aliens out there, mean ones too." His shoulders stooped. "And we're not the heroes you need with you."

Riff turned away, facing the window. Trees swayed outside, and colonists were already gathering to point at the newly arrived vessel.

"I can't believe this," Riff whispered. "I . . . I can't."

Steel grumbled and clutched the hilt of his sword. "We've been betrayed."

Nova snarled and bared her teeth. "This whole thing has been a sham." The gladiator cracked her whip, raising sparks of electricity. "Just a sham!"

Piston and Twig were staring at their feet. Romy curled up on the floor, crying silently.

"Giga, you knew?" Riff whispered, turning toward her. "Even you knew and you didn't tell me?"

The android lowered her head. She spoke in a shaky whisper. "I . . . I'm sorry, Captain, I . . ." Giga could say no more. She covered her face and fled back to the bridge.

The deck seemed to sway around Riff. His world seemed to crash around him. A skelkrin ship hovered above. A pirilian girl who could possibly just save the universe was hiding somewhere outside. The fate of the cosmos came down to here, to this planet, and the rug was pulled out from under his feet.

What do I do? Riff thought and closed his eyes. *Oh, Dad, I wish you were here. What do I do now?*

In his mind, he could see his father again--a kindly old magician with a white beard and sad smile.

You were never a hero, my son. His father seemed to speak in his mind. *But you can become one. So can they. The courage in your heart is true. So is the courage of your friends.*

The vision vanished. Riff opened his eyes. He took a deep, shaky breath and turned back toward the others.

"Piston." Riff knelt before the gruffle and clutched his shoulder. "Piston, you might have been pretending back on Earth. But you weren't pretending when you rigged the spool and dragged out the tardigrade." He turned toward Twig. "Twig, you were perhaps only daydreaming on Earth. But you were a real heroine when you got into the space suit and let that beast nearly swallow you."

The diminutive mechanic wiped away tears. "Really? A heroine?"

Riff straightened and nodded. "Yes. You are all heroes and heroines today. I need to go out there, and I need to face the skelkrins, and I need to find the missing pirilian. And I need my friends. I need your wrench, Twig."

The halfling bit her lip, raised her wrench, and let electricity crackle on its head. "You've got it, Captain."

Riff turned toward Piston. "Piston, I need your hammer."

The gruffle blinked away tears, raised his chin, and hefted his massive hammer. "You've got it, sir."

Next Riff turned toward Romy; the demon was still curled up into a ball. "Romy, I need your pitchfork."

Sniffling, the demon rose to her feet, raised her pitchfork, and managed to snarl. "It's yours." She handed it to him.

Riff rolled his eyes. "Romy, I mean I need *you* to use it."

Her eyes widened and she wagged her tail. "Okay!"

Next Riff turned toward Steel. His brother stared back, eyes hard, and raised his sword.

"By my honor," Steel said, "my sword is yours."

At last, Riff turned toward Nova. The woman he loved. The woman he would always fight for. Sunlight gleamed on her golden armor and golden hair.

"And I need your whip, Nova," he whispered. "And I need you by my side."

She nodded, green eyes soft. "My whip is yours."

Riff drew his gun from his holster. He stared at them all, one by one. "I don't care who we used to be. I don't care if we were failed musicians, gladiators, outcast knights, outcast demons, refugees, or relics. Right now, here, today--we are Alien Hunters."

They nodded. They pinned on their badges.

"Alien Hunters," they whispered, one by one, and their eyes gleamed.

Giga's head appeared from around the doorway. Hesitantly, the android stepped back into the main deck. "Am . . . am I one too?"

Riff couldn't help but grin, a huge grin that hurt his cheeks. He took a badge from the table, and he pinned it to Giga's kimono. "I know that you can't leave the ship, Giga, no more than a heart can leave a body. You are the heart of this ship. And you are the heart of the hunters. You are always one of us."

He hadn't known androids could cry, but right now, tears flowed down Giga's cheeks. She saluted him.

"Happy to comply, Captain," she whispered. "Always."

The damn tears were now stinging Riff's eyes too. He turned and walked toward the airlock. "Now come on! We've got aliens to hunt."

"Yeah!" Romy shouted and whooped.

Riff opened the hatch and lowered the staircase. One by one, the Alien Hunters stepped off their ship and onto a new world.

CHAPTER TWENTY-TWO
THE PURPLE ONE AND THE RED ONES

Skrum was moving through the forest, sniffing for his prey, when his communicator buzzed.

He growled and snorted. Around him, his fellow skelkrins hissed and snapped their teeth. They had been following the trail for days now, traveling from farm to farm, leaving a wake of destruction. Across the planet of Cirona, barns burned, livestock lay slaughtered, and the bones of farmers lay in heaps. And still Midnight evaded them. Still the purple-skinned vermin stayed always one step ahead, vanishing whenever Skrum caught sight of her, porting from hilltop to hilltop, fading into shadows.

The pirilians are sneaky bastards, Skurm thought and licked his chops. *And this one will scream for decades, scream with a million tortured clones.*

His communicator, a bulky metal box, buzzed again upon his chest. Skrum howled in frustration and slammed his fist against the red button that shone there.

"What?" he snarled.

A staticky voice came from the speaker. "My lord Skrum!"

Skrum recognized that voice. It was Kur-Ta speaking, pilot of *The Crab*, their warship. The fool was useless in a fight. Skrum had left him in the vessel above the planet, his eye in the dark.

"Why do you disturb my hunt, Kur-Ta?" Skrum hissed into the communicator.

"My lord, a starship approached the planet. A human starship. I did as you instructed. I did not engage the enemy in battle. I let the ship land."

Skrum's lips peeled back in a snarl. "What class human ship? A division-class destroyer? A dreadnaught? A starwolf?"

Kur-Ta hesitated. "It . . . it looks like a dragon, my lord. Not a military vessel. Barely spaceworthy, my lord. It bore Earth letters on its hull. Couldn't hold more than a dozen human vermin."

A small blue bird fluttered toward Skrum. He crushed it in his palm, watched the blood leak, and considered. A novelty ship. Human by design.

"Aminor," Skrum whispered.

The old fool was known by many names. The traveler. The wizard. Old Man Sky. To some in the galaxy he was a hero, to others just a myth.

To Skrum, he was only the human who had freed Midnight from his prison.

He spoke into his communicator. "Feed me this ship's coordinates, Kur-Ta. Inform me if it moves again. The humans are here to hunt the same prey." Skrum licked his lips. "This will be more fun than I had imagined."

"Yes, my lord."

Once the coordinates were fed through, Skrum slammed his fist against his communicator again, shutting it off.

Some predators, Skrum knew, hunted with brute strength, no cunning to them. Not him. Skrum was an apex-predator, and he hunted with guile, with deception, with slow stalking before the pounce.

"It is time to stalk," he said to his fellow skelkrins. They gathered around him, tongues hanging low, eyes burning bright. "Soon the girl will be ours. And then . . . then every planet between here and Earth."

* * * * *

The Alien Hunters, toughest mercenaries in the galaxy, stormed out of their dragon starship, weapons raised, snarling and ready for battle.

A little girl gaped with wide eyes and dropped her teddy bear. A duck quacked and waddled off.

Riff cleared his throat and holstered his gun. He waved down his comrades' weapons.

So much for a skelkrin ambush, he thought.

The town was small, its roads unpaved. Several buildings rose ahead: a saloon, a barbershop, a funeral home, and a large building with a clock tower that looked like town hall. Beyond the buildings, Riff could see forests, distant mountains, and even fields--real fields where crops grew from the soil, not inside boxes.

Two moons hung in the sky, one deep blue and the other pale white.

"Are you the Alien Hunters?" the little girl asked. She leaned down and picked up her doll.

Romy's eyes widened. She rushed forward, holding her own teddy bear. "Oh hai! You have a teddy too! Maybe they can be friends."

The girl stared at the demon, then at the others. "You're not strong enough."

Riff stepped forward and knelt by the girl. "It's all right, child. You're safe with us here. We've come to get rid of the alien."

The girl shook her head. "You came here for the purple alien. But there are other ones. Bigger. Red aliens. Aliens who will kill you. You should leave. You will die."

With that, the girl clutched her doll to her chest, spun around, and fled into a home.

"Thank goodness you're here!"

Riff turned to see a tall man with a yellow beard hurry forward. He wore fine clothes of brown and tan fabric, tall boots, and a cowboy hat.

Romy growled and raised her pitchfork. "An alien!"

Nova had to grab the demon and tug her back. "Human, Romy. Human!"

The bearded man hesitated, then turned toward Riff and shook his hand. "Name's Efrom. Mayor Efrom. I run this here town and, gosh, we're glad to have you here. Bunch of aliens come to this planet, and they've gone to killing." Efrom lowered his head. "First the purple one, then the red ones." He glanced up at the demon, gruffle, halfling, and ashai. "And now all manner of 'em come to Cirona."

Romy wagged her tail. "I'm a demon, not an alien."

Nova pulled her farther back. "Romy, shut your mouth or it's to the attic with you again."

Riff looked around him, waiting for the "red ones"--no doubt the skelkrins--to leap out at any moment.

"Efrom, you called us here for the purple one. The pirilian. Where is she?"

Efrom dabbed his forehead with a handkerchief. "Come inside. Into the shade. So hot here in the light of Vega, hotter than old Sol back on Earth. Let me pour you some cold sweet tea."

Nova slammed her palm over Romy's mouth before the demon could ask about poodles.

They entered the large stone building with the clock tower, and they sat at a long table covered with maps. A butler served the tea, which was very cold and very sweet, and Efrom spent a long while talking, pointing at the maps. Some locations were marked with a purple dot: places where they had spotted the pirilian stealing food or sneaking into barns. Other places were marked with red dots: places where the skelkrins had attacked, killing settlers and burning down farmhouses.

"The last place we saw the pirilian is here." Efrom pointed at a location on the map. "This was just this morning, only 'bout five kilometers away. Old Farmer Grog called in the report. Said the creature's skulking around, stealing his fruit. Tried to call out to her, but she won't answer. He's scared to death now, Grog is. Last few places the purple one showed up, the red ones showed up only hours later." He shuddered. "And the red ones are worse."

Riff nodded. "We'll head over there now. We'll take the *Dragon Huntress*."

Efrom tsked his tongue. "Farmer Grog be mighty upset if you land on his fields. Treats his corn better than his children. You can take the horses. Come with me."

They stepped back outside. Efrom whistled, and six horses rode over, their manes long and flowing.

"Fine steeds," Steel said, nodding with satisfaction.

Romy's mouth watered and she licked her lips.

"Can I just take one bite?" the demon begged, only for Nova to scowl and crack her whip.

They mounted the horses. Little Twig nearly vanished into her saddle, while Piston nearly overflowed his; the poor horse below the stocky gruffle whined in protest. Despite having wings, even Romy rode a horse. The demon wore an oversized cowboy hat she had found indoors, pushing it back whenever it slipped over her eyes.

"Just head down that road." Efrom pointed. "And may Vega's light bless you."

Steel kneed his horse, leading the group. Riff rode close behind, and the others followed. As the Alien Hunters rode out, leaving the town behind, Riff looked over his shoulder and stared back at the *Dragon Huntress*. Giga stood at the windshield, looking out at them, standing still and sad.

Riff felt sadness fill him too. They were six here on their horses, but they should be seven.

Giga is one of us, he thought, *yet she's trapped forever in the ship, a part of its hardware, doomed to die if she ever leaves.*

It somehow felt wrong to think of Giga as hardware. She had become to him almost like a living woman. Already Riff missed her. As the *Dragon Huntress* vanished from view behind him, he felt a pain in his chest at being apart from her. Once more, he could feel her falling into his lap, the warmth of her body, the softness of her lips kissing his cheek--

He shook his head wildly. Foolishness!

Giga is an android, Riff, he told himself. *A machine. Not a living woman. Besides, you love Nova. You've always only loved her.*

He turned to look at Nova and felt some of his doubt fade. The warrior-princess rode on a white mare, and her armor gleamed in the sun. She seemed a goddess of gold. Her hair flowed in the wind, her eyes shone, and she smiled at him, a bright smile, a smile so rare these days. She used to smile like this so often in the old days. She was beautiful, strong, wise, a woman he had lost once, a woman he could not bear to lose again.

She saw him staring, gave him a nod and crooked smile, and mimicked tilting a hat. "Howdy, partner."

He nodded back. "Howdy, little lady."

He added words he could not bring to his lips, not here: *I love you, Nova, always.*

Nova, strong and proud. Giga, shy and fragile. Life and machine. Fire and silk. The part of Riff that admired women . . . and the part that wanted them to admire him.

He was so lost in his thoughts he barely noticed that they were nearing Old Grog's farm.

Riff was used to the farms on Earth. To him, a "farm" was a massive building of concrete and metal, hundreds of stories tall, within whose walls meat, grain, and produce grew in glass boxes. The farm before him looked like something out of a history book. Fields of corn and wheat spread across the land--real fields of grain that grew in the open. Cows, horses, and sheep grazed in a sward of grass. Farther back rose a red barn, several silos, a few sheds, and a farmhouse.

The farmhouse windows and doors were boarded up. A man Riff assumed to be Farmer Grog peeked between two boards on a window, then quickly vanished from view.

Steel rode up close to Riff. The knight stared around, frowning. "You reckon the pirilian is still out there?"

Riff passed his gaze across the farm from silo to barn to fields. "If Farmer Grog's hiding, he obviously believes there are aliens about." He looked back at his motley companions and sighed; Romy was busy whispering to her teddy bear, while Twig was cleaning her ear with her wrench. "I don't think anyone in their right mind would be scared of this lot."

Nova rode up to him too. The ashai nodded and unfurled her whip. "We split up. We search every nook and cranny of this place."

"No." Riff shook his head. "We stay close together. We don't know if Midnight is hostile or not. She's a pirilian. If she's hostile, she's powerful enough to kill us all."

He kneed his horse, riding closer toward the farm. The others rode around him, and dust rose from the dirt road. The fields rustled at their sides.

She could be anywhere, Riff thought. *Hiding in the fields, in the barn, in the farmhouse attic . . . or maybe even long gone, fled to the mountains.*

"Midnight!" he called out. "Midnight, we're here to help you! If you can hear me, come and talk to me!"

The fields rustled. A large black bird, similar to a crow but beating eight wings, fled into the distance.

No pirilian.

No skelkrins.

Riff rode on, his gun raised and loaded. His companions rode around him, weapons ready. Even Romy had finally ceased her blabbering and raised her pitchfork.

"Midnight!" Riff called. "I know you're here. Come and talk to me. Come--"

Stalks of corn creaked at his right side.

The air popped.

A flash of purple appeared on the barn's roof.

A ball of golden light hurled down toward him.

Riff shouted. His horse reared and neighed. The light missed them by inches, slamming into the dirt road, digging a hole.

Nova shouted and lashed her whip, sending sparks of electricity toward the barn. Steel shouted and pointed his sword, and light blasted out from the blade.

"No!" Riff shouted. "We want her alive, don't--"

The air popped again. The purple figure vanished from the barn. Purple flashed again to Riff's left. She stood in the field of wheat! He glimpsed yellow eyes, a lavender face, a black hood and cloak. She raised her palm and more *qi* energy flew his way.

Riff winced. He tried to dodge the blast of light, to ride away, knowing he was too slow, knowing the *qi* would hit him.

A whip cracked.

Nova's lash swung through the air, faster than the speed of sound, and slapped the ball of *qi* away. The energy slammed into a rock on the road, shattering the stone.

Nova winked and gave him a crooked smile. "Watch your back, pilgrim."

He groaned. "Cowboy talk later. Catch her!"

Nova nodded. "Let's rustle up that varmint."

"I said no cowboy talk!"

The air popped again as Midnight ported, now appearing on top of the silo. Her *qi* blasted down, screeching through the air. The blast hurtled toward Steel. The knight swung his sword, parrying the blow.

Midnight vanished.

Riff heard her shout behind him.

He spun around--too late. Her light blasted forward, heading toward Nova.

And Nova was facing the wrong way.

"Nova!" Riff shouted. He rode his horse toward her, leaped from the saddle, and tried to grab her, to pull her down.

He was too slow. Midnight's *qi* slammed into Nova's golden armor, knocking the ashai from the saddle. She slammed onto the ground, screaming in pain, her armor cracking.

Steel screamed too. Riff turned his head to see Midnight appear a hundred meters above in the sky, her light blasting down onto Steel. The knight's armor cracked, and he fell too.

Before Midnight could fall down to her death, she ported again, now appearing upon the farmhouse roof, and her light flared out.

Twig was screaming. Piston leaped off his saddle, placed his hammer's head against his shoulder, and began firing bullets through the hammer's shaft. The fire riddled the farmhouse.

"No firing!" Riff shouted. "We need her alive!"

"She's killing us, Captain!" Piston shouted back.

"There she is, in the sky again!" Romy cried out. The demon snarled, leaped off her horse, and beat her wings. She soared into the sky, claws stretched out, fangs bared. Before the demon could reach Midnight, the pirilian vanished again.

This time, Midnight appeared on the road only several feet away from Riff.

She raised her palms and pointed her light at him.

"Wait!" Riff shouted. "Midnight, wait!"

She shot her light toward him.

Riff grimaced and fired his gun.

Blood splashed.

The air popped.

Midnight vanished.

Riff found himself lying on the ground by his horse. He grimaced in pain; an ugly burn covered his thigh. Purple blood speckled the road. He had hit Midnight. Stars damn it, he had hit her, the very woman he needed alive, the very woman whose life might just save the cosmos. Yet perhaps she still lived. He saw no corpse.

"Midnight!" he shouted, struggling to his feet. His wound smoked and sizzled. "Midnight, listen to me! Stop fighting us. I'm here to help you. My name is Riff Starfire. My father, Aminor, sent me here. Can you hear me?"

The fields rustled. Nova moaned on the road, still alive, her armor cracked. Twig was leaning over the ashai, bandaging her wound. Steel struggled to his feet; his breastplate had shattered, but it had saved his life.

No Midnight.

No more *qi* light.

Piston slowly lowered his hammer. "She ported off to die, Captain." The gruffle spat. "Probably lying dead in the fields."

Twig gazed around with wide eyes, then covered her face and trembled. Romy flew back down to the ground, stood beside her horse, and looked around with huge, haunted eyes. Groaning,

Nova struggled to her feet and came to stand beside Riff. She raised her whip; the lash crackled with electricity.

"Midnight," Riff said again, speaking softly now. "Midnight, we're putting down our weapons." He knelt slowly and placed his gun down on the ground. "You're safe."

He looked at the others, gesturing for them to do the same. Romy put down her pitchfork, and Twig tossed down her wrench. Piston grumbled but let his hammer drop with a thud. Nova growled and clung to her whip, but at a glare from Riff, she spat and let it fall to the ground; it coiled up like a snake, its electricity dying.

"Steel, you too," Riff said.

The knight stared back, sword in hand. Riff knew that Solflare was a part of the knight as much as his arm, heart, and soul. But finally Steel tightened his lips, put down the antique sword, and took a step back.

"Midnight, our weapons are down!" Riff stepped farther away from the pile of weapons. The others joined him. "Now come out. Let us tend to your wound. Let us help you."

For a long moment he heard only the rustling fields.

And then, slowly, Midnight emerged from between the corn stalks.

Riff's plasma blast had grazed her hip; her purple blood dripped. She gazed at him with huge, luminous eyes like those of a cat. She pulled back her hood, revealing a purple face, indigo hair, and long ears.

"Riff?" she whispered, and those eyes flooded with tears. "Riff from Earth? Aminor's son?"

He smiled tremulously and reached out to her. "It's me. You're safe. We're here to help. We--"

Roars tore the air.

The earth shook.

Twenty creatures rose from the field, towering giants of crimson skin, blazing white eyes, fangs and claws.

Skelkrins, Riff knew at once.

"Midnight, behind you!" he shouted, racing toward her, trying to grab her.

He was too slow.

One of the skelkrins, a beast of horns and warty red skin, fired a massive iron gun the size of a man.

A black web blasted out, tipped with metal shards, and wrapped around Midnight. The pirilian fell, screaming, thrashing as the web tightened around her, constricting her, sealing her within a cocoon.

"Kill them!" Riff shouted to his companions. "Shoot them down!"

The other Alien Hunters raced toward their pile of weapons. Riff clenched his jaw and ran forward instead, trying to reach the trapped Midnight. She was still thrashing within her cocoon, her screams muffled. A shining black membrane was growing along the web, thickening into a shell, sealing Midnight until her screams died, until she couldn't even thrash.

Riff reached the cocoon and leaped forward, trying to grab the encased Midnight.

The skelkrin who shot her stepped forward. He was a massive, towering creature. Easily over eight feet tall. Easily a thousand pounds of muscle and jagged black armor. The creature's fangs shone, longer than daggers. His white eyes swirled like exploding suns. The beast swung his arm, and a fist the size of a frozen chicken slammed into Riff's head.

Riff flew through the air.

He slammed against the ground, seeing stars, tasting blood.

"Riff!" Nova shouted.

He blinked, trying to see through the haze. He managed to push himself up to his elbows. The world spun, and he made out twenty skelkrins or more looming above him. One of them--the brute that had hit him--lifted Midnight in her black encasing. He held the bundle to his chest; Midnight seemed small as a baby in swaddling clothes against him.

"Midnight!" Riff shouted and pushed himself to his feet. His jaw screamed in agony.

The ground shook as the skelkrins turned on their jet packs. Smoke rose in clouds. Fire raged across the fields. The skelkrins blasted up into the sky, carrying Midnight with them.

At his side, Nova lashed her whip again and again, sending up lightning bolts toward the fleeing skelkrins. Piston growled, grabbed his hammer, and began blasting bullets out of its shaft. Steel lifted his sword, pointed it skyward, and shot up beams of light.

"Wait!" Riff shouted. "Stop! You'll hit Midnight."

One of the weapons--Riff wasn't sure which one--hit a skelkrin above. The beast's jet tank exploded in the sky, raining down sparks and bits of red flesh. The other skelkrins kept soaring.

"Stop!" Riff shouted. "We can't hurt Midnight!"

He stared upward, wincing. The skelkrins rose higher and higher, leaving trails of smoke and fire . . . until they vanished.

Riff turned to stare at the others. They looked back at him, some grim, others gasping. Romy shed tears. Dust and blood covered them all.

"They're taking Midnight back to their starship." Riff's heart banged against his ribs, his fingers shook, and blood dripped down his leg. He gritted his teeth and leaped back onto his horse. "Hurry! To the *Dragon Huntress*. Ride!"

They all leaped onto their horses. They galloped down the road. Dust flew, stinging Riff's eyes, and he could barely breathe, and fear colder and darker than the depths of space flooded him.

* * * * *

Skrum blasted up through Cirona's atmosphere, clutching the wriggling Midnight in his arms.

Fire and heat blazed around them. Midnight screamed inside the fleshy membrane he had wrapped her in. The cocoon would protect her frail body from the vacuum of space. As his jet pack roared, thrusting him into the emptiness, he held her close to his chest.

"You are safe, precious." He licked the cocoon, savoring its sticky sweetness. "You are safe inside your shell. It is when I open your shell that you should scream."

They shot through the last layers of atmosphere, twenty skelkrins and their prey. Of course, they needed no space suits like humans, no sticky cocoons like the one that engulfed Midnight. They were skelkrins. They were the galaxy's strongest predators. Their hard skin could withstand even the vacuum of space. Their lungs could last without air for hours, even days.

"We are the galaxy's most evolved hunters," he said to the cocoon. Midnight still writhed inside. "And soon you, Midnight, will lead us to every corner of the galaxy on our conquest. Yes, precious. I'm going to break you into a million shards. I'm going to clone each one into a new you. And I'm going to thrust you into a million starships. You will become the engines of our fleet, porting us across the universe. As our enemies still use fuel or hyperjets, we will use Midnight-engines." Skrum licked his chops. "You, precious child, will bring about a skelkrin cosmos."

She screamed. She wept. He smiled.

The skelkrins kept blasting upward, moving through open space now, leaving the planet far below. Skrum looked up and saw his warship there, a massive crab with iron claws. He directed his flight toward the ship.

The hangar doors opened above, a mouth to swallow them. Skrum shot toward the entrance, flew through the hangar, and finally landed on the hard metal floor. The others entered behind him and the hangar doors slammed shut with a thud.

Skrum tossed Midnight down. She clanged against the floor. The other skelkrins laughed, kicked her, spat on her shell.

"Enough!" Skrum shouted. "She's not to be harmed. Not yet. She must reach the emperor alive."

He shoved the other skelkrins aside. They hissed and snapped their teeth at him, but they withdrew. Skrum stepped toward the hardened, black shell and knelt before it. He tore open a rent with his claws, exposing Midnight's face.

She gasped for air. She screamed.

Skrum spat on her face.

"You thought you could escape me." He trailed a claw across her cheek, cutting a thin line. Purple blood beaded. "My sweet Midnight, it's time to go home."

He rose to his feet. He turned to face the others. "We go to the bridge. We bomb this planet into desolation. And then we fly home in victory!"

Their roars shook the warship, and Midnight screamed again.

CHAPTER TWENTY-THREE
THE CRAB'S CLAWS

"Giga, fire up the engines!" Riff shouted into his communicator, riding his horse back into town. "We got to fly!"

Dust rose around him in clouds as he galloped. The skelkrins were gone into the sky. His fellow Alien Hunters rode around him, eyes dark.

Riff tugged the reins, and his horse reared and halted. He leaped from the saddle and ran, kicking up dust, toward the *HMS Dragon Huntress*. The ship stood in the yard. Several children had been coloring with chalk on its facade; they fled as Riff approached. He yanked the airlock's outer door, raced upstairs, opened the second door, and barged into the main deck. Steel ran close behind, and the others soon leaped in too.

Riff made for the bridge, shouting all the while. "Giga, fly! Fly into orbit!"

Her voice rose from the bridge ahead. "Happy to comply!"

Smoke blasted out the windows. The ship shook madly. They were soaring into the sky before Riff even reached the bridge. He stumbled up the last few steps, falling and banging his knee. The ship rattled madly, roaring as it ascended. Riff fell again, dragged himself into the bridge, and somehow made it to his chair. Blood kept seeping down his leg.

"Captain!" Giga said. "You're hurt. Are--"

"Just keep flying! Find the skelkrin ship. They have Midnight."

Giga gasped, shut her mouth, and nodded. At his sides, Nova and Steel made it to their seats and sat down. The ship kept shaking madly as it soared through the atmosphere. The bulldog fell again. Finally they found themselves in open space, Vega shining in the distance.

Ahead flew the skelkrin warship.

Riff had seen the vessel on his monitor before, but now it loomed before him. The massive ship dwarfed the *Dragon Huntress*. Its metal claws reached out, each large enough to crush the *Dragon Huntress*. Its spikes gleamed in the sunlight. And its guns were blasting out plasma, raining death down onto the planet below.

"They're killing the colonists," Nova whispered. Tears filled her eyes. "They're burning them all."

Slowly the skelkrin ship began turning toward the *Dragon Huntress*.

Its guns fired.

"Giga, dodge!" Riff shouted.

The *Dragon* swerved in the sky. Riff nearly fell from his seat. They dodged one blast of plasma, but another blast slammed into them.

Sparks flew. Fire raged across the bridge. A thousand lights blinked and warning sirens wailed.

"Fire back!" Nova shouted, leaping to her feet.

"Wait, no!" Riff said. "Giga, cancel that order. We can't hurt Midnight."

More enemy fire flew. Plasma blasted all around them. The *Dragon Huntress* flew madly, dodging blast after blast until another bolt hit them. The windshield cracked and nearly shattered.

"Captain, we've lost an engine!" Piston shouted through the communicator.

"Riff, we might have to kill her!" Nova shouted. "We have to blast them out of space, Midnight or no Midnight."

Giga turned toward Riff. She stared, awaiting his orders. "Captain?" the android whispered.

Riff clenched his jaw. He couldn't flee--not with Midnight aboard the enemy vessel. He couldn't fire back--not without killing her.

"Giga," he said, "fire at their cannons and engines. Not their main hull." He clenched his fist. "We're going to cripple the bastards."

Giga's eyes flashed and her lips peeled back into something almost like a snarl. "Happy to comply, Captain," she hissed . . . and fired.

Searing red plasma blasted from the *Dragon Huntress* like dragonfire.

The inferno slammed into the enemy ship's cannons.

Explosions filled space.

The skelkrin ship rocked madly. Shards of metal flew out. Flames blasted through the escaping air. Riff caught his breath, suddenly sure the entire warship would crash down to the planet, taking Midnight with it.

But the great metal crab remained flying. Its main plasma guns had shattered. The cannons thrust out in broken shards, reminding Riff of those old cartoons where the villain fired a shotgun with a rock in the barrel. But the *Crab*'s smaller guns, a dozen of them across its hull, had survived the assault. They now turned toward the *Dragon Huntress* and shot out smaller bolts.

"Evasive action!" Riff shouted. He was sure he had heard that term somewhere before. It seemed to work. Happy to comply, Giga raised the *Dragon Huntress* higher. The blasts shot beneath them.

The skelkrin vessel came charging toward them.

"Giga, fly beneath the bastard." Riff stood at the windshield, staring at the warship barreling forward. "Fly under it, and we're going to cripple its engines. We can't blast it apart, but we can make sure they're not getting away with Midnight."

Giga nodded and the *Dragon Huntress* dipped in orbit, then charged forward. Enemy lasers flew above them. Streaks of light filled the sky.

"Lower!" Riff shouted. "We're going to slam together!"

The Crab came charging forth. Soon the two ships were only a kilometer apart, then only meters apart.

Nova screamed.

Giga snarled.

The *Dragon Huntress* dipped in space. Riff grimaced, grabbing onto the dashboard.

The Crab charged forth above them. The two ships rubbed together. Sparks flew from the instruments. Metal screeched and banged together.

"It'll open us like a tin can!" Steel shouted.

"Giga, lower!"

The *Dragon Huntress* sank deeper. They reached the end of the enemy ship.

"Blast their engines apart!" Riff shouted.

The *Dragon Huntress* flew deeper into space, then spun around to face the *Crab*.

The dragon blasted out its fire. The plasma slammed into the enemy's backside, blazing across its rear engines.

Those engines exploded with heat and light that washed the *Dragon Huntress's* bridge.

The enemy ship kept flying.

Its hyperdrive engines were shattered. They were in ruin. They were in shreds. Yet somehow, they were lighting up. Coils of blue light flowed across them.

"Captain, the enemy vessel is prepared to shoot into hyperdrive," Giga said.

"Fire again! Tear the engines apart!"

"Cannot compute, Captain. Their engines are heating up. A blast from us now will tear their entire ship apart, Midnight included."

Riff clenched his fists. "Warm up our own hyperdrive engines. We're going after them."

"Cannot compute, Captain. Our fuel tank sustained damage and is leaking its contents." Giga turned to stare at him. "We have barely enough fuel left to remain in orbit, Captain."

The enemy hyperdrive engines were sputtering. One went dark, coughed, and reignited. The *Crab*'s engines were obviously struggling but getting brighter. Riff had a sudden memory of his father's old lawnmower which always took several yanks on the cord to kick-start.

The skelkrins are going to escape with Midnight, Riff realized. *And we can't stop them.*

"Get them on speakers, Gig." He returned to his seat. "Put them on."

"Happy to comply, Captain." Giga nodded. "Hailing enemy vessel . . . hailing . . . hailing . . ."

With a crackle of electricity, the head-on display in front of Riff sprang to life.

Onscreen leered the ugly, fanged face of the brute that had kidnapped Midnight and struck Riff. The pain in Riff's jaw flared again.

"Captain Raphael 'Riff' Starfire." The skelkrin grinned and licked his chops. Saliva dripped down his chin. "Yes, I know your name. This is Captain Skrum of the Skelkrin Empire. Called to say goodbye, Starfire?"

"I called to tell you that you're a coward." Riff snorted. "Running from a fight?"

The skelkrin growled, then laughed. His milky white eyes seemed to burn with inner fire. "There is no more fight, Starfire. Your ship is leaking fuel. Your engines are shattered. Your puny weapons could not cripple us."

"So why are you fleeing, dog?" Riff balled up his fists. "I thought skelkrins were apex predators. I thought you were the greatest hunters in the galaxy. And yet you flee from me, a puny little human. If you leave now, I'm going to spread the word across the galaxy. Everyone from Vega to Sol will know that Skrum the skelkrin is a yellow-bellied coward who fled from me." Riff forced himself to grin. "You want to prove your strength? Finish what you started. We're both hunters. Come and hunt me."

Riff swiped his finger across his throat. Giga understood the signal and cut off the connection.

"Riff," Nova whispered. She was pale, and her hand clenched around her whip. "We can't defeat them in a fight. What are you doing?"

Riff grinned savagely, clutching his armrests. "I'm hunting aliens." He turned toward Giga. "Same maneuver as before. We fly under them. Once their hyperdrive engines have cooled off, can we blast them without making their whole ship explode?"

The android nodded. "Aye, Captain."

"Good. We do that. Now. Now!"

The *Crab*'s hyperdrive engines were going dark again, but its thrusters were blasting. The ship was turning back toward them.

"Giga, under them!" Riff said. "Blast those hyper engines!"

The *Dragon Huntress* flew.

The *Crab* charged toward them.

This time, the enemy vessel did not fire its guns. Instead, one of its great, iron claws swung downward.

"Evasive ac--!" Riff began.

Before he could complete the word, the claw slammed into the *Dragon Huntress*.

They tumbled through space. Sparks flew. A panel caught fire.

"Captain, we can't take much more of this!" Piston's voice rose from the communicator.

"Giga, fire at their engines!" Riff shouted. "Fire, fire! Point us up and fire!"

The *Crab* loomed above them. The *Dragon Huntress* steadied itself below, raised its head . . . and belched out smoke.

Riff cursed. "Why aren't we firing? Blow our dragonfire!"

Giga tilted her head. "Cannot compute, Captain. Weapon ignition requires fuel. Our tank has leaked out its last drop."

Riff cursed every foul word he knew. *The Crab* came swooping down toward them again, claws snapping.

"Pull back!" Riff stared in horror at the approaching enemy. "Use thruster power!"

The *Dragon Huntress* blasted out gas. They shot backward in space. The enemy vessel flew in pursuit. The two ships streamed through orbit.

Riff spoke into his communicator. "Piston, we need more fuel. Hook up the reserve tanks."

"I can't do it, Captain!" The gruffle's voice rose through the speaker. "The damn demon drank our spare tank. Drank every last drop, she did."

Gods, Riff thought. *We might die because of the damn demon.*

"Piston, we have to fire our plasma!"

"I cannot fire without fuel, Captain!"

Giga turned toward him. "Captain, thruster power is running low. We have only a few more minutes of flight left, and then we'll be sitting ducks, sir."

No. Riff stumbled toward the windshield. *Gods, no, it can't end like this.*

He stared out into space. The skelkrin vessel came charging toward them, claws opening wide, ready to tear them apart.

CHAPTER TWENTY-FOUR
OF WARRIORS AND WRENCHES

Steel stood on the bridge of the *Dragon Huntress*, staring at the enemy vessel approaching. He raised his chin.

There is a damsel in distress on that ship.

He took a deep breath.

Midnight needs me. She needs a knight.

Riff was shouting at Giga to fly, shouting at Piston to find more fuel, shouting at the enemy warship in a rage. That enemy warship kept charging forth, claws clattering.

My brother is losing control, Steel thought. *But a knight remains calm. A knight always maintains his honor, his duty, his chivalry, even in the face of death.*

He stepped toward the side of the bridge, opened a cabinet, and pulled out a space suit.

"Steel, what are you doing?" Riff said, turning toward him.

Calmly, Steel began removing his ancient knightly armor and pulling on the space suit. "I'm going after the damsel, brother," he said calmly. "Midnight needs me."

As the *Dragon Huntress* kept orbiting the planet on thruster power, and as the enemy approached, Riff marched toward Steel and grabbed his arm.

"What are you talking about?"

Steel gazed at his brother. He reached out and clasped Riff's shoulder. "My honor demands it, brother. There is a damsel in distress within their vessel. Our ship is crippled. I will go fight for her with sword and chivalry."

Riff slapped his forehead. "Steel! Damn it! This isn't a game anymore. You're not back on Earth in your fake castle. You can't pretend to be some knight anymore like from the fairy tales. This is real battle, Steel. And the fate of the cosmos itself hangs in the balance."

Those words dug deep. They twisted inside Steel.

A relic, some on Earth had called him. A dinosaur. A madman. A modern Don Quixote.

No.

Steel squared his shoulders. "I am a Knight of Sol, brother. You are right. This is no game." He zipped his space suit shut, put on his helmet, and lifted his sword. "Yes, the fate of the cosmos hangs in the balance. So does my honor. I pray we meet again." Steel clasped Riff's arm. "I love you, my brother. Always."

Riff laughed mirthlessly and turned toward Nova. "Can you believe this, Nova? Can you--Nova? Nova, what the hell are you doing?"

The ashai princess too was pulling on a space suit. She glared at Riff. "I'm going with your lump-headed brother. I'm not letting him die in glory without me. The poor bastard has no idea what he's doing." She flashed Steel a crooked smile. "Needs a real warrior with him."

Steel wanted to object. To tell Nova to stay. The woman was an abomination, not a true lady. She was crude, rude, a woman who spat, who drank, who--

A woman I need with me, he thought. *A true warrior.*

He lifted a jetpack from the cabinet and handed it to her. He placed another across his back.

"So we fly together, Nova of Ashmar. We fight together."

She spat into her palm and slapped his shoulder. "We hunt aliens together."

They turned toward Riff--a knight and a gladiator.

"You can't leave," Riff whispered. "You'll die."

Nova stepped toward him and touched his cheek. "According to your dad, if the skelkrins get away with Midnight, we'll all die." She leaned forward and kissed his lips.

Riff growled and stepped toward the cabinet where a third space suit still hung. "Then I'm going with you."

Steel reached out his arm and stopped him. "No, Riff. You are captain of the *Dragon Huntress.* A captain does not abandon his ship in battle. Besides--I will need this third space suit." He lifted it, placed it under his arm, and smiled thinly. "How else am I to bring Midnight back here?"

Riff stared back at the windshield. The enemy vessel was flying forth, its engines sputtering, its claws snapping. The *Dragon Huntress* raced along its orbit, down to fumes, its weapon crippled. Riff turned back toward Steel, stepped closer, and embraced him.

"Go kick their asses, brother."

Steel groaned. "Do you have to be so crude?" Then he tightened his lips, wrapped his arms around Riff, and held him tight. "Goodbye, brother. I will see you again, in this life or the next."

With that, Steel spun around. He marched off the bridge, down the stairs, and into the main deck. Romy was huddled in the corner, staring with wide eyes. Steel tilted his head toward her.

"Guard the ship while I'm away, my friend," he said.

Romy sniffled and her eyes filled with tears. Trembling, she leaped to her feet and saluted him.

Steel stepped toward the airlock. Nova walked with him.

They tugged the first door open and closed it behind them.

They stepped down the stairs.

They opened the outer door, exposing the vacuum.

Steel and Nova, knight and gladiator, Alien Hunters, friends . . . shot into the emptiness of space.

* * * * *

"Twig, we've got to go faster!" Piston said. "Gods old and new, lassie. We've got to do something or that giant space crab will tear us apart."

The engine room was in shambles. Pipes had cracked and blasted out steam. Electricity buzzed across the switchboard. Part of the hull itself had cracked; Piston had sealed it just in time before losing their air. Worst of all, the fuel was gone, leaked out into space. Romy had drunk the spare tank. They were coasting along their orbit; without fuel, they couldn't change course, couldn't speed up, and couldn't ignite their plasma cannon.

"Oh, it's a right mess." Piston leaped toward a cracking pipe and began to tape it shut. "We've got to move faster! We've got to get away from those claws. We can't take another hit."

Twig was busy climbing a ladder, welding together shattered fuses. "Piston, the throttle engines are down to fumes! We can't coast much longer. We're going to slip out of orbit soon and crash down to the planet. That is, if the skelkrins don't catch us first."

Piston stared out the porthole at the skelkrin warship that was charging toward them, claws snapping. "There's got to be some way to go faster."

Twig tightened her lips. "We can compress the air from the attic. Blast it through the vents and out to the thruster engines."

Piston groaned. "It'll never be enough air! Will shoot us maybe a few meters forward before gravity or skelkrin claws grab us. What we need is *power*. More engines!"

Twig hopped off the ladder. "We've got a ship full of engines, Piston! The motor in the vacuum cleaner. The motor in the fridge. The motor in the furnace and air conditioner. We can rig those together."

Piston waved his hammer at her. "Blast it, you clod! You'll never propel a starship with a vacuum cleaner."

"I will!" She raised her chin. "As a little girl back on Haven, I used to always tug motors out of our vacuums, fridges, and other contraptions and build robots and rockets. Used to drive my old gaffer crazy. I can do it."

Piston clutched his head. "I must be going insane! Taking ideas from a damn halfling." He groaned. "Well, all right! Off we go. Let's find some bloody motors."

They raced off, leaving the engine room, and burst into the main deck. Romy was standing there, looking helpless.

"Romy, help me dig for motors!" Twig shouted.

The demon nodded. "All right!"

They raced through the ship--gruffle, halfling, and demon. Piston tore the motor out of the microwave. Romy ripped out the motor from the fridge, pausing to grab a last slice of cake. Twig plundered the attic for the vacuum cleaner. They rushed back down into the engine room where Piston grabbed the motor out of the furnace.

"Going to get mighty cold in here soon," he said as the heating systems died down.

They piled up the motors on the floor, and Twig worked in a fury, mumbling to herself, welding.

"Piston, get me some screws! And an Allen key!"

He was going insane for sure. Taking orders from a halfling! Yet when he glanced out the porthole, the enemy vessel was nearer. The claw reached out and grazed the *Dragon*'s hull, and the metal screamed.

"Hurry!" Twig shouted.

"Piston, we need more speed!" Riff shouted over the communicator.

Piston returned with the supplies, and Twig worked at mad speed, forming a single great motor out of the many smaller parts.

"Got it!" she said. "Piston, help me attach it to the main engine thrust!"

They worked together while Romy watched with wide eyes, icing on her face.

"Done!" Twig shouted and flipped the switch.

Outside the porthole, the skelkrin claw reached toward them.

Twig's motor sputtered, roared to life, and blasted out sparks, feeding energy into the main engines.

With a great bolt that shook the room and dropped Piston to the floor, the *Dragon Huntress* blasted forward.

They streamed through space, roaring around the planet, leaving the enemy vessel behind.

Riff's laughter sounded through the speakers. "We're blasting like a bullet, Piston!" The captain whooped. "You're a genius, man. A genius!"

Piston puffed out his chest and spoke into his microphone. "Aye, Captain! Thank you, Captain. I--Well . . ." He lowered his head. "Truth is, it was all Twig, sir. Little beast is a maverick with the engines."

"Twig, I love you," Riff said. "I'm going to give you another bonus if we get out of this. We're well out of skelkrin range now, and . . ."

Riff's voice faded.

"Captain?" Piston said. "Captain, are you all right up there?"

For a moment, silence. Then a whisper. "Another vessel."

"Another vessel, Captain?" Piston raced toward the porthole. "What other--" He gasped. "Oh no, sir. Oh no. This can't be. This can't be, sir!"

Piston sank to his knees. His heart sank deeper.

Outside in space, roaring toward them and firing its guns, came a great silver warship, its hull sporting the Cosmian sigil.

CHAPTER TWENTY-FIVE
THE ENGINEER

Steel and Nova shot through open space, jet packs roaring out flame.

The planet of Cirona spread below, a great green ball. The *Dragon Huntress* flew away behind them. Ahead loomed the *Crab*, the massive skelkrin warship.

Be with me, light of Sol, Steel prayed silently. He clutched his sword in one hand, the spare space suit in the other. *By my honor, I cannot fail today.*

"I'm coming for you, Midnight," he whispered.

Nova flew at his side, her whip coiling like a string of gold. The skelkrin warship tilted overhead. Its guns pointed downward, and it blasted out its lasers.

Steel and Nova scattered and soared. The beams shot between them. They rose higher.

"To the hangar!" Steel said. "We'll blast through the hatch."

Nova's voice rose through the speakers in his helmet. "Race you there, old boy."

More weapons blasted out from the ship. One laser beam slammed into Steel's sword, bouncing off and down toward the planet. He stormed forward, jet pack thrumming on his back.

Nova swung her whip before her as she flew, knocking back blasts of laser. They charged toward the hangar doors, and Steel readied his blade.

Swing true, Solflare, he whispered.

A meter away from the ship, he swung his sword.

The blade slammed into the hangar door with a shower of light, slicing through the iron. Nova laughed at his side, swung her whip, and cracked open another chunk of metal. With another swing of his blade, Steel tore the door open.

They blasted into the hangar, shooting fire from their jet packs, and landed on a metal floor. They let their engines die.

The hangar was vast, large enough that the *Dragon Huntress* could have fit inside. Three skelkrins stood here. The towering crimson beasts howled, baring their fangs. They charged forward, swinging their claws.

"For Sol!" Steel shouted and ran to meet them.

"For fire and venom!" Nova cried--the words of her people--and ran forward.

The gladiator swung her whip. The electric lash sliced through a skelkrin's arm, severing it. Steel reached the beasts, swung his blade, and cut off another creature's leg.

The skelkrins screeched. One roared, grabbed Steel, and leaned in to bite. The creature's fangs gleamed. His eyes were smelters.

Steel drove his sword forward, slamming the crossguard into the alien's face.

A fang snapped and fell.

The creature stepped back, howling, and Steel swung his sword. Light flashed. The blade sliced through the creature's torso, cleaving it in two, leaving a trail of smoke.

The skelkrin slammed down dead.

Steel turned his head to see Nova swing her whip, cutting through the last living skelkrin. The creature fell down dead, black blood spurting across the floor. More blood pooled around Steel's feet.

He frowned.

He knelt and pressed his finger against a small, purple splotch. He examined the liquid.

"Purple blood." Steel's heart twisted. "Midnight was here."

"There!" Nova pointed. "A trail of purple blood. It leads deeper into the ship."

Steel straightened and began walking. "We follow. We find her."

They left the hangar and entered a long, black corridor. Scattered lights flickered on the ceiling.

Shadows stirred. White eyes cracked open.

Four more skelkrins came charging their way, howling.

Steel pointed his blade forward, blasting out beams of light. Nova cracked her whip, sending forth lightning bolts. The skelkrins roared and fell. Steel and Nova kept walking. One skelkrin on the floor reached toward Steel, trying to grab him. A thrust from Steel's sword cut through his heart.

"More purple blood." Nova pointed to a splotch ahead. "This way."

They ran down another dark corridor. The walls were jagged iron. The ceiling towered above them. Gears spun in the walls. There were no windows. It felt to Steel like walking through the dungeon of some ancient, medieval fortress of evil, seeking a princess to save.

I will find Midnight. I will find my princess.

They kept moving through the iron labyrinth, following the trail of purple blood. A great archway rose ahead, twenty feet tall; the trail led through it. A stench wafted from beyond, acidic, rotted. A low growl sounded.

Steel paused and looked at Nova. She stared back.

"There's something in there," Steel whispered.

Nova raised her chin and gave him a crooked smile. "Let's go kill it."

It felt like years since Steel had smiled, but now he smiled with her.

They raised their weapons and stepped through the archway.

They found themselves in a great hall, large as a cathedral. Many gears and levers covered the walls, floor, and ceiling, some of them larger than men. A narrow bridge spanned the length of the chamber, stretching over a chasm toward another doorway. Steam blasted out. Fires roared in pits. It was some sort of engine room, Steel realized.

And below in the chasm lived the engineer.

The creature was massive, larger than Steel's old castle on Earth. Ten of its tentacles spread out, turning gears, tugging levers, rearranging pipes, keeping the ship moving. Its many eyes blinked, and its mouth opened wide in the pit, ringed with teeth, screeching.

Nova's eyes widened. "Calamari!"

Steel grimaced. "Never could abide the stuff." He pointed. "Midnight's blood trails along the bridge. We pass."

He stepped onto the walkway. Nova grabbed his arm and held him back. "Let me walk first. I need room to swing my whip."

He stiffened. "I am a Knight of Sol. I will not let a woman walk before me while I trail behind. I will walk ahead, defending you."

Nova tugged him closer to her and snarled. Her eyes flashed. "I am a princess of Ashmar, a planet of proud warriors. I am a gladiator. I tamed a thousand beasts. I wield a whip of pure energy. I will walk ahead." She tightened her grip on his arm. "We are equal here, Steel Starfire."

He stared into those burning green eyes. For many years, when Steel had looked at Nova, he had seen a shameful sight. A woman who acted like a man, who cursed and spat, who confused him. Who scared him.

Looking at her now, however, he saw a proud warrior. He saw a partner. He saw a sister-in-arms.

He nodded and bowed his head. "Forgive me, Nova." He looked back up at her. "Forgive me for everything. I've been a fool."

For an instant something damp and sad filled her eyes, but then she nodded. She smiled crookedly. "Let's go save your princess, Steel. Together."

She stepped onto the bridge. Steel walked behind her.

They had taken only ten steps into the engine room when the creature below squealed. Its tentacles--each one was as long as the *Dragon Huntress*--left the gears and levers they held. Its suckers smacked, each one full of teeth. The creature's eyes glared up from below, and the tentacles came flying toward Steel and Nova.

With a roar, Nova lashed her whip. "Down, beast!" she cried and burst into a run. "Down!"

One tentacle came swinging down above Steel. He ran, and the digit slammed into the walkway behind him, denting the metal. Another tentacle swung ahead, and Steel thrust his sword, lashing out light. The bolt slammed into the tentacle, knocking it aside, but another swung from his other side. It crashed against him, knocking him sideways.

Steel fell from the bridge.

He reached up and caught the ledge.

A tentacle grabbed his leg, biting, squeezing. Below in the pit, the creature's mouth smacked, ready to devour him.

Ahead on the bridge, Nova was swinging her whip in circles, holding back several other tentacles. Steel shouted in pain, kicked madly, and lashed down his sword. He cut through the tentacle that grabbed his leg, tugged mightily, and pulled himself back onto the bridge. He thrust his blade again, knocking back another of the creature's arms.

"Nova, keep running!" he shouted.

They raced along the bridge. The creature bucked below, reaching out toward them. Nova sliced through one tentacle with her whip; the severed digit slammed down, sank between two gears, and spurted blood as the gears crushed it.

They were almost across the bridge when a tentacle thrust up, grabbed Nova around her waist, and lifted her into the air.

She screamed, kicking madly. The creature pinned her arms to her sides; she could not swing her whip.

"Nova!" Steel cried.

He leaped toward her, sword flashing. He was too late. The tentacle tossed Nova through the air, and she went plunging down toward the great mouth below.

Steel gritted his teeth and jumped off the bridge.

Nova fell.

The creature's mouth opened, ready to swallow her.

As he plunged down, Steel thrust his sword before him, blasting light into the alien's maw.

The creature squealed, the light cutting through its palate, and closed its mouth an instant before Nova hit it. She slammed against its closed lips and rolled to the floor.

Steel hit the floor an instant later.

"Nova, I'm here." He grabbed her. He lifted her. She wrapped her arms around him.

The creature's blobby head rose ahead of them on the floor, massive, larger than both of them. Its mouth turned toward them, snapping its teeth.

"Hold me tight!" Nova said and swung her whip. The lash wrapped around the bridge above.

They leaped up, rising just before the creature's jaws could snap around them. They climbed the whip and tugged themselves back onto the bridge.

Blasting their weapons, they ran the last few steps and leaped through the far doorway.

They landed in a shadowy corridor.

Behind them, the great octopus squealed. When Steel looked over his shoulder, he saw the beast stretch its remaining tentacles toward the instruments. It continued its work, wounded and hungry, its prey gone.

Steel and Nova paused for only a moment, panting. The trail of purple blood stretched ahead. Steel raised his sword and Nova raised her whip. They kept following.

CHAPTER TWENTY-SIX
INTO THE FIRE

Riff stood on the *Dragon Huntress*'s bridge with Giga, staring out the windshield at the new starship approaching.

Out of the frying pan and into the fire, he thought as cold sweat trickled down his back.

With Twig's makeshift engine, they had blasted out of the skelkrins' range. The massive, crablike warship was now many kilometers away, Steel and Nova invading its bowels. But this new warship that approached terrified Riff just as much.

The vessel was several times the *Dragon Huntress*'s size, built like a great barracuda. It stormed forth through space, its jaws opening to reveal cannons. Its hull was shimmering silver, smooth, fluid. Its headlights blazed like eyes. Upon its hull appeared the words: "*SS Barracuda*, Holy Cosmian Order"

Riff grimaced and clutched his gun as if he could fire through the windshield and blast the enemy ship apart.

"Captain, message coming in from new vessel." Giga stepped toward him and held his hand.

"Put it on screen."

Giga nodded, suddenly not so happy to comply. With crackling static, a hideous countenance appeared on the HUD--a face half man, half metal.

"Grotter," Riff whispered.

The cyborg smiled a twitching smile. Gears clicked upon his face. "Riff Starfire. Did you think me dead? You've run far, boy. But now your running days are over. I will kill you now--the way I killed your mother thirty years ago." He raised his snapping claw of metal. "Die like she did--squealing like a pig."

The transmission died.

The *SS Barracuda* fired its guns.

Riff didn't even waste time shouting for Giga's help. He grabbed the manual controls and yanked the ship up. The clatter of counter-squares pieces, Twig's wrenches, and Romy's bottles of juice rose from the decks below. The blasts of Grotter's fire blazed under the ship. One grazed the hull, and the *Dragon Huntress* rattled madly. Sparks flew across the bridge, and the crack on the windshield stretched longer.

If that glass shatters, we'll all be sucked out into space.

"Piston!" Riff shouted into his communicator. "Piston, have you fixed our gun yet? We have to fire. Now."

"No can do, Captain!" rose the gruffle's voice through the speakers. "We can't fire without fuel."

"Rig the motors up to the gun! Come up with something, I don't care, but we need our dragonfire!"

"Aye, Captain!"

Riff yanked at the controls, trying to steer away, to escape. The fuel lights beeped. Empty. Empty.

The *Barracuda* fired again.

Riff yanked the *Dragon* sideways, moving closer to the planet. He dodged a few blasts of Grotter's fire. Another blast slammed into the *Dragon*'s wing, tossing it into a spin.

Even Giga, always composed, screamed and squeezed his hand.

"He's tearing us apart, Captain," the android whispered, turning toward him. Fear filled her eyes.

The *Barracuda* fired again. Blasts pummeled the *Dragon Huntress*. Steam and fire blazed across the ship.

Riff winced, pulled Giga into his arms, and held her so close he almost crushed her.

* * * * *

"Twig, we've got to blow our dragonfire!" Piston cried. "Can we connect your motors to the plasma gun?"

Twig raced around the engine room, leaping over shattered pipes, fallen engine coils, and tools that swept across the swaying floor like jetsam. "It won't work! The gun needs fuel, Piston! No motor will work."

Piston ducked and leaped aside as wrenches and hammers fell from a shelf. Another blast of enemy fire hit the *Dragon*. Alarms blared. The attic hull was breached. Romy screamed and raced to hide behind Piston, tears in her eyes.

"What about your electric wrench?" Piston said. "Can we rig that?"

Twig shook her head, her long black hair in disarray. "It's no use, Piston. Without fuel, we can't fire our gun. Period." She turned to look at her rigged engine made of many smaller motors. "And this contraption is going to be out of battery power any moment now." She paused from running around, stared at Piston with wide eyes, and her voice dropped to a whisper. "We're done for."

Behind Piston, Romy wailed.

Piston spun around toward the blubbering demon, grabbed her shoulders, and shook her. "This is all your fault, you beast of Hell! If you hadn't drunk the fuel from the reserve tank, we'd have a chance, damn it."

Romy's lips wobbled, and tears poured down her red cheeks. "I was thirsty!" The fire on her head crackled like a guttering torch. "It's not my fault."

More blasts shook the ship. The alarms blared. A monitor displayed air blasting out of another breached room, this one the ship's washroom.

"Of course it's your fault!" Piston dug his fingers into Romy's arms. "You've doomed us all. You've doomed us to death! You-- You-- Why are you dancing?"

Romy was leaping from foot to foot, hands clasped between her thighs. She bit her lip. "Because I have to go to the bathroom!"

Piston groaned and rolled his eyes. "This isn't the time, Romy! You're not a toddler. The bathroom's blasted to bits. Hold it in!"

She hopped around, hands thrust between her thighs as if struggling to seal a dam. "But I drank too much fuel! I have to goooo."

"You can't! Unless you want to be sucked out of the bathroom hull into space, you--" Piston froze. He spun toward Twig, then back to Romy. "The . . . the fuel's still inside you?"

Romy whined. "So much it's about to come out of my ears!"

Piston spun toward Twig. The halfling stared back with wide eyes, her jaw hanging open.

"It might work," Piston whispered.

Twig covered her mouth. She spoke between her fingers. "It can't . . ."

Piston tightened his lips. "Get a funnel and a hose!"

They raced through the engine room. As Romy hopped about, biting her lip, Twig ran a hose into the fuel pipe, and Piston found a funnel and connected it to the other end.

"Piston, we need that dragonfire!" Riff shouted through the speakers.

More enemy fire blasted outside. The ship shook again.

Twig raced toward Romy and held out the funnel. "All right, Romy. Time to go wee-wee."

The demon's eyes widened. "That's not a bathroom."

"It is now, go!" Piston shouted.

The demon whined. "I can't! Not like this."

Piston rolled his eyes. He grabbed a chair and slammed his fist into the seat, punching a hole through it. Twig placed the funnel inside.

"There, it's a potty now," Piston said. "Sit down and go."

Romy sat on the seat. She looked around. "I can't go when you're watching me!"

Piston rolled his eyes and turned his back. Twig stood at his side, also turning her back to the demon.

Nothing happened.

"Romy?" Twig asked. "Are you going?"

The demon sounded miserable. "I can't go like this! You can still hear me. Play some music or something."

Piston trembled with rage and fear. "Romy, hurry!"

"I need music!"

Piston's hands shook. He hit the button on his wrist's communicator. "Giga, we need music! Play something!"

The android's voice sounded through the speakers. "Happy to comply!"

Electric blues filled the engine room. A moment later, Romy sighed.

The blaring empty fuel lights shut off.

Piston laughed and jumped about. "We're in business, Captain! Dragonfire ready to blow!"

Romy stepped off her seat and grinned. "That's better."

* * * * *

Riff stood on the bridge, leaned against the windshield, and uttered one word: "Fire."

Giga snarled and clenched her fists. "Very happy to comply."

The *Dragon Huntress* turned in the sky, faced the *SS Barracuda*, and roared out its dragonfire.

The plasma blasted out of the *Dragon's* mouth, streaming toward the enemy vessel, a raging white, red, and yellow inferno.

Grotter tried to dodge. The *Barracuda* made an attempt to rise higher. It was too slow. The dragonfire slammed into the enemy ship with the rage of a supernova.

The *Barracuda* cracked. Its fuel and plasma tanks ignited.

"Fire again!" Riff shouted. "Fire everything!"

The dragonfire blasted out. The fuel gauges sank back to empty. The blaze slammed into the *Barracuda*, shattering its hull. Explosions rocked the Cosmian ship. A fuel tank shattered and blasted out flame. Then the explosions tore *The Barracuda* apart into a million pieces.

Riff stared, holding his breath.

A single escape pod, round and hard like a bullet, flew out from the inferno and dived down toward Planet Cirona below.

Riff dug his fingernails into his palms.

"Grotter's in there." He ground his teeth. "He escaped. Giga, chase that pod and bathe it with more fire."

"Cannot compute, Captain. Fuel tank is once more empty. We've barely got enough to stay afloat."

Riff stared down at the capsule. The pod was now streaming into the atmosphere, wreathed in fire. Grotter was in there. Riff knew it.

"I have to face him," he whispered. "I have to stop him." His fists shook, and he turned to stare into Giga's eyes. "I have to go down there, to kill him, to put an end to this. Or he'll always hunt me." His voice dropped to a whisper. "I have to avenge my mother."

"We can't even land, Captain," Giga said. "We don't have the fuel. And . . . what about Steel and Nova? We can't leave them."

Riff turned to stare toward the skelkrin ship. It was still flying toward them, claws snapping, but with its crippled engines, it couldn't catch up with the *Dragon Huntress*. Steel and Nova were gone. A hole gaped open in the *Crab*; the knight and gladiator had gone in there.

Riff looked back at Giga. "You're right, Giga. The *Dragon Huntress* can't leave orbit. Not with Steel and Nova there. They'll be flying back soon--with Midnight. I need you to take command of this ship."

Her eyes widened. "Captain?"

He turned. He walked off the bridge, climbed downstairs, and headed toward the *Dragon*'s escape pod.

"Captain, wait!" Giga said. She raced down the hallway and grabbed his arm. "You can't do this. He'll kill you."

Riff stood with one foot in the escape pod. He turned to face Giga. "If he does, you have to save Steel, Nova, and

Midnight. You have to take charge of this ship. And I have to face Grotter. I have to do what I should have done years ago."

Footsteps padded up the corridor. Twig came running toward them, her hair in disarray. Soot covered her clothes and face, and tears streamed down her cheeks.

"Captain!" the little halfling said. "I heard over the speakers. I . . ." She leaped toward him and hugged his leg, clinging to him. "Please don't go."

He stroked her hair. "I must do this, Twig. You'll be fine without me. Keep helping Piston."

Twig pulled back, sniffing. As her tears fell, she drew her electric wrench from her tool belt and held it out toward him. "Take this, Captain. My lucky wrench. The best one I have. It'll help you."

Riff smiled and slung the wrench into his belt. "Thank you, Twig. My little heroine."

She sniffed again, then turned and fled back into the engine room.

Riff turned back toward Giga. The android stared at him, face blank.

"Goodbye, Giga," he whispered.

The android hesitated for a moment, then pulled him into her embrace, and she kissed his lips--a deep kiss, a kiss that tasted of lavender. When she finally pulled back, her eyes were damp.

"I will wait for you, my captain," Giga whispered. "Always."

He squeezed her palm, then stepped into the escape pod. The door whooshed shut.

Riff pressed a few controls, and the capsule blasted out into space, leaving the *Dragon Huntress* and streaming down toward the planet below, toward the man he must kill.

CHAPTER TWENTY-SEVEN
STEEL AND LIGHT

The trail of purple blood led their way. Steel and Nova stepped down the dark corridor and through an archway. They found themselves entering the *Crab*'s command bridge.

The chamber was massive, as large as the hangar. Floor-to-ceiling windows afforded an open view of space. In the distance, still too far to reach, flew the *Dragon Huntress*; the escape pod was streaming down from the starship toward the green planet below. Vega's light gave a last flicker, then vanished behind the planet's horizon, and shadows fell. Only the red lights of the bridge now cast their glow.

An oozing black cocoon hung from the ceiling, swaying gently. A rent in the cocoon revealed a purple face and gleaming yellow eyes--Midnight. Her eyes widened to see them, then filled with tears.

Steel inhaled sharply and raised his blade. Nova hissed and readied her whip.

Between them and Midnight rose several seats of jagged spikes, each as large as a throne. Upon them sat the skelkrins.

One of the beasts saw them enter. The alien rose to his feet, pounded his chest, and roared. The creature stood eight feet tall, covered in black armor, and his eyes burned white with hatred. The other skelkrins heard the call, turned toward the door too, and bellowed in rage. Their saliva dripped to the floor, and their fangs gleamed, long and sharp as daggers.

Nova gave Steel a crooked smile. "Bet I can kill more than you."

Steel raised his sword. "Good! Kill them!"

The skelkrins ran toward them.

Steel snarled and thrust his blade, casting out light. Nova swung her whip, blasting lightning. One skelkrin fell. Then another.

The others reached them.

Steel was a tall man, taller than most humans, but the skelkrins made him feel small as a child. Yet still he fought. He fought in a fury. For his honor. For Midnight. For all Earth. His blade swung, shedding the black blood of the beasts. He knocked aside claws. He stabbed at their armor. He roared as he fought, and his light streamed from his blade into their flesh.

A claw slammed against him, knocking him down. Blood seeped down his side. Fangs bit into his leg, and he roared but kept swinging his blade, cutting the enemy down. He rose to his feet, blasting out more light, ignoring the pain.

I was banished from the Knights of Sol, he thought as he fought. *But I found a new order.*

He roared out his cry, "I am an Alien Hunter!"

Nova laughed at his side. "We are Alien Hunters!"

The gladiator cracked her whip, slicing through a skelkrin. Steel thrust his sword, knocking another beast down. The corpses of the enemy piled up at their feet. With a swing of Solflare, Steel cut the last creature down.

Steel and Nova stood panting. Blood dripped down Steel's leg and arm, and his space suit was punctured. He ignored the pain, ignored the fear, and took steps toward Midnight.

The pirilian stared at him, eyes wide, and cried out, "Watch out!"

Steel froze.

Before he could take another breath, one of the jagged iron thrones spun around.

A massive skelkrin sat there, larger than the others, holding a gun larger than Steel's arm.

The creature fired.

Steel thrust his sword.

The enemy blast hit him, and Steel fell.

He didn't even feel pain. For a moment, he didn't even think he was hit, not until he saw the blood pooling below him.

He shot me in the stomach, Steel realized. Beneath his space suit, he was bleeding. His body was broken, leaking out his lifeblood.

The skelkrin laughed. "Welcome, Steel and Nova! I am Lord Skrum. I am your destroyer. I will feast upon your flesh."

Nova screamed and charged forward, whip lashing in a fury.

"Die, Skrum!" she shouted. "I am Nova of Ashmar. Gladiator of the Alien Arena. Warrior-princess. The woman who will kill you."

Her whip shot out bolt after bolt of lightning, but the blasts ricocheted off Skrum's armor, doing the skelkrin lord no harm. The alien stepped toward Nova, nearly twice her height, and swung his fist.

The blow slammed into Nova, tossing her into the air. She flew, hit a wall, and slumped down.

Trapped in her cocoon, Midnight screamed.

Steel tried to rise. He tried to cry out for Nova. The gladiator wasn't moving, only moaning on the floor. Slowly, savoring every step, Skrum stepped toward the wounded Nova. His gun smoked. He slammed his boot down, crushing Nova's wrist, pinning down her whip. Nova screamed.

"Good," Skrum said. "I like it when you pests die screaming."

The skelkrin lord pointed his gun toward Nova's head.

His blood pouring, his head swimming, Steel rose to his feet.

He thrust his sword.

A blast of light shot out, slammed into Skrum's gun, and shattered its barrel.

Steel raised his blade again. "By my honor, Skrum, I challenge you to a duel."

The skelkrin lord howled and tossed aside his ruined gun. Strings of saliva dangled between his fangs. His claws thrust out.

"I will slay you, worm."

Steel raised his chin. He held his sword with one hand, and he kept his second hand pressed to his wound. "You will fight me. But not here. Not among the wounded and dead." Steel allowed himself a small, tight smile. "Let's take this outside."

He turned and left the command bridge.

Skrum roared behind him. "Do you flee from a fight, coward?"

Steel kept moving, heading down the corridor. At first he limped. His blood dripped behind him--not a light trickle like Midnight's blood but a thick trail. He was moments from death, perhaps. He kept moving, soon running.

Skrum roared behind him and followed.

I have to get him away from Midnight and Nova. I have to protect them, to lure him off.

Steel raced through the dark corridors of the skelkrin ship, the beast howling in pursuit.

He was dizzy, struggling for every breath, when Steel made it back to the engine room.

The great alien octopus still lurked below the overpass. Several of its tentacles were severed, but the others were still turning dials and gears across the walls, keeping the starship flying. As Steel limped onto the bridge, the creature below snapped its great jaws and hissed, still hungering for his flesh.

Skrum's roars rose from the corridor behind Steel.

The knight trudged onward, weaker now, feeling close to death. Finally he could move no farther. He had lost too much blood.

In the middle of the bridge that spanned the chasm, Steel turned around, stood still, and waited.

With a roar, Skrum emerged from the corridor and raced onto the bridge. The skelkrin snapped his teeth and reached out his claws.

"Die now!" Skrum cried. "Die now, filthy human. Die knowing that your race failed. That humanity will perish. That the Earth will be mine."

The alien thundered onto the bridge as the octopus roared below.

Steel stood calmly, bleeding, and stared into the skelkrin's white eyes.

"Earth stands." Steel raised his blade of light. "Humanity will not fall. Not so long as I defend it. By my honor, skelkrin, I send you to the abyss!"

Skrum raced toward him, howling.

Steel slammed his blade down onto the bridge.

Light blasted out. Metal bent and snapped. With a crack, with showering shards of iron, the bridge shattered.

As the walkway collapsed around him, Skrum stared at Steel. For an instant, terror filled the skelkrin's eyes.

Then Skrum fell.

Steel clung to his section of the bridge, holding on with all his might. His feet dangled. Below him, Skrum tumbled down toward the waiting octopus. The great beast opened its jaws wide, caught Skrum in its mouth, and chomped down.

Black blood spurted. The octopus chewed. Skrum roared . . . then fell silent. The massive jaws on the floor closed. A great tongue slipped out, licked up the last skelkrin crumbs, then slunk back in. The octopus closed its eyes, satisfied with its meal.

Steel's feet dangled over the pit. His hand clung to the section of bridge that still stood, but the metal was bending. His blood still dripped. Any moment now, he knew, he would fall into the pit and join Skrum in the beast's belly.

He was too weak to hold on.

His grip loosened.

He fell through the air.

He saw something purple appear at the corridor above. Midnight! With a pop, she vanished.

She reappeared in midair as Steel fell. She wrapped her arms around him. She popped out of reality.

Steel, held in her arms, saw a world of flashing, coiling purple lights.

They snapped back into existence across the bridge, back in the corridor above the pit.

"Steel!" Midnight cried. She laid him down on the floor, holding him. Her tears fell. "Steel, can you hear me?"

"My lady," he whispered. He could speak no louder. He reached up a shaky hand and caressed her indigo hair. "You are safe, my lady."

Nova raced forward and knelt above Steel too. "Steel, damn it! Don't you die here, you bastard." She clutched his hand, and her tears fell. "Don't you leave me here."

Steel looked down at his wounds. There was barely any blood left to spill. He would die here, he knew. But he had saved Midnight. He had saved the world.

I can rest in peace. I protected my honor.

He closed his eyes.

Warmth filled him, and through his eyelids, he saw a soft light. It filled him with warmth, with healing, with comforting joy. It was calling him home.

The light of the afterlife.

His eyelids flicked open.

He gasped.

It was no heavenly glow! The light came from Midnight's palms. Like down on the planet, she had summoned balls of luminous *qi*. But this light was not a weapon; it was soft, golden, soothing him, healing him. Midnight placed her glowing hands upon him, and her *qi* energy flowed through him, filling him with strength.

His wounds closed.

The light faded.

He was healed.

Midnight smiled softly.

"Thank you, Steel," she whispered.

She seemed exhausted. She fell to the floor, smiling, her breath soft.

Tears in his eyes, Steel lifted her in his arms. She weighed almost nothing.

"You gave me some of your life's energy," he whispered.

Midnight smiled up at him, eyelids fluttering. "Use my strength, Steel Starfire. Use my gift. Use it to keep fighting."

"I will, my lady!" Tears flowed down his cheeks. "Always."

Strobe lights flared across the wall. A siren wailed. A deep, metallic voice boomed through the ship, speaking in the skelkrin language.

Midnight gasped and covered her mouth.

"What's the voice saying?" Nova asked, staring around, whip raised.

"All skelkrins are dead on the ship." Midnight's eyes widened. "It's going to self-destruct. In sixty seconds. Fifty-nine. Fifty-eight."

They ran.

The ship shook around them. Pipes cracked and steam blasted out. Fire raged. A hunk of ceiling fell down, slamming against the floor only a foot behind them. They ran on. The voice kept booming.

"Thirty seconds!" Midnight shouted.

They raced along cracking corridors, through smoke, through flame, until they reached the hangar.

Nova shoved the spare space suit at Midnight. "Put this on!"

Steel cursed and looked down at his own suit. "There are holes in this."

Nova groaned, reached into her pocket, and tossed him a roll of duct tape. "Never go hunting aliens without duct tape. Tape yourself up!"

"Ten seconds!" Midnight shouted, shoving herself into the suit. She placed her helmet on. "Two! One!"

They ran together.

They leaped out the hangar door.

Fire raged and the ship collapsed, metal shards blasting out.

Their jet packs roared.

The silence of vacuum fell.

Flames and heat and metal blazed around them, and they charged forward, soaring through the fire, emerging from the inferno, screaming, singed.

A second explosion flared behind them, the light as bright as a sun. A shockwave blasted out, hitting them. Steel, Nova, and Midnight tumbled through space. The planet spun madly around them. The stars streaked.

When finally they settled their flight, Steel looked behind him.

The skelkrin ship was gone. Nothing but shrapnel remained.

They floated through the silence, three souls--a knight, a gladiator, and a girl who would no longer destroy the universe.

Steel closed his eyes and breathed.

CHAPTER TWENTY-EIGHT

ELECTRICITY

The pod roared through Cirona's atmosphere, engulfed in flame. Riff dug his fingers into his seat, gritted his teeth, and prayed.

Let me live, old gods and new. Let me live so I can kill.

He shot through the fire, emerging into open sky. He breathed a shaky breath of relief, looked out the porthole, and saw a vapor trail in the sky.

Grotter's capsule, he knew.

Riff snarled and grabbed the pod's controls. He curved his flight, heading toward that vapor trail. To the man who had killed his mother. To Grotter. The man Riff would kill today.

The forests raced up toward him. The vapor trail led to a patch of shattered trees. Riff shot forward, deployed his parachute, and began to glide.

He was moments away from the forest when the gunfire started.

Riff cursed.

The gunfire blasted up from between the trees, slamming into Riff's pod. The bullets ricocheted off the surface. The pod was built to withstand reentry and it could withstand bullets, but the parachute was not as lucky. With holes in the chute, the pod plummeted.

Riff grimaced and prepared for impact.

Branches snapped and shattered. Trees collapsed. The pod shoved through the canopy and slammed against the forest floor, rattling every tooth in Riff's mouth.

For a moment, silence.

Riff sat still in his seat. Every part of him ached. No more gunfire sounded.

Slowly, he reached into his holster and drew old Ethel.

Silence.

He looked toward the porthole. Branches swayed there, thick with leaves. A bird with eight wings fluttered by. The light of Vega fell in a warm, golden glow, rich with pollen.

Riff reached one hand toward the door handle.

He leaned back.

He pulled the handle, letting the door swing outward.

Gunfire roared, slamming into the pod. Riff leaned back, wincing, and thrust his gun out the door. He fired. Again. Again.

The gunfire outside died.

Riff caught his breath. He ripped off his chair's armrest and held it out toward the door.

Gunfire blasted, tearing the armrest apart.

Riff cursed.

I can't step out without Grotter blasting me to bits.

The gunfire faded outside. Grotter's laughter sounded across the forest, followed by his raspy, metallic voice.

"Are you bleeding to death in there, Starfire? Come out when you want me to end your pain."

Riff cursed. He couldn't hit Grotter from in here. He stared ahead at the control panel across from him.

Oh bloody hell.

He sucked in breath, fired a blast of plasma out the doorway, and kicked.

A bullet grazed his leg.

Riff shouted and slammed his foot against the controls.

The engines on the pod roared, shoving him forward. The pod rolled. Riff screamed. He blasted across the forest, slammed into a tree, and raised a shower of dirt and wooden chips.

He leaped out of the pod, rolled across the ground, rose to a crouch, and fired his gun.

Grotter stood ahead between the trees. One of Riff's plasma blasts slammed into the cyborg's metallic half, shoving him back.

Riff fired again. He hit Grotter's mechanical arm. The cyborg hissed, raised his machine gun, and began spraying more bullets.

Riff rolled across the forest. Bullets slammed into the soil and trees around him. He hid behind a tree as bullets peppered the trunk.

Grotter laughed again. "You've already lost, Riff Starfire! You cannot defeat me. Your plasma cannot hurt metal. You will die here, far from home."

More bullets flew. Riff cursed, reached around the tree, and fired again.

This time, he aimed for Grotter's gun.

A bullet whistled and slammed into Riff's shoulder. He grunted but kept firing, blast after blast. Grotter screamed. The plasma washed over his human arm, wilting the skin, charring the bone. Grotter's machine gun fell to the ground.

Riff stepped out from behind the tree. His leg bled. His shoulder spurted blood. He limped forward, woozy, losing more blood every step.

"You are only half metal," Riff said and raised his gun again. He fired.

Ethel's blast of plasma slammed into Grotter's head, melting skin.

Grotter screamed. A horrible sound. The sound of a butchered animal. But the cyborg did not fall. The creature charged forward, screeching, half his face burnt.

"I only need my metal!" the cyborg shrieked. Riff grimaced to see that even beneath the charred flesh of Grotter's human half, gears turned and clicked.

Before Riff could fire again, the cyborg reached him and swung his claw.

The hand of metal slammed into Riff's head, knocking him down.

He thudded onto the forest floor and tasted blood. He saw stars. He raised his gun.

Grotter's claw swung again, hitting Riff's hand. Riff yowled, his fingers crushed, and Ethel thumped to the ground. Grotter kicked the gun away.

No. No! I can't die here.

Riff rose to his feet, blood in his mouth. "You killed my mother, you bastard. Prepare to die."

Riff swung his fist.

Grotter grabbed his hand in his claws, tightened his grip, and crushed Riff's fingers.

Pain shot through Riff. He screamed. He fell to his knees. The claws kept tightening. Riff heard a finger bone crack. He could barely breathe, barely cling to consciousness. His lifeblood drained away, and all turned to haze.

"Yes," Grotter hissed, further tightening his grip. "Die slowly. Bleed out here as I crush you, bone by bone. Bleed out minute by long minute. I'm going to make it last."

Still clutching Riff's hand, the cyborg kicked, driving his boot into Riff's stomach.

All Riff knew was pain, darkness, stars. All he saw was shadows and light.

It's like looking at space, he thought, eyelids fluttering. *It's like being up there again.*

Before him, through the haze of encroaching death, he saw them again. Steel, his brother, the only family Riff had. Giga-- sweet, gentle, loyal Giga, perhaps the dearest friend he had. Nova- -the woman he loved, the woman he had loved for years.

I can't die. I can't part from you.

He would even miss Piston with his grumblings, Romy with her silly board games, little Twig with her smiles and wrenches and--

Riff's eyes snapped open.

He drew a shaky breath.

"Still alive?" Grotter said. The cyborg glared at him. The human half of his face had melted away, revealing the gears within. In the metallic half of his face, his bionic eye blazed with red hatred. "This is taking longer than I thought. Good. Good."

The cyborg still crushed Riff's right hand in his claw. With his shaking left hand, Riff reached to his belt and drew Twig's electric wrench.

"What's that?" Grotter asked. "Need to tighten a screw?"

Riff clicked the button on the wrench. Electricity crackled to life between its prongs.

"Screw you," Riff whispered hoarsely and drove the wrench forward.

He slammed the prongs against Grotter's face.

Electricity crackled, racing through the cyborg's gears and circuits.

Grotter screamed. His claw loosened, releasing Riff. The electricity raced over the cyborg, driving down his body, along his limbs, burning, blasting out smoke.

"What have you done?" Grotter screeched, an inhuman sound, impossibly high-pitched.

Riff struggled to his feet. "Won our little game. Avenged my mother. Rid the universe of scum. All the above, really."

He drove the wrench forward again.

Electricity crackled, and the cyborg screamed . . . then fell silent.

Grotter thumped down onto the ground. A few last gears turned, then stilled. Riff kicked the creature, scattering bolts.

Between the rising smoke, a light flickered.

Riff caught his breath.

A part of Grotter was still working. Metal clicked. A lens shutter opened. The light intensified and blasted out, forming a hologram in the forest.

Riff stumbled a few paces back, fell to his knees, and stared.

A hologram of a towering skelkrin stood before him, flickering, fading, appearing again. This was no skelkrin warrior in armor. This creature wore a black cloak, and a dark crown topped his crimson head.

"Emperor Lore," Riff whispered, on his knees before the apparition.

The hologram stared at him with white eyes. The emperor's face twisted with fury.

"Riff Starfire," the creature hissed. "It is you. The human my slave told me of. I will remember your name and your face, Starfire. When my hosts arrive at your world, you will be the first to scream, the last to die. I will break you slowly. I--"

Riff rose to his feet and slammed his heel into the hologram projector. The light died.

"Enough of that rubbish," Riff whispered. He could speak no louder.

He managed to take a few steps away, then fell. His face hit the ground. Soil filled his mouth. He was tired. The birds fluttered above, and sunlight fell upon him, warming him, and the pain faded.

CHAPTER TWENTY-NINE

HOMECOMING

Riff's eyes fluttered open.

He found himself staring into yellow eyes set in a purple face.

He blinked.

"Hello," he whispered.

Midnight smiled down at him, her teeth very white, her smile very warm. "Hello."

Riff moaned and looked around him. He still lay on the forest floor. The trees rustled around him. Midnight knelt above him, wearing one of the *Dragon Huntress*'s space suits. Her helmet rested in a patch of grass.

"I'm sorry I shot you," Riff said. "Just want to get that out of the way."

She laughed. "I'm sorry I blasted you with *qi*. That makes us even."

He pushed himself onto his elbows and looked down at his body. His wounds were gone; only scars remained. He whistled softly. "I must be the world's fastest healer."

"No, but I might be." Midnight raised her palms; they were glowing. "I saw the trail your capsule left through the sky. I ported down here. I found you in the forest, and I healed you with my energy, whatever energy I could muster." She blinked and sat down heavily. "I'm a bit woozy. Healing two Starfires in one day takes a lot out of a woman."

Riff's breath caught. "Steel! Nova! Are they . . ."

"Back on the *Dragon Huntress*." Midnight pointed to the sky. "They're still up there, looking down at us. Ship's badly damaged. Holes all over. Can't even land." She grinned. "You're lucky I know how to port. Within the blink of an eye, I can travel anywhere that I can see. All pirilians can."

He nodded, feeling woozy too. He pulled himself toward a tree and leaned against the trunk.

"That's why they wanted you, isn't it?" he whispered. "The skelkrins. Not because of the light you can blast from your hands. Not because of the healing. Because of the teleporting." He swallowed. It hurt. "My father said something about that in a letter to me, how if they caught you, they'd gain power to destroy the cosmos."

Midnight lowered her head. She wriggled closer to him and leaned against the same tree. She spoke softly, her voice still afraid, still pained.

"The skelkrins attacked my planet." A tear streamed down her lavender cheek. "For a long year, we fought them. We fought them well, but they were too many, their weapons too horrible. They burned our world from the sky. They bombed us until they realized that we're worth more alive than dead, that we carry a magic inside us they can use." She trembled. "By then only I was alive."

Riff reached out and held her hand. She was trembling. "I'm sorry, Midnight."

She closed her eyes. She kept speaking as if she hadn't heard him. "It was Skrum who caught me. He took me to a skelkrin laboratory. And he cut me, experimented on me, trying to learn how to use my magic." She took a shuddering breath, for a moment unable to speak. "His scientists developed a plan. They were to clone me--a clone for every ship in the skelkrin fleet. They were to place me into their engines. They were to turn me into a creature half pirilian, half warship, to use the power inside me to port their ships across the stars. Even in hyperspace, it would take the skelkrins months to reach Earth. But with my clones inside their ships . . . all they'd need is a line of sight. They could send their entire armada to Earth in an instant, then to every other world in this galaxy. They would have been unstoppable, appearing and disappearing, bombing worlds, blinking out of reality, appearing again with more ammo, more troops. The galaxy would have fallen to them, while I screamed inside a million of their engines."

Riff felt the blood drain from his face. "God," he whispered.

Midnight nodded, sobbing softly. "It was the Traveler who saved me. An old man with a long white beard. He is known in myths and legends in my world, known by many names. I always thought him only that--a legend. Until he appeared in the skelkrin lab. Until he freed me, placed me on a starjet, told me to fly and find his son." She looked at Riff and touched his cheek. "To find you, Riff."

He blinked, then laughed. "My father? Midnight, my father is nothing but a street corner magician, pulling rabbits out of hats for the amusement of children. True, he often vanished on long trips. It would sometimes be a year or two before he returned home. But . . . he just traveled as part of his show. To perform as a magician in distant worlds. He's not a legend."

Midnight stroked his hair. "He is greater than you know, Riff Starfire. You are the child of a hero." She kissed his cheek. "*You* are a hero."

He groaned and struggled to stand up. "A hero who can barely stand. God, I feel like a tenderized steak." He helped Midnight to her feet too. "I saw the town a few kilometers north. From the air, it looked like the skelkrin fire hadn't hit it. What say we mosey on in, head to the nearest saloon, and order an actual steak?"

She raised an eyebrow. "I thought they hired you to remove me, not walk with me into their capital city."

He snorted. "Oh, they'll see how lovely you are, and they'll feel even worse when they hand over my payment. It'll make things all the sweeter."

They walked through the forest, leaning against each other. The trees rustled. The birds sang. No explosions, no *qi*, no bloodthirsty aliens, no killer cyborgs. For the first time in long days, things felt all right.

* * * * *

The Cironan shuttle soared through the atmosphere and out into space, carrying a team of mechanics, a dusty beat-up captain, and a young pirilian.

As they flew toward the *HMS Dragon Huntress*, Riff stared out the window and rubbed his eyes.

"Bloody hell," he whispered.

The dragon ship looked awful. A large hole, large enough to lead a horse through, gaped open on the roof, exposing Romy's attic. One wing was torn to shreds, and the dragon's snout--right below the bridge--was crumpled up. Soot and scratches covered the hull.

"It's amazing that the damn boat's still afloat." Riff patted his wallet and looked at Midnight. "It's going to cost me everything I earned to remove you to fix the ship."

The pirilian smiled. "Aren't you glad you found me then?"

Of the two other vessels that had orbited Planet Cirona--the skelkrin *Crab* and Grotter's *Barracuda*--not a trace remained, only bad memories.

The Cironan shuttle slowed its flight, approached the *Dragon Huntress*, and entered orbit beside it.

Riff, Midnight, and the mechanics put on their helmets.

"All right, boys!" Riff said. "You know what to do. Patch up the holes, smooth out the dents, a new paint job would be nice . . . oh, and can you take a look at the left hyperdrive engine? Makes a strange rattling noise."

The team headed out, floating into space, their tools ready. They got to work at once, hovering around the *Dragon Huntress* with welding tools, bolts, and wrenches that Twig would have drooled over.

Riff remained for a moment in the shuttle with Midnight, and sudden sadness seeped into him. He stared out at the *Dragon* and sighed.

"She's a good ship." He nodded. "She's home."

Riff cleared his throat; it was suddenly scratchy. He rose to his feet and floated out into space, and Midnight floated with him. They opened the *Dragon Huntress's* outer door, floated inside onto the staircase, and closed the door behind them. Once the air was repressurized, they climbed the steps, opened the inner door, and stepped into the main deck.

Everyone was waiting there.

His shipmates. His friends. His family. They all stood facing him, their Alien Hunters badges pinned to their chests.

Romy gave a huge wail and leaped forward. She wrapped her arms around Riff, squeezed him, and gave him endless kisses. Her tears streamed.

"Oh, Riff! I was so worried. So worried for you." She sniffled. "Welcome back." Suddenly her eyes brightened. "Did you bring me any presents?"

He nodded, reached into his pocket, and handed her a new counter-squares piece carved from wood. It was shaped like a poodle. Romy squealed in delight and raced toward her board game.

Piston approached Riff next. The gruffle cleared his throat, stared down at his feet, and mumbled something about the engine coils and a job well done, but then a tear filled the engineer's eye.

"Ah, curse it all!" Piston said and tugged Riff into a crushing embrace, lifting him off his feet. "Welcome back, laddie! I mean, Captain. I mean . . ." He had to put Riff down, pull out a handkerchief, and blow his nose. "It's good to have you back, sir."

Twig leaped onto Riff next, hugging him tightly. "Did my wrench help?" the halfling asked.

Riff laughed and handed it back to her. "It's deadlier than my gun, little one. It saved my life. Keep it handy."

She nodded, chin raised. "I will!"

The halfling stepped back, and Giga approached Riff next. The android stared at him hesitantly; she seemed unsure of herself, awkward, embarrassed. Riff remembered their kiss, remembered holding her close as fire burned around them.

He pulled her close again, embracing the android. He whispered into her ear, "I'm back, Giga."

She held him tightly, and he felt her android tears on his shoulder. "Welcome back, sir. I waited for you." She sniffed and gave him a salute. "I'm yours, my captain. Always."

Riff stepped deeper into the main deck and came to stand before his brother.

Steel Starfire, the noble knight, stared back at him, tall and strong and proud as always. The knight stroked his drooping mustache, his pride and joy.

"Welcome back, brother," Steel said, chin raised. "You performed admirably. You--"

"Oh shut it, you big tinman." He pulled Steel into his arms and squeezed him.

Steel stiffened for a moment, then relaxed and hugged Riff back. "Welcome back, brother," the knight said again, and this time his voice was soft and warm.

Finally Riff turned toward the last member of his crew. To Nova.

"You look awful," the ashai said.

He looked at her. As always, she wore her golden gladiator suit, the material as strong as any armor. Her whip hung at her side, coiled up. Her pointed ears thrust out from her mane of blond hair, and her green eyes stared at him with humor, mockery, and love.

He pulled her into his arms and he kissed her. He kissed her like he'd never kissed her before, not caring that the others saw. He never wanted to let her go.

"I love you, Nova," he whispered. "I love you and I'm sorry. I'm sorry for the man that I was." He touched her cheek. "Do you forgive me?"

She sighed, rolled her eyes, then grinned and pinched his cheek. "You did well today, Riff. Consider yourself redeemed."

She raised her fist. "For now! Don't you screw up again, or I'm going to bash you more than an army of skelkrins and cyborgs."

Romy hopped up toward them, grabbed Riff's arm, and tugged. "Riffff . . . come on and play with me! I have the counter-squares pieces all set up. The poodle's right in the middle. Come on!"

He sighed but let the demon tug him over. She wagged her tail and made a move on the board. Her poodle captured his dragon and she squealed with joy.

* * * * *

Steel stood in the *Dragon*'s crew quarters between the bunk beds. He stared out the porthole at the mechanics floating around the ship, welding and patching and painting.

The other Alien Hunters were on the main deck, laughing and hooting around a rousing game of counter-squares. But Steel had never cared much for games, for social gatherings, for noise or laughter or fun. He stared down at the planet below, thinking of the planet he had left behind--of Earth, of the home he had vowed to defend. And he wondered if he even still had a home there.

I saved the world, he thought. *I slew Skrum, the warlord who would have destroyed Earth like he destroyed Midnight's home. Yet when I return to Earth, what awaits me there?*

His throat tightened. The Knights of Sol had banished him. The Cosmians had destroyed his castle. His mother was dead, his father missing. He had no wife, no children, no friends but for his horse and sword. He would return to Earth, its savior . . . only for nobody to know, nobody to care, nobody to believe him. He would be like he had been, a relic, an outcast.

He lowered his head.

A voice rose behind him.

"Howdy, partner."

He spun around. He saw Nova standing in the doorway, smiling softly.

"Hello," he said.

She stepped into the chamber and stood with him between the bunks. She looked through the porthole down at Planet Cirona.

"Beautiful, isn't it?" Nova said.

Steel nodded. "A pristine world. A world like Earth was thousands of years ago. Perhaps . . . perhaps a world more suited for a rusty old relic like me."

She turned back toward him. "You're not a relic. I'm sorry, Steel. I'm sorry I always called you that."

He took her hand in his. She was a proud warrior, a great gladiator, a slayer of many enemies, yet her hand felt so soft, so small in his.

"And I'm sorry too." He bowed his head. "I always scorned you. Belittled you. I am ashamed."

Nova bit her lip, then squeezed his hand and grinned. "We sure killed a lot of skelkrins together, didn't we?"

A smile tingled below his mustache. "I believe we're more or less even."

"Even?" She gasped and playfully slapped his chest. "I killed way more!"

"We killed them together." Now his smile widened. It was a real smile, a good smile. And he felt young. "We make a good pair of warriors."

She nodded. "We do, Steel." Her voice softened. "We do. Stay with us here. Stay with me. I need another warrior on this ship. I need another friend."

They stood together, staring out the window at the green world below.

CHAPTER THIRTY
THE TRAVELER

The mechanics' shuttle was heading back to the planet, their work completed, when Riff saw a new vessel approach.

He still stood in the main deck, gazing out the window. Romy was passed out on the couch, snoring. Piston and Twig had returned to the engine room, where they were performing last repairs and calibrations of their own. Giga and Nova were both on the bridge. Only Steel and Midnight stood here with Riff when he saw the flying saucer outside.

"Look!" He pointed.

Steel and Midnight came to stand at his side. They gazed out with wide eyes.

The vessel was unlike any Riff had ever seen. It was deep blue, limned with light, spinning toward them. A dome rose upon its crest like a cockpit, glowing golden.

Riff frowned and spoke into his communicator. "Giga, can you hail the incoming vessel?"

Her voice rose through the speaker. "Captain? The mechanic vessel is leaving, not incoming."

"The saucer," Riff said. "The blue one."

"Cannot compute, Captain. No other vessel is in range."

Riff rubbed his eyes and stared outside again. He could definitely see the flying saucer there. When he turned toward Steel and Midnight, he knew they saw it too; they were gaping as if disbelieving.

A few meters away from the *Dragon Huntress*, the saucer halted its flight. A covered walkway stretched out from it, connecting with the *Dragon*.

The airlock on the main deck began to open.

Riff hissed and drew his gun. "We're being boarded."

Steel frowned and drew his sword. Midnight let *qi* gather in her palms.

The airlock door swung open.

"Hello, hello!" rose a voice. "Oh, nice place you've got here. A couch! I love couches. Counter-squares! Love that game." Light flowed around the figure, revealing only a silhouette. "What are you doing with your weapons drawn? Is that any way to welcome a guest?"

Riff knew that voice. He lowered his gun, barely able to breathe. Steel gasped and lowered his sword.

The figure closed the hatch, sealing the light outside.

Riff gasped.

It was him.

"Dad!" he shouted.

"Father!" Steel cried.

Midnight covered her mouth, eyes wide.

The old man nodded and stepped deeper into the main deck, holding a wooden walking staff. The magician wore his long white robes, and his white beard was just as long and flowing. A pointed hat rested on his head. He looked around, nodding. "Just needs a good vacuuming. Too bad there's no motor in that vacuum cleaner over there."

Riff raced forward and embraced the old man. "Dad! What are you doing here?"

Steel joined them, seeming unable to speak, too overcome for words.

Old Aminor looked at them and laughed. "I've come to visit my boys! So shocked that your old man should stop by?" He snorted. "You two never learned any hospitality. Now shove aside! Move!"

The magician elbowed his way between them, approached Midnight, and turned solemn. The old man took her lavender hand and lowered his head.

"Forgive me, Midnight," he said softly. "I should never have left you. I know how much you suffered, my child." His eyes brightened. "But I see you found my sons after all."

She hugged him, and tears flowed from her eyes. "Dear Traveler. Thank you."

"Dad!" Riff said. "What . . . what is this 'Traveler' talk? Where have you been all this time?"

Aminor squared his shoulders and rapped Riff with his staff. "I was off on an adventure! Not that it's any of your business. I was seeking a new home for our lovely lady here." He turned back toward Midnight, and once more his voice softened. "It lies very near, yet very far. Only a few kilometers away, yet many dimensions away. A new world, Midnight. A world where others of your kind have sought shelter. A world where the skelkrins can never reach you." He reached out his hand. "If you take my hand, child, I will take you there."

She trembled, crying softly. "There are . . . other pirilians? Others who survived?"

Aminor nodded. "A few, child. I managed to save a few. They wait for you now. Wait for you beyond the stars, beyond the dimensions, a place where no enemy can reach you. Will you come with me now?" Suddenly the old man's eyes gleamed with his own tears. "I'm sorry, Midnight, that I could not save your world. The pain of that tragedy will forever fill me. But if you will travel with me, I will take you to a new world. A new beginning."

She sniffed and nodded, unable to speak. She took his hand. They walked together toward the airlock.

"Wait!" Steel said. The knight's voice was hoarse. "Midnight! Wait."

He stepped toward her and knelt.

Midnight gently released Aminor's hand and turned toward the knight.

"My sweet knight," she whispered. "My savior. My hero."

Tears flowed down Steel's gaunt cheeks and into his mustache. He took her hand in his and kissed it. "My lady."

She kissed Steel's forehead, smiled warmly, and needed to say no more.

"Goodbye, Riff," she whispered, turning to look at him.

Riff stared, not sure what to say, what to do, how to feel. He stepped toward her, and he too kissed her hand. "Goodbye, Midnight. Will we ever see you again?"

She turned to look at Aminor, her eyes questioning, then back at Riff. She nodded. "I'm sure of it." She kissed his cheek. "Until we meet again."

Aminor smiled, wiped his eyes, and escorted Midnight to the doorway. She stepped into the light, heading toward the flying saucer, vanishing in its glow.

"Dad, wait!" Riff said. "Don't . . . don't go. Not yet." His voice caught in his throat. "There's so much I don't understand."

Aminor stood at the doorway between the two vessels, between space and light. The old man looked around the deck, looked at his sons, and nodded.

"I'm proud of you, my sons. Last time I saw you, you were both languishing away. You were both lost. I've seen you grow. I've seen you become heroes." He winked. "Keep being heroes, my sons. This is where you belong. I will always be proud of you. I will always love you."

The old man tipped his hat.

With that, Aminor turned and left the *Dragon Huntress*, closing the door behind him.

"Dad!" Riff cried. "Wait!"

Yet before he could open the door again, Riff heard the saucer detach. He turned toward the porthole to see the strange, glowing vessel fly farther away, spin, and vanish with a gleam of light.

Steel came to stand beside him. He inhaled deeply. "He's off to another dimension, I suppose."

Riff nodded. "Off on another adventure we'll probably never hear anything about."

"And Midnight goes with him." Steel lowered his head. "I will miss her."

Riff stretched and yawned. "I miss sleeping. And eating. And taking long showers. Did Piston fix the shower yet?" He sighed. "I suppose our own adventure is over, brother. For now. We saved Cirona. We saved Midnight. We probably saved Earth and the rest of the cosmos."

Yet even as he spoke those words, a chill filled him. He remembered Emperor Lore's hologram emerging from Grotter's corpse, remembered the skelkrin threatening to attack again. There was still evil out there. There were still aliens who wanted to hunt him.

There was still work to do.

He patted Steel's shoulder. "Come on, brother. Let's go look for something to eat."

* * * * *

With a belly full of Cironan fruit and bread, Riff left the kitchen and stepped back into the bridge. Steel came with him, clad as always in his armor, his sword at his side.

"Konnichiwa!" Giga greeted Riff with a salute. "Welcome back to your bridge, Captain."

Nova was already in her seat, facing the repaired windshield--or, as Giga would no doubt call it, the front fused silica viewport pane. The bobbleheads were now bolted onto the dashboard, ready to withstand any bump on the road. Riff sank into his captain's seat, and Steel sat at his right-hand side. Planet Cirona rotated slowly below.

"Well," Riff said. "I suppose we . . . have lives to get back to." He looked at Steel. "A castle to rebuild." He glanced at Nova. "The Alien Arena to compete in. The Blue Strings to play in."

Yet his words tasted stale in his mouth. The others stared at him, silent, saying nothing. Steel bowed his head.

Somehow, after everything they had lived through, Earth itself seemed a little stale.

"Captain!" Twig's voice rose from behind, and she raced onto the bridge, holding a sheaf of papers. "Captain, a whole slew of work orders just came in! Turns out worlds for light-years around heard about how we saved Cirona. They want to hire us, Captain!" Twig's eyes shone. "What do we do? Where do we go next?"

She paused, panting. Her trusted wrench hung from her tool belt again.

Riff glanced at Steel, then at Nova. "Or . . ." he said, ". . . we can take one more job. Or two. Just to make enough money so I can buy my guitar back. And maybe then a little more."

Steel nodded. "We are, after all, the Alien Hunters."

Riff took a deep breath and rose to his feet. He walked toward the windshield. "Twig, what's the nearest star that needs us?"

The halfling shuffled through the papers. "That would be . . . Alpha Draconis, sir. In the Draco constellation. Says here they're having a devil of a time with a . . . oh stars. Not a snot-monster!"

Riff smiled thinly and turned toward Giga. "Giga, chart a course to Alpha Draconis please. Hyperdrive engines should be back up and running. And . . . don't fly us there too fast. I think we all need some time to relax on the way."

The android smiled and raised her chin. "Happy to comply, Captain. Nice and easy pace."

The engines revved up, purring like comfortable cats.

With a blast of light, the *HMS Dragon Huntress* shot into deep space, heading toward the stars.

THE END

NOVELS BY DANIEL ARENSON

Alien Hunters:
Alien Hunters
Alien Sky
Alien Shadows

Misfit Heroes:
Eye of the Wizard
Wand of the Witch

Dawn of Dragons:
Requiem's Song
Requiem's Hope
Requiem's Prayer

Song of Dragons:
Blood of Requiem
Tears of Requiem
Light of Requiem

Dragonlore:
A Dawn of Dragonfire
A Day of Dragon Blood
A Night of Dragon Wings

The Dragon War:
A Legacy of Light
A Birthright of Blood
A Memory of Fire

KEEP IN TOUCH

www.DanielArenson.com
Daniel@DanielArenson.com
Facebook.com/DanielArenson
Twitter.com/DanielArenson

Made in the USA
Middletown, DE
30 April 2017